CAMDEN COUNTY LIBRARY
203 LAUREL ROAD
VOORHEES, NJ 08043

MAR 0 2 2017

The Coaster

Books by Erich Wurster

The Coaster

The Coaster

Erich Wurster

Poisoned Pen Press

Copyright © 2016 by Erich Wurster

First Edition 2016

10 9 8 7 6 5 4 3 2 1

Library of Congress Catalog Card Number: 2015957975

ISBN: 9781464205651   Hardcover
       9781464205675   Trade Paperback

All rights reserved. No part of this publication may be repro-
duced, stored in, or introduced into a retrieval system, or
transmitted in any form, or by any means (electronic, mechani-
cal, photocopying, recording, or otherwise) without the prior
written permission of both the copyright owner and the pub-
lisher of this book.

Poisoned Pen Press
6962 E. First Ave., Ste. 103
Scottsdale, AZ 85251
www.poisonedpenpress.com
info@poisonedpenpress.com

Printed in the United States of America

For Trish

Acknowledgments

Thank you to Bill Roskens. This book would never have been written without his contributions, and he deserves much greater credit/blame than the typical, perfunctory acknowledgment. People would sometimes say to the two of us, "Hey, you guys should write a book." For unknown reasons, we took those half-hearted, insincere suggestions at face value and proceeded to do just that. We traded Word documents back and forth and our wives allowed us to go on a couple of "writer's trips," which we spent drinking and watching European golf. Although universally acclaimed for his wit, Bill believes his writing to be wooden and hamhanded. This is correct. Nevertheless, he contributed mightily to the writing of this book, including supplying the details of his own life, many of which are superficially shared by the protagonist. Special thanks to Bill's wife, Lisa, for allowing that to happen against her better judgment. Bill and I are already working on the next book as he continues to try to weasel his way into a coauthor credit.

Thank you to all the great people at Poisoned Pen Press for believing in the book and doing everything possible to ensure its success. Barbara Peters and Annette Rogers each edited the manuscript several times and their corrections and suggestions were invaluable. Whatever flaws remain are on me.

Thank you to my parents, Rick and Mary Wurster. Everyone thanks their parents, but mine truly have provided nothing but unconditional love and support since the day I was born. My sister, Wynne, and brother, Tom, too. Also thanks to my in-laws, Ron and Nancy Jones and Pat and John Russell, for all of their support over the years.

Thank you to my wife, Trish, for her tremendous patience throughout this long process. See? I wasn't just screwing around on the computer. I was writing a book!

Finally, thank you to my children: Will, Charlie, Henry, and Mary. Think of this as sort of a virtual hug.

Chapter One

I didn't know it at the time, but everything started in late December, that week after Christmas when everybody is just kind of half-working. A regular week for me. This particular morning was memorable only because at 6:05 am, forty minutes before the alarm was set to go off, my wife reached over and gave me the sex tap on my shoulder. Sex is mostly a morning activity for us. At night, we're too tired. Well, I'm not. But my wife is "fucking exhausted" every night.

The sad thing is we used to have sex all the time, even spontaneously. Once the kids were born, the frequency declined but there was still mutual interest. Now I let her decide. It's easier that way. Under our current implied contract, when enough time has elapsed, duty calls and she gives me the tap. Almost always first thing in the morning.

Morning sex, for my wife, is "get it out of the way" sex. She's crossing it off her to-do list, like picking up the dry cleaning or calling the cable guy: *Let's knock this out before breakfast and get on with our day.* An added bonus for her is at that time of day I haven't had a chance to annoy her yet so her feelings for me are generally positive. Sarah enjoys it once we get started, though sex for her is one of those things that's often more trouble than it's worth. I can relate. That's my attitude about everything *except* sex.

This particular morning, the normal process was underway. Our dogs had taken up their usual positions of prime viewing, which is disconcerting, but as we were finishing (or I was), I rose far enough off the mattress to look out the window and make eye contact with a guy sitting in a pickup truck not thirty feet from my bedroom.

"Sarah, I think the roofers are here." They apparently arrive early and watch their customers have sex until their work can properly begin at seven.

We dove onto the floor and crawled naked together toward the bathroom. When we were a few feet from safety, our bedroom door opened and there stood nine-year-old Emily with her blanket and favorite stuffed animal, Justin Beaver.

"Hi, Mommy," she said. "What are you guys doing?"

"Daddy lost a contact lens," Sarah said from all fours.

"Didn't Daddy have Lasik surgery a couple of years ago?"

"It's been lost for a long time, honey," I said. "Now go get your brother up for breakfast."

By the time I'd showered and fixed breakfast, Emily had forgotten the naked contact lens search. Like gunslinging quarterbacks, kids have short memories. They don't worry about that interception they just threw. They take another shot downfield. I dropped the kids at school and then spent a normal day at the office doing whatever it is I do there. It seems impossible that whatever minor tasks I accomplish could add up to a full day, but they always do.

Around two, my cell phone rang. More often than not, it's my wife, and it was.

"Is now a good time?"

Not really. By her standards, I'm not doing anything. By my standards, I'm very busy. "Not really. I've got a—"

My wife thinks "Is now a good time?" is a rhetorical question. "This'll just take a second. You remember we've got Mom and Dad's charity thing tonight?"

Sarah likes to pretend we've already discussed something that she's springing on me out of the blue or mentioned months ago. She's afraid I'll try to get out of it if I have advance warning. Still, this was a command performance. The "charity thing" was a benefit gala for the art gallery or the natural history museum or whatever, a black-tie event her parents were involved with.

"It's not that I don't remember. You haven't said anything about it."

"Well, it's on the board." Every Sunday night, my wife carefully updates the weekly family calendar to keep track of all our events. Apparently she'd buried "Benefit Gala" in the middle of a week of basketball practices, haircuts, and dentist appointments on the calendar. I would argue that an entry as horrifying as "Benefit Gala" should not be simply written in ordinary script in the middle of the calendar but delivered to me verbally.

Sarah interrupted my reverie. "Why aren't you saying anything? Do you have a gun to your head?" Whenever either of us acts weird on the phone, the other asks if there's a gun to our head in case we sound strange because we're trying to send a coded message without alerting our abductors. It hasn't happened yet, but you never know. It's best to be prepared.

"Not this time," I said with a frustrated sigh. "But I wish I had known sooner."

Good god! A benefit gala! A cold trickle of sweat dripped out of my armpit and down my rib cage at the mere thought of it. Mingling for hours with a bunch of do-gooders. I would have to be on my A game, which required just the right mix of various alcohols. I really needed one of those pumps that keeps an ICU patient constantly medicated at the appropriate level. Instead, I would rely on my years of experience with scotch and tequila.

"You're not fooling me. I saw you checking your tux this morning. Anyway, the tickets are still at Dad's office. Can you stop by on your way home and pick them up?"

Sure I could. I looked at the calendar on my computer. Completely blank. "I guess I could move a few things around and make some time."

The truth is, I spend my days pretending to be "a hardworking businessman" and "a pillar of our community." Even though I'm not that smart or successful, everyone thinks I am. My entire life feels like a lie. Not a big, interesting, book-worthy lie, as if

I've got a secret family locked in the dungeon under my house. Just a series of small, meaningless deceptions to hide my true self from others. Maybe "lie" is a little strong. Let's say people only know the me I pretend to be.

"Thanks, honey. You're the best. Be home by five so you have time to get ready. We can't be late for this." Sarah worries about whether I'll be on time despite my DiMaggio-esque streak of being ready before her 847 times in a row (all numbers approximate).

"Okay. Love you."

"Love you, too."

Our phone *I love you*'s outnumber our in-person *I love you*'s about a hundred to one. It's easier to say if you can't see the other person.

Sarah's father, Sam, helped me get set up in business. My little company manages a number of properties owned by his various businesses. I am nominally in charge.

Sarah is the president to her father's chief executive officer of The Bennett Company. Like America, their business is business, which is another way of saying I don't really know what they do. But I do know that Sam built the business up from nothing, and now he was grooming his heir apparent, who also happened to be his actual heir and my lovely wife, to someday take his place. So Sarah is our family's primary breadwinner; I am its soccer mom.

Sarah spends most of her time at the company's newer offices across town. They ran out of space at their original location, but Sam insisted on keeping the office where he started Bennett Capital forty years ago. He told me he didn't need some fancy office to impress people, but I think he wanted to give Sarah the freedom to do her job without his constantly looking over her shoulder.

Sam's executive assistant was sitting at the desk outside his office. Her name is Harriet Buchanan and she had been with Sam from the beginning. Harriet isn't a secretary. She has her own secretary. She is a gatekeeper and a scheduler and Sam's right-hand woman. Harriet never married and the cliché would be that she was in love with Sam and married to her work, but I have no idea if that's true. For all I know, she's married to Melissa Etheridge and has as many adopted children as Rosie O'Donnell.

Harriet, I like. I am always glad to see her. She looked up and smiled when she saw me.

I nodded in her direction. "Moneypenny."

"Mr. Bond. What brings you down to headquarters?"

"Important business, Moneypenny. A man like me doesn't have spare time during my busy week to waste on social visits."

Harriet raised an eyebrow. "At least not social visits where both your wife and father-in-law work."

"Accurate but hurtful, Harriet," I said. "I'm actually here on an errand for said wife. She left the tickets for tonight here."

"You're going to need those," Harriet said. "I'll go look on her desk."

"Thanks," I said. "Is the big man in his office?"

"Sure, go on in. He's alone."

I knocked on Sam's door and stuck in my head. He was on the phone but waved me to a chair in front of his desk. He literally made more phone calls in a week than I made in a year. Even when we played golf, he'd often skip a hole to take an important call. He wasn't being rude and no one was offended. He is that important to his business. The decision couldn't be made without him. Very few decisions required my input, at work or at home.

Sam is nearing seventy, but you'd never know it. Sure, he'd lost a little hair, and what he had was gray, which he cut himself with clippers on the eighth-inch setting. He would never take the time to hide his male-pattern baldness by shaving his head completely, and he lost respect for those who did.

Sam has the vitality of a much younger man. He only needs glasses for reading and he is in better shape than I am, even though he never seems to work out. His passion for life keeps him fit. Early to bed, early to rise, work his ass off in between, pretty much the opposite of me. But I love him and respect him. Probably *because* he is the opposite of me.

When he hung up, I said, "I just stopped by to get our tickets and wish you good luck. We probably won't get much of a chance to talk tonight. Everybody's going to want their time with the guest of honor."

"Thanks, Bob. I'm glad you're here. I've been meaning to set up a time for us to get together."

"Oh? Well, I'm sure whatever's good for Sarah is fine with me."

"No, I mean just the two of us. I've got some things I want to discuss with you."

Just the two of us? I didn't know whether to be frightened or flattered. "What about?"

"There's no time to get into it today," Sam said. "I'll have Harriet schedule something for next week. I've got a speech to give tonight and I'm sure you have work to do."

I looked at my watch. "Not really. I just have to go home and get ready for the gala."

"All part of the job of being my son-in-law and my daughter's husband." Sam stood up, shook my hand, and eyed me with the steely gaze that had won a thousand negotiations. "And believe me, Bob, I know it's not an easy one. I probably don't say it enough but I appreciate all you do for the family."

What was going on? All I could think of was the scene in *Goodfellas* when they told Joe Pesci he was going to become a made man right before they shot him in the back of the head. "Thanks for saying that, Sam. It means a lot coming from you." It really did.

◇◇◇

Sarah and I have been married for nineteen years. We met in college, a classic Hollywood "meet cute." I was protesting outside Planned Parenthood and she tried to cross our picket line to get an abortion. We hated each other at first, but I won her over....Okay, that didn't happen. We met at a party for the rich and privileged. She liked me right away, or we never would have gotten together.

Sarah is a beautiful woman, with dark hair and a killer body even after two children. She's too good-looking for me. They say a man has outkicked his coverage when his wife is better than he deserves. Well, I kicked the ball clear out of the end zone for a touchback.

We decided to cap the family at four after Nick and Emily were born. If I were the mother, we could have had more, but Sarah needed to get back to work. Plus, our friends who have more than two kids find that with the third child, the parents are constantly outnumbered. They're up against a permanent power play where the other side always has a one-man advantage. Those parents have no choice but to go to a zone defense and we're a man-to-man team all the way. In fact, at this stage of our lives, Sarah and I are more like child-rearing partners than a romantic couple. Getting married is basically forming a two-person company with the craziest person you've ever worked with. And it's a lifetime fucking contract.

Anyone who knows us would consider us "rich," and in a way we are. My wife makes a hefty salary and I make more than I deserve. The shadow of my wife's family money looms over everything. People want to be in business with my father-in-law, and by extension with us, despite our less than favorable personal balance sheet. True, we spend a shitload of money, but we don't actually *have* any money. I'm afraid to sit down and run the numbers, though I'm confident our net worth is negative. On a monthly basis, there's more going out than coming in. We're as nervous and anxious about money as people who are barely making ends meet, but on a grander scale. We're still in debt. We still worry about paying the bills every month. They're just a lot bigger bills: ten-thousand-dollar mortgage payments instead of five-hundred-dollar rent checks.

We live on a substantial piece of land in the country, just outside of Kansas City. That's Missouri, not Kansas, a distinction that is lost on the national media. Not that it matters. Names and places have been changed to protect the guilty.

The property is more a non-working farm than an estate. Our house is spacious, but lived in. We're not hosting a lot of fancy dinner parties out in the country. We have horses, a barn and stable to house them, and a couple hundred acres of grassy fields for them to roam. There's a pond where my son and I like to pretend to fish to get out of chores assigned by his mother. We also have a little guest house where ranch hands might have bunked back in the day, but our wrangling needs are currently minimal. Still—and easy to say when you've always had plenty—I've never cared about money. But I do want to be respected as someone who is earning his own way instead of riding on his wife's coattails. Or her father's.

Chapter Two

I got home promptly at five as requested and fixed myself a drink. As I sat down to relax, I heard a truck pull up our gravel driveway. I walked over to the kitchen window and looked out to see what my wife was up to now. Nothing really would have surprised me, but almost anything would have annoyed me.

I heard a piercing whinny and saw a horse trailer headed for our barn. Most of Sarah's financially ruinous boondoggles involve horses. She can't bear to see one put down, so we're generally running an old folks' home for horses. We could have fed and clothed ten villages in Africa for every horse we've ushered gently over to the other side.

One time Sarah brought home a horse so old my dog, Max, tried to drag him into the house and put him in his bowl. His back was so swayed, your feet would touch the ground if you tried to ride him, not that anyone would. You could walk faster. The few remaining strands of hair that passed for his tail couldn't even knock a fly out of the air. Instead of his name, it should have said *Do Not Resuscitate* over his stall.

The poor creature was miserable. So naturally Sarah wanted him to undergo an expensive medical procedure that would extend his wretched existence a few months or years. If he were lucky, it would kill him. It's always difficult to tell the vet something is a little too expensive for a mere animal, especially when your sobbing wife probably told him to do whatever it takes to save Gluey. I always assume the vet is an animal lover or he wouldn't have become a vet in the first place, so I tread carefully.

The vet put a hand on my shoulder, looked me in the eye and, perhaps blinking back a tear, said, "Don't worry, Bob. I know how much you love Gluey, and I can assure you he'll receive the best equine medical care in the world." And that's what he got. Those last two weeks hooked up to one-hundred-thousand-dollar machines may have been the best of Gluey's life.

I drained my scotch, washed out my glass in the sink—it was nice to get one in before Sarah started counting—and headed outside. When I got to the barn, Sarah and her trainer were wrestling a big black stallion out of the trailer. I could tell it was a stallion because I know a lot about horses. And it was wild and aggressive. And it had a big black cock.

Sarah was struggling to get the beast into a stall.

"What do we have here, honey?"

Sarah turned and smiled sheepishly. "Bob, this is Oedipus Platinum. He's going to be staying with us for a while."

"That's good. We need some more aggressive, violent animals around here. The kids are getting too comfortable."

"They'll be fine."

"By the way, didn't the original Oedipus screw his mother and kill his father?"

"I have no plans to screw the horse, Bob."

"So you're leaving open the possibility that he might kill me."

"I'm not his mother and you're not his father. Oedipus is his show name. His barn name is Rex."

"What's Rex doing here?"

"It's a pre-purchase trial. Gives me a chance to check him out before leasing or buying him."

I stared up at Rex. He was massive, completely black except for a flash of white like a lightning bolt between his eyes. He looked like a horse superhero. "What kind of horse is he?"

Rex leaned down and snorted as Sarah patted his muzzle. "He's a Dutch Warmblood, bred in Holland to jump. Seventeen hands. Nearly fifteen hundred pounds. Big, powerful, graceful, and athletic. To put it in terms you would understand, he's the power forward of the horse world."

"An impressive animal, to be sure. But do we really want a stallion around here?"

"If you geld him, he'll lose his aggressiveness as a jumper. Not to mention giving up any chance at breeding him if he's a champion."

I reached up and tried to rub his muzzle as Sarah had. He snorted and yanked his head away. "I sympathize with you there, boy. I'm not a champion, but I still like to breed."

I turned to Sarah. "Seriously, a stallion will try to kick you in the head every chance he gets."

"It will be good for the kids to learn caution around dangerous animals."

"Weren't there any tigers or crocodiles available? We might as well be running a fucking zoo."

Sarah stared at me like I'd suggested getting a pet that wasn't a rescue. "You know I would never force an animal to live in a cage."

"Are you kidding? Every wild animal would love to live at a zoo. You think they enjoy hunting for their food? Have you noticed you never see a fat predator? That's because they hunt just enough to stay alive."

"An animal should be free to roam in its natural habitat."

"All the animals would run for the front of the line if they were offering zoo placement. Food and mates are brought to you while you lie around all day. It's like a fucking luxury spa for animals. Hell, I'd like to live in a zoo."

"If you don't shut up, you're going to find out what it's like to live in the barn."

We managed to get the stallion in his stall and calm him down when he suddenly reared to his full height as a flying object buzzed past his head.

"Goddammit, Nick," I yelled. "You're freaking the horse out."

I ran out of the barn and found my son, Nick, holding the remote control to his drone spy-plane. "Hi, Dad."

"Jesus, Nick, what are you doing? Your mom's going to kill you for spooking the horse."

"Sorry, I lost control."

The toys kids have today are incredible. This thing can fly for an hour on one good charge and record audio and video to Nick's computer. When I was a kid, we'd spend all day putting together a balsa wood plane with a rubber band propeller and then it would fly two feet and crash. But, then again, when my father was young, he had to play with a football made out of a pig's bladder. Nick's kids will probably fly jetpacks to school.

Chapter Three

Inside, I was showered and dressed by six. My pre-game routine for one of these command performances is a couple of tequila shots. I find shots to be the most effective method because they don't fill your bladder and they can be downed quickly enough that your wife won't see you carrying a drink around. Sarah tends to frown on my drinking before we leave the house because she knows I might hit it pretty hard during dinner. What she doesn't know is that I could barely make it *to* the event without at least a couple of pops.

I tossed back the two tequila shots and sat down to wait. Despite repeatedly badgering me to hurry, Sarah herself is invariably thirty minutes late. It doesn't matter what she needs to do to get ready. If by pure chance she happened to be ready right at the appointed hour, she would somehow fill the time with a randomly selected activity until we're thirty minutes late. She doesn't even wear a watch. Like a veteran quarterback who knows instinctively when the rush is about to get to him, she has a clock in her head that tells her when we're the right amount of late. When she reaches that point and she's ready to go, she's instantly annoyed the rest of us aren't already sitting in the car with the motor running.

Sarah only has two settings: (1) obliviously holding everyone else up and (2) impatiently hurrying others. She expects everybody to be on high alert until she's ready to leave. The family waits silently, only communicating through hand signals like a

SWAT team waiting for the "go" signal from their chief hostage negotiator. It might be fifteen minutes, it might be an hour, but we maintain our readiness. LIVES ARE AT STAKE, PEOPLE! The second Sarah herself is ready, she expects the entire family to spring into action. If one makes the mistake of going to the bathroom right at that moment, she'll call our names in an agitated voice, and then finally say with a sigh, "I'll be waiting in the car!"

"Bob, Let's go!! We're going to be late!! What are you doing?"

"Sitting on my ass waiting for you, like I do every time we leave the house."

"Well, hurry up!! I'll be in the car!" *See? Back off, fellas, she's all mine.*

After she went outside, I waited five extra minutes just to piss her off. I knew that somewhere inside that layer of wife-insanity even she had to realize her anger was completely unreasonable. Like a psychiatrist, I was trying to get her to examine and confront her feelings. Or I was just being a dick.

When I got in the car, I said, "Sorry. I didn't mean to hold you up." I don't think Sarah could tell if I was being sarcastic, so to her credit, she didn't respond. I drove and Sarah sat in the passenger seat, scrolling through texts or e-mails or something on her iPhone. I would be more than happy to suffer through the entire ride in blessed silence, but Sarah feels like she has to make conversation at times like these, even though she is clearly more interested in what she's doing on her phone. I don't know if this is one of the many ways she completely misunderstands me and what I might want, or more likely, she doesn't care what I want but is trying to live up to some ideal in her mind of what happy couples do when they're alone in the car. She figures they ask each other about their day and, you know, talk to each other. I wouldn't know about any of that. I don't know any happy couples.

Tonight, for whatever reason, Sarah wanted to pretend to talk, so without looking up from her phone, she asked me, "What's going on in your life?"

I actually do think we're pretty happy, but I also think we should be secure enough in our happiness not to force conversations and pretend to be interested in each other's lives just because Sarah failed a relationship quiz in *Cosmo* this month. Plus, even if I had any small talk to offer, I needed to save it to fill in the awkward silences at the living hell of a cocktail party we were heading for.

But I'd been feeling a little depressed about my lack of a satisfying career. I even briefly went to a psychiatrist to sort through my feelings on the matter. The doctor didn't think I had a problem.

"Don't be so hard on yourself," he said. "Not everyone is cut out to be a worker bee or a grinder."

"Isn't that just an excuse for being lazy?" I asked.

"People are different," he said. "Not every personality variance is a problem to be fixed. We could give you drugs to make you a hard worker who would focus like crazy on a task. But then you wouldn't be you anymore. Would you want that?"

"No, but my wife would," I said. "I don't think she likes the original me anymore."

I'd never discussed this with Sarah, and the ten-minute car ride to the party was probably not the optimal time to bring it up, but for some reason I blurted out, "I feel like I'm in a rut."

Sarah murmured a "Hmmmm" and continued to thumb through her e-mails.

"Yeah, I'm thinking about a career change. I don't have a plan or anything, but—" I glanced over at Sarah and it was clear she was still scrolling and not listening, so I just stopped talking. She didn't notice and continued to utter listener feedback noises like "uh huh" and "yeah." After another minute or two, she must have realized I was no longer speaking and said "That…sounds… good…." as she was putting the finishing touches on what was no doubt an important text reminding her personal assistant to pick up her dry cleaning—except I pick up her dry cleaning.

Sarah doesn't alternate between talking and listening. She alternates between talking and waiting to talk again. She closed her phone and said, "Well, I had a great day. We had an early meeting on the blah blah blah…work-related bullshit…yada yada yada….” *So now that you're done with your work and will be paying attention, you'd like to talk? By all means, go ahead, honey, I'd love to hear about your day.*

I leaned across Sarah, pulled the passenger door handle and kicked her out the open door. She bounced once on the street and then went up over the curb and tumbled down a steep, rock-strewn incline, like when someone jumps off a moving train in a movie. That's what I wanted to do. What I really did was tune her out, which I accomplished by thinking about my current work life. I'm normally not one to bring my work home with me. Why would I? There's nothing to bring. I don't have enough work to fill my days, much less my nights. But now I was spending my evening worrying about work I didn't even have, suddenly concluding I was wasting my life like a walking midlife crisis cliché. It's too late, Bob. *I like to address myself by name in my internal monologues like people who chastise themselves verbally after a bad golf shot. Come on, Jim. Finish your swing!* That ship sailed about twenty years ago.

As we pulled into the parking lot, Sarah was finishing up her story. “…and it turns out, thank God, Sharon had a backup disk in her office.”

I helped her out of the car, kissed her on the cheek and said, “Well, I'm glad everything worked out. Now if we find out terrorists are holding everyone hostage inside and won't let anyone else in, it'll be a perfect day.”

I was feeling good, buzzed enough to survive the gauntlet of the “important” people in our fair city for the two minutes it would take me to make my way to the open bar. I had to be on my best behavior because my in-laws were the co-chairpersons or whatever they call it now when they insist on honoring a powerful man and his faithful wife as if they were equally responsible for giving millions of dollars to the cause. And maybe they are. These events would never happen without an aggressively charitable wife trying to justify her privileged existence.

I was in my custom-tailored tuxedo purchased for just such an occasion and Sarah was wearing a beaded gown and brand new high-heeled shoes that would make her feet bleed before her second drink. If she'd told me how much her ensemble cost, I probably would have divorced her on the spot.

My in-laws are "honored" as chairpersons at a lot of these events. This is a high society mechanism for extorting a huge donation from the "chair couple." If you say you'll be the honorary chairman of an event, there is an implied offer to give a "seed" donation. The organization in question can then say, when people ask how much they should give, "Well, the honorary chairs gave fifty thousand dollars." It's all a scam.

The breakdown is usually as follows: a young, societally inbred couple or two are named the event's co-chairpersons. They are responsible for actually doing a few things to get the event on solid ground. They may have to make a few fundraising visits, often to their place of employment or their father's law firm, or the like. Their wives will be responsible for stocking the silent auction with donated vacation homes and what women think passes for sports memorabilia. There will also be the Honorary Chairs, and these are always the heavy-hitter names, your Old Bulls and Silverbacks. They are really expected to do nothing in terms of tangible "work," but they are expected to cough up their Christmas card lists and make a sizeable donation to the cause.

Then there are the events that are true honoraria. These might be such things as So and So Charity's Woman of the Year, Hall of Fame honorees, and so forth. The person or persons being honored are always expected to make a giant donation to the group celebrating them. My in-laws have spent a fortune being celebrated as a power couple, giving both time and money, in our town. For several years, my wife and I dutifully trooped to event after event celebrating her father. Then after he had been feted by every conceivable organization, here came the next group of 501(c)(3)s who were primed and ready to celebrate the wonderful contributions of my mother-in-law. It truly takes a shitload of money to be honored for your selfless acts.

I hope one day to be the first nominee for one of these awards to say, "I'm sorry, I'd love to be your Man of the Year, but we just can't afford it."

◇◇◇

Sarah was stopped every ten feet as we made our way across the ballroom. We got ambushed by an attractive woman who engaged Sarah like they were old friends.

"Sarah! It's great to see you. I've missed our weekly meetings when we were on the Shymana Committee."

I may have the name of that committee wrong.

"I know, Karen! That was so fun! Have you met my husband, Bob? Bob, this is Karen Summers."

The woman stuck out a hand expensively manicured in one of the gothy dark colors that are popular now with the middle-aged.

It's always seemed to me it would be difficult to be taken seriously in business or government with painted finger- and toenails. All the men in their conservative blue suits and red power ties would think to themselves, *You're playing with the big boys now. My time is worth thousands of dollars an hour and this chick spends her time trying to decide whether or not to put a flower on her big toe.*

Karen eyed me mischievously. "So we finally meet. I've heard so much about this mysterious husband of Sarah's but I'd never even laid eyes on him. I was beginning to think Sarah made you up."

I'd heard this one before, the accusatory jab about how I never showed up to anything, so I had a ready reply, which I never used. *"Sarah keeps me locked in the basement and only lets me out for special occasions like sex and charity events. Unfortunately, mostly charity events."*

"They're really one and the same from my point of view," Sarah might have replied.

"Charity begins at home, honey," I'd have answered. We would all laugh.

Truthfully, I gave a fake chuckle, but it was the best I could do. An actual laugh at an event like this would be a rarity for me. Or any time, really. I'm not an easy laugher who makes everyone feel like they're engaged in hilarious banter at a cocktail party. I'm the guy you're never really sure is kidding—I almost always am—but you can't tell from the expression on my face. Many successful people are humorless and literal to a fault. As a rule they're not sure what I mean, so they move on to a new topic. Great. The last thing I want is some old society matron leaning in close to me and shouting over the noise, "I'm sorry. I don't understand." I'm not equipped with witty, pleasant small talk.

Back to Karen. I seldom hear the other person's name when I'm being introduced. I'm too busy searching my brain for something clever to say to register information about my verbal sparring partner.

Sarah turned to me and said, "Have you ever met Karen's husband, John?"

I gave my standard reply. "I'm sure I have." I *am* sure I have. He's the kind of guy I've most certainly met but don't remember, which would apply to the majority of the upper crust of this city.

Karen said, "You guys should get together. I'm sure you'd hit it off."

"Of course you're sure," I muttered under my breath. "You've known me all of ten seconds."

"She's right," Sarah said. "John's a lot of laughs. He's always telling jokes." Although I might gain some insight into the current level of racism in the Midwest, the thought of hanging around with a noted joke-teller makes me ill. Guys who tell jokes aren't funny. They memorize jokes because they've got no material of their own.

Karen said, "You guys should play golf. Do you play, Bob?"

Sarah jumped in and answered. If she thinks she knows the answer, she can't help but interrupt me. She's like the little girl in class everybody hates because she raises her hand for every goddamned question. If Sarah were married to Albert Einstein and someone asked him "So how's your theory of the universe coming?" she would answer for him. "He figured it out. It's e = m something." Remember, Einstein is standing right there.

"Bob loves golf. He plays every chance he gets. He'd love to play with John." I do not *love* golf. I play golf. I do not play every chance I get. I enjoy it, but a huge part of my pleasure is wrapped up in the group I'm playing with. I'm not one of those guys who's just happy to be playing, even with someone like John. Of my ten most enjoyable activities, my love for golf would rank about seventh. I would absolutely not love to play with John.

"I'll have John call you."

"Great. Or have him e-mail me." I much prefer to deal with people I'm trying to avoid by e-mail. It's a lot easier to craft the perfect turndown of their invitation in an e-mail than it is on the phone. I can slow the game down. There's no quick thinking required.

Karen moved off and we made our way through the crowd.

Once I'm seated at dinner, I can easily converse with my tablemates, no matter who they are, but I'm terrible at making casual "cocktail hour" conversation. I'm reasonably comfortable among people I know well and people I don't know at all. I'm most uncomfortable among people I should know but really don't or can't remember. Like everyone at tonight's party.

The best minglers are the confident types who don't hyperventilate upon entering the joint. They casually go from one person to the next, knowing all the names and conjuring up the perfect comment for each encounter. They remember a connector for each new person. Maybe it's something about their kids or their job or a charity thing they are working on, but whatever it is, it's GOOD.

The frustrating thing about all these events is they never change. As she always does, my wife continued to greet and converse with people with whom I was only vaguely familiar. I stood, dumbly, behind and beside her, reading the "program" for the auction items as though it contained the escape route out of this hellhole. We encountered a fat middle-aged woman in what looked like a low-cut, flowered housecoat but was probably a designer gown that cost five thousand dollars. She topped it all off with dyed red hair, the kind people used to think was sexy when they talked about dating a redhead.

Sarah said, "Sheila, have you met my husband?"

Sarah turned to me. "Bob, this is Sheila Banks. She got us those excellent tickets when we took the kids to *Wicked*." Then to Sheila, "Bob cried like a schoolgirl when he thought both witches were dead."

I gave Sarah the evil eye and stuck out my hand. "Pleased to meet you." When we're at these kinds of events, Sarah says or does things all night long that make me cringe, but criticizing her would be like a fan in the upper deck bitching about Peyton Manning.

I had no recollection of Sheila or the play. "The play was great, thanks!" By this point, I was actually sweating on the crown of my head. I could feel it start to pool and I feared a drip might cascade down my nose, causing someone to ask me if I was feeling all right. We moved on into the party, Sarah excited and talkative, me socially exhausted after ten minutes.

Reading from my scripted list of the first fifteen plays of the "game," number one is always straight for the bar. But it's a Catch-22. I need immediate cocktails to get through the evening, but the line at the bar is a horror of acquaintances who might challenge me on any number of topics that I'm totally unequipped to respond to. I managed to untangle myself from Sarah and Sheila, who had no doubt been having a fascinating conversation of which I had heard not one word. At this point I would've crawled through broken glass for a scotch and water.

The guy at the end of the line looked kind of familiar from behind, but then everyone at these events looks the same. Custom tuxedoes in basic black, hundred-dollar haircuts or completely shaved heads, expensive watches. I couldn't even pick myself out of a group photo. He turned around and stuck out his hand.

"How are you, sir?" he said. The "sir" is an obvious clue that he doesn't know my name either.

Who the hell was this guy? I went into the storage room in my brain to search through the various file cabinets and drawers of my mind. The place was filled with stacks of manila file folders, haphazardly torn-out sheets from yellow legal pads, and post-it notes. I tossed the room like a drug dealer looking for his stolen coke. Finally, it came to me. He was from the club. Mark or Brad or one of those names that doesn't fit once you get over a certain age. And he was definitely over it.

"Not bad," I said and shook his hand with my best approximation of a friendly smile. "Thought I'd find you near the bar." Har har. I always find it's best to act like whoever you're talking to is a real booze hound, especially when you really *are* always at the bar. It turns the focus back on them and includes them as one of the fun guys in a room full of stiffs.

I recalled I had been in Mark/Brad's foursome a couple of years ago in one of those club tournaments where you're paired up randomly with other members. I made about a fifty-foot putt on the last hole that allowed us to finish in the money. And by "in the money" I mean a twenty-five-dollar gift certificate to the pro shop, which might buy you a sleeve of Titleists or a pair of socks but certainly not both. It was also a scramble where everybody plays each shot from the same spot, so I'd already seen the putt three times. People hole tons of putts during scrambles. You have to shoot like ten under par to win one. And it was still just blind luck. Nevertheless, I was doomed from that day forward to discuss it with Brad/Mark every time I saw him for the rest of our lives, mostly because we had nothing else to say to each other.

I waited for it.

"That was some putt you made on eighteen the last time we played."

"Never up, never in," I said, which is a golfing phrase about not leaving putts short that gets a snicker whenever you say it because it sounds dirty. Mark/Brad responded with the appropriate chuckle and I knew we would eventually repeat this conversation verbatim every afternoon during bingo at the Shady

Acres Rest Home. By that time, it would rarely be up again for either of us, and almost certainly never in.

To change the subject from something to nothing, I asked, "What are you drinking?"

"Oh," he smiled, "Bud Light."

"Excellent. I'll buy."

"Thanks," he said with genuine gratitude and then realized it was an open bar. "I'll get you next time." This is what passes for banter for the modern American male. It's like someone in your office who likes to say "Let me buy you a cup of coffee" as he pours you a mug out of the community pot. It was lame, but when in Rome…

"How's the family?" I asked to fill the void. Before he answered, I saw my old buddy Lang swimming near the bar and made a lunge for him like he was the last helicopter out of Saigon. I pulled Lang into line as Brad/Mark swallowed his reply and turned to place his order. I now had a life preserver to stand next to in the bar line and I wasn't going to let him do the polite thing and get us into a tiresome three-way conversation.

"I've got a serious legal question for you," I said to Lang and then leaned in and whispered in a voice too low for anyone else to hear, "Just babble on about *res ipsa loquitur* and *habeas corpus* and shit until this guy gets his drink." Lang, an attorney, can filibuster with the best of them and before we knew it we were at the front of the line. I ordered two shots of tequila and two scotch and waters.

I turned to Lang. "You want anything?" He just laughed.

It's not exactly the Algonquin Round Table around here, but I do what I can. I didn't specify a brand because at a function like this they only offer one choice and it's always plenty good enough for me.

Lang and I threw back our shots and wandered off into the party with our drinks. The night began to hit its stride and became tolerable like all the others. Alcohol and a safety pal always get the job done.

◇◇◇

Dan Langham and I have been friends for over twenty years, since we met as incoming freshmen pledges in the Phi Fakea Namea fraternity house. Lang was one of those guys who would change his personality with every new fad. As a freshman, he was kind of a nerd at first, but when he came back for the second semester he was really into music. I think he had a couple of months where he was leading the fraternity Bible study (not a huge group) because he was dating a super-religious girl. For a while he was a granola-eating hippie/liberal, and now he makes Bill O'Reilly look like Sean Penn. We weren't really good friends, we just shared the bond of people who have been subjected to the same hazing rituals.

Then Lang graduated to his drinking stage. This was my one and only college stage, so fortunately when he finally decided to make the move, I was available to work closely with him. In pretty short order, he was a passable drinking companion. Not great—you wouldn't want it to be just you and him—but he helped fill out the group. Lang was what the baseball stats guys call replacement level. If you brought up the next guy in line from Triple A, he'd be about as good.

One of my guiding principles in life is that people don't fundamentally change, but Lang could do it. He had completely reinvented himself several times. I was impressed. Who wouldn't want to reinvent himself? I know I would.

Late in the evening, when the crowd was beginning to thin a little, Lang found me out on the balcony smoking a cigarette I had bummed from a waitress. In the old days there would have been twenty people out there. Tonight it was just me.

"You'll never guess who's here."

"You're right. I won't."

"Let me give you a hint. *Don't worry, that's a one-way window.*"

I almost spit out my drink. "Corny's here? And I've spent all night talking to upstanding citizens? What the hell is he doing here?"

"Let's go find out."

◇◇◇

Dave "Corny" Cornwallis was another fraternity brother. Most frat guys aren't really like the guys you see stealing the nerds' girlfriends in teen comedies, but Corny actually was. He was right out of central casting for Fraternity Asshole. He was the first guy I knew who did coke, who got into real fights, and who would gladly perform any sexual act in front of the whole house. One night Corny talked a girl into having sex in the laundry room in front of half the fraternity. He told her you could only see out the window, not in, and she believed him.

I followed Lang to a back bar that I hadn't known was there. How did I miss a whole bar? There was a group of three or four early-thirties *American Psycho* types surrounding a slightly older guy who had their rapt attention.

"And the woman says, *You're Thor? I'm tho thore I can hardly pith.*" Raucous laughter, drinks spilled, backs slapped, the whole nine yards. Corny joined in the laughter at his own joke. When he looked up, he spotted us and broke into a huge grin. "It's like a goddamn fraternity party in here! I'd give you losers the secret handshake if I could remember what it was."

Corny separated himself from the crowd and joined Lang and me leaning on a stand-up table. We swapped old stories for a while and at some point, Lang said, "You know, Bob, Corny's doing some business with Sarah's dad."

Corny was making big deals with *my* father-in-law? Shouldn't that be me? "Good for you, Corny. Who did you screw to get into that league?"

"That list is too long to enumerate, Bobby," Corny said. "But it's not what you know, it's who you know, and the people I know swim in the same waters as Sam."

"That doesn't explain how you get to swim with them. Why are you here tonight?"

"You gotta come down and kiss the ring before the business gets done." Corny looked at his watch. "Listen, Bobby, I've got to run. There's a cocktail waitress at my hotel with my name on her. But I'll be back in town in a couple weeks. Let's get together and I'll tell you all about it."

"Did you see Corny tonight?" I asked Sarah as we undressed for bed. I was out of my clothes like I was wearing a tear-away tuxedo. With a little help from me, Sarah managed to extricate herself from her gown, a job originally designed to be handled by a team of courtesans and ladies-in-waiting.

"No, but I heard he was there," she said. "I wasn't really looking for a reunion with him. Frankly, I'm kind of embarrassed you still like to hang around him. He's such an asshole."

"I wouldn't want to see him every day, but he's still a fun guy to run into. Hell, he told me he's working with your dad on something. He can't be *that* bad."

"What could Daddy possibly be doing with him? We need to tell him to back away from whatever Corny is selling."

"I don't want to screw Corny's deal up for him. Your father doesn't need any help from us. He knows what he's doing."

The telephone rang early the next morning. Sarah answered from bed in an I'm-doing-a-poor-job-of-masking-that-I-was-just-awakened-from-REM-sleep voice.

"Hi, Mom."

I pulled the pillow over my head so I couldn't hear what I assumed would be a recap of last night's activities, including analysis of my possibly inappropriate behavior. But there was none of that.

Sarah always has something to say, but she was eerily silent. Finally, she said."How did it happen?" and then listened some more. By now I was on full alert and I tried to catch her eye but it was like she was catatonic. A blank stare.

"I'll be right there." Sarah hung up the phone. She looked at me and said in a flat voice, "Daddy had a heart attack last night. Mom couldn't wake him up this morning. He's dead."

I held my arms out and she fell into me, her chest heaving with great sobs of anguish. Despite the fact I need her more than she needs me, my manly instinct to protect her kicked in and I felt helpless. All I could do was whisper "I am so sorry" over and over until the spasms finally subsided.

Chapter Four

A young death is tragic. An old death is just the cycle of life. Nature makes an elderly death tolerable because it's simply the order of things. The body deteriorates, the memory goes. There's even occasional joy in reminiscing over a life well-lived. But there's no joy at the death of a child or a young parent. A human being could hardly go on if every death was as devastating as the death of a young person close to you. Sam's death was in between.

Sarah should have been able to slowly say goodbye to her father as he gradually aged. Sam worked his ass off his whole life. He deserved to enjoy the fruits of his labors in retirement and die peacefully in his sleep. And his daughter deserved a "he lived a good long life" send-off for her father. Hell, Sam was still more active and productive than I am in my prime.

The next week was a blur. Sam's death wasn't only a loss for our family, but the entire community. Every would-be power broker in town, minor and major, wanted to be seen expressing their condolences personally. We had so many comfort dishes of lasagna and tuna casserole in the refrigerator, we had to start giving them away. We were exhausted. It was the first time I've ever looked forward to a funeral. I was hoping Sarah and her mother could finally get out of the public eye and grieve in peace once it was over.

It seemed like half the community told Sarah they were praying for her. Should you tell someone you're praying for them even if you're really not? I realize it's supposed to make the other person feel better. But what if they're counting on that prayer? Some people really do organize groups and apparently believe prayer's benefits are cumulative, the more the better, like maybe it needs to be loud enough for God to hear, or there's some minimum caring threshold that you have to hurdle before God will listen to your prayers. *What a pathetic effort, St. Peter. This guy could only get twenty-seven people to pray for his life? Let's give the miracle to someone else. If only a couple of those no-shows had come through…* That just makes no sense to me. Either God cares or He doesn't. It's not an *American Idol* vote. And in this case it was too late anyway. Sam was already dead.

It's not that I don't want to believe in something. It's that I don't understand how anyone does. Give me a sign, any sign. An oral history of a couple of "miracles" that happened two thousand years ago isn't going to cut it.

◇◇◇

Sam's funeral was held in an enormous church of some denomination or another. Presbyterian, maybe. You'd think I'd be familiar with this particular church because my wife and I got married here twenty years ago, but that memory is a haze for me.

I hadn't seen the minister much since my wedding. His name was Jonathon Wright. His most interesting feature was his utter blandness, which I think is the main requirement for the job. If you had a lot of passion for something, you would never be a minister. They're not like priests, who have so much heavenly zeal they're willing to remain celibate—at least the heterosexual non-pedophiles are. A vow of celibacy takes a real commitment to God. But a minister is just a guy. He's married. He has missionary sex once a week like everybody else. The church is just a job to him. He could just as easily have been a teacher or a middle manager in a big company.

Wright had wire-framed glasses a little too big for current fashion, and brown hair parted on the side, a little too long for my tastes, like a guy trying to look youthful so he could relate to "the kids," which he could not. He was too friendly in a mild and inoffensive way, the kind of person who won't leave you alone even though you have nothing to say to him. Frankly, Sam never liked him much and mentioned it every time his name came up. But there was no one else to handle a service of this magnitude.

The Rev was a little more animated than usual because this had to be a huge opportunity for him. Sam was a big deal in this town. The minister was like a D.A. who got a high-profile murder case or a local reporter who happened on the scene of a tragedy. He was going to milk this for all the publicity he could get. If people found out a bigwig like Sam went to church here, maybe some other high rollers who needed a few charitable write-offs would give it a try. The collection box doesn't fill itself every week.

Sarah's an only child, so for purposes of providing the minister something to say about a man he barely knew, the "family" was only the two of us and her mother. The three of us sat down on a couch in what I assumed was the nave, since most of my church knowledge comes from crossword puzzles. Sarah was between me and her mother. They were both holding tissues and sniffling, but not crying openly at the moment. Wright sat across from us and leaned forward.

"If there is anything any of us here at the church can do to help you at this difficult time, please don't hesitate to ask." We nodded and he continued. "Now if you don't mind, I'd like to ask you a few questions to help me prepare my remarks. Do you have any favorite stories about Sam? Did he have any hobbies he was particularly passionate about? Did he have some distinctive personality traits I should mention?"

I hate it when the minister pretends he had a relationship with the deceased by sprinkling a few specifics he learned from the family into his generic sermon. It's no different from a hack comedian who uses the same jokes in every city but changes the name in the punch line to the local mayor or sports team. Why fake it? Who cares if you didn't know him? You're not fooling anybody. Just admit it and give your best funeral speech. But I didn't say that. I didn't say anything. I wanted whatever Sam's wife and daughter wanted.

◇◇◇

As the service started, I left Sarah and her mother and went to the back of the church to meet up with the other pallbearers. It was a who's who of the titans of industry in our city. And me, the lucky son of a bitch who married the deceased's daughter. I was also the only one under seventy, so I was worried I might have to pretty much carry the damn thing all by myself. And this wasn't some cheap, easy-to-lift coffin. The funeral director recommended a solid mahogany model with a bunch of special features and assured us that Sarah's father would be comfortable. I wanted to say, *"You understand he's dead, right? He's not going to be living in there like* I Dream of Jeannie. *We're going to bury him in it underground."* This coffin was nicer than my car.

Fortunately someone realized that five old men and one middle-aged man in country club shape were not going to be able to carry a coffin the size of a school bus. The coffin was sitting on some kind of wheeled contraption and we were able to guide it down to the front of the church with no trouble. I shook the hands of the other pallbearers, who each gave me a look that said "Goodbye, family fortune." Or maybe the look said "I'm sorry for your loss." I couldn't tell. I sat down in the front row next to Sarah and the kids.

The church was packed with mourners. Everyone who was anyone in our city was at this funeral, plus all the people angling to become someone. They even set up several extra rooms where people could watch the proceedings on video monitors. There had to be at least a thousand people in the church and I heard many more were turned away.

Reverend Wright approached the podium and began to speak. "Our Lord, we come into your presence this day to mourn the passing of Samuel Bennett, grandfather, father, brother, and husband. We are also gathered here today to give thanks for the life of Samuel Bennett, whose time on earth was a blessing to us all. We have come to honor a life well-lived, a life that has touched many and served even more. We come to be comforted in our sorrow and pray that your spirit would cover us with peace that passes understanding. We know that just as you walked with Samuel throughout his entire life, you are walking with him now in his new home, his true heavenly home. We are here today to celebrate the passage that Samuel has made into the greater wholeness, the loving arms of God."

When I was a kid, a teenager who was a family friend killed himself over the Christmas holidays, the worst thing you could do to your parents unless you took a couple of siblings with you. But at the funeral, the minister suggested the deceased was happy now that he was spending Christmas with God. Excellent holiday message for the kids: suicide is the answer.

The minister gave way to Sam's oldest friend, Henry Miller, a golfing buddy and fellow pillar of our financial community. Miller was choking back the tears, but he was the kind of guy who could give an eloquent, off-the-cuff speech in his sleep, and he regaled the crowd with stories of Sam's generous spirit.

"Sam Bennett grew up poor, but he was raised to believe that if you worked hard enough and smart enough, you could achieve anything. And that's what he did. But he never forgot what it was like to be poor and he used all of his success to create for others the same kinds of opportunities he'd received. Sam's philanthropic efforts have raised literally tens of millions of dollars for…"

Sam truly was a great man. He started with nothing and look at all he accomplished. And I was born with the world at my feet and what have I ever done? How many lives have I touched? What would people say at my funeral?

Of course, when someone dies at my age, everyone always speculates about the reason. In my case, I'm sure they'd have a town meeting to discuss it. *Was he still smoking? He's always been overweight. Was it drugs? I'll bet it was drugs!*

Sam's passing isn't a murder investigation. We don't need to find the identity of the killer. Just extend sympathies to the family and shut the fuck up.

Obviously, Sam was of a previous generation, but I'd been attending a lot of funerals lately, including people my age or even younger. The older you get, the more you encounter death on an increasingly regular basis. Every year your group gets smaller. Eventually you're either going to be dead or the only one left.

Chapter Five

We had to go to Lang's office for the reading of the last will and testament, as they say. That's lawyers for you. Never say something once if you can say it twice. Never say "stop" if you can say "cease and desist." Never say "I give to my wife" when you can say "I hereby give, devise and bequeath to my surviving spouse."

Lang's father had handled all of Sam's legal work for over forty years. When Don Langham retired a few years ago, the firm divvied up Sam's business among the partners. Sam had gotten too big and the law had gotten too complex for any one lawyer to handle it all. Or at least any one lawyer of this generation. If you plopped a young Don Langham down in today's world, he could probably do it. But they don't make 'em like Don and Sam anymore.

Estate planning fell to Langham the Younger, which worked out nicely for all concerned. Lang was an expert in the field, and Sam only felt comfortable confiding his intimate personal business to friends of the family who had his complete trust. As far as I could tell, Sam had always been happy with the work Lang was doing for him. He clearly didn't treat the son with the same deference that he used with Langham the Elder, but it was as much respect as Sam gave to a "next generation," as he called us.

The law offices of Legal-sounding-names-I-made-up-so-you-couldn't-tell-what-firm-this-really-was and Langham are exactly what you'd expect. Expensive but understated. Mahogany every-where. The impression you got was *We know what we're doing and we're professional and discreet. In exchange, we charge you the same hourly rate as a high-class call girl.*

The receptionist, who could have been a high-class call girl herself, ushered us into a conference room with a large rectangular table and a bunch of expensive chairs around it. Again, the mahogany. The bookshelves in the room were filled with row after row of tan legal volumes with red and black bands that a Hollywood set designer would use to fill a lawyer's office. The classic "generic law book," purely for show in the modern computer age.

Of course the dinosaurs at this firm may actually be using those law books. Lawyers in old firms are slow to adopt the new customs. I worked in a firm right out of law school that still used typewriters and carbon paper. If you wanted to make a minor change to a fifty-page contract, your secretary had to type the whole damn thing over again or type additions in the margins and draw arrows to where they should go. Something you billed a client five thousand dollars for looked like a rough draft for a seventh grade term paper. The senior partners would dictate something, hand the cassette tape to their secretary, she (yes, it was always a she) would type it up (with carbons for extra copies), give it to him (almost always a him) to review, he would make changes on the hard copy with a pen (probably fountain), and give it back to her for re-typing. Repeat as necessary. The whole thing could take weeks. Or he could type it himself now on a computer in about five minutes.

The receptionist brought in a silver tray with coffee for us and we sat around the conference table to wait for Lang. Despite being with my wife and mother-in-law under the somber circumstances of the reading of the will of my deceased father-in-law, I couldn't help noticing she looked like a porn actress pretending to be a receptionist.

She left us alone with our thoughts. This was not a classic "reading of the will" setting. There was no extended family all gathered in a room gnashing their teeth and hoping to be remembered fondly by the dearly departed. And there would be no gasps in surprise when it turned out the entire fortune would go to his cat or the illegitimate son we didn't know about. I was pretty sure Sam's will would not specifically mention every greedy relative who had been sucking up to him in hopes of being rewarded with a bequest, only to then skewer them from the grave. *And to my niece, Gwendolyn, who showed so much interest in my collection of priceless sculptures, I bequeath a month's worth of pottery lessons at the local community college.* It would be fun if they did, but most people write their wills without putting much thought into the dramatic possibilities at the will reading.

So it was the three of us. I wouldn't even call it an official "reading of the will." Lang had just told us to meet with him so he could explain some things to us about Sam's estate.

After a few minutes, Lang came in carrying an accordion file. He was like a completely different guy when he was in lawyer mode. Pinstriped charcoal suit, maroon silk tie, gold cuff links. He even had his initials embroidered on the shirt cuff, an affectation I've never understood. *We know it's your shirt. You're currently wearing it. Are you worried you'll get it mixed up with another guy's shirt at the gym?* If you want to send the message that you're an arrogant prick, message received. But we were going to figure that out pretty quickly anyway.

Lang spoke in that careful, deliberate way lawyers talk, like he wanted to make sure the court reporter got every word down on paper, not his usual bantering style when hanging out with the guys. "First of all, let me express my deepest condolences personally, and on behalf of the firm, to the three of you on the tragic loss of Mr. Bennett. As I'm sure you are all aware, Sam was a client of this firm before I was even born and, more importantly, a great friend to me and my family. If there is anything I can do for you, please don't hesitate to ask."

He opened the folder and handed us each a document. At the top it read *Last Will and Testament of Samuel E. Bennett.* "The document before you is a copy of Sam's will. As you can see, there's not much to it. The will simply leaves everything he has to a trust that we created a number of years ago. Joan, you of course were involved throughout this process, so please forgive me if I explain something you already know, but I want to make certain we are all on the same page here."

"Of course, Daniel," Joan said. "My memory definitely needs refreshing. I signed the documents, but Sam handled everything. He didn't need any financial advice from me." She did not say *financial advice from poor little ole me*, but she might as well have. Joan downplayed her business expertise, but some of the charities she's been in charge of moved more money around than Fortune 500 companies. For people Joan's age, it was seen as unseemly for a woman to get her hands dirty in the business world. She was taught to give all the credit to her man, but pull as many strings as possible behind the scenes.

"Okay," Lang said. "When you die, your property is subject to an estate tax. Absent some careful tax planning, you're going to be giving most of the fruits of your labor to the government instead of passing it on to your loved ones, which is why you've been working so hard in the first place." *Or not, as the case may be.*

Lang continued. "The good news is you can transfer an unlimited amount of your assets to your surviving spouse upon your death, as well as an exemption amount to anyone else. So on the death of the first spouse we create two trusts, a marital trust for the benefit of the surviving spouse and a family trust for the benefit of the children, or in this case only child…"

I listened to Lang's spiel with one ear. He meandered through the mechanics of the trust document. "…the marital trust would be under the complete control of the surviving spouse…" yadda yadda yadda "the spouse would receive the income from the family trust…" this is why I don't practice law "…in the best interests of the beneficiaries."

Lang paused and looked us over for a second. "Is everyone following this? Bob, you must remember all this from Wills and Trusts class, right?"

"Right," I lied. "So Joan gets everything in the marital trust but only the income from the family trust, right?"

"That's right," he replied. "And when Joan dies, it all goes to

Sarah." Sarah glanced at me with a tear in her eye. The last thing she wanted to think about was her mother being gone as well.

"So," I said, continuing to show off my limited and out-of-date legal expertise, "are you the trustee, specifically, or did Sam just name the whole firm?" The latter was a typical thing to do in case your personal lawyer dies before you do (if only!).

"That's what I wanted to explain to you today," Lang said. "You see, Sam didn't name me or the firm trustee."

I knew that it's fairly common to name the surviving spouse herself as trustee. Joan could maintain control of her personal finances and Sam knew she would still rely on all of their advisors. "So did he name Joan?"

Lang was scanning our faces again. He looked like a guy with a story to tell who was afraid to tell it. He leaned forward. "No, Bob, Sam didn't name Joan as the trustee, either." He looked straight into my eyes for what seemed like an inappropriate length of time for a heterosexual man.

"He named you."

Both Sarah and her mother audibly gasped.

◇◇◇

"Why me?"

"Why not you? You're his son-in-law. He trusted you. You're a lawyer."

"I'm not a lawyer. I just went to law school. There's a difference."

"Okay. Let's just say you have a legal background. Why wouldn't he pick you?"

Because I know nothing about wills or trusts or business and now I'm in charge of Sam's entire fortune? Because I can barely get through my meager workday as it is?

"I don't know. He'd want an expert to handle it. Somebody with experience in these kinds of things."

"He wanted family, Bob. And you'll have the entire firm at your disposal. Maybe you don't know what you're doing, but we do."

It still made no sense. Was it possible a savvy businessman like Sam didn't know I was clueless? Am I that good at faking it? Sure, random acquaintances around town mostly bought my act, but Sam was the smartest person I'd ever met. He didn't make it from a small farm in the middle of the prairie to being the head of a multinational company by not being able to read people. I always assumed Sam saw through me. I figured he tolerated me because Sarah loved me and I was a good husband and father, but I never got the idea he respected me professionally. I used to tease Sarah about the fact that she, Sam, and Joan were all on the boards of directors of his various companies, but I was conspicuously absent. Since he apparently never considered me director material, it made no sense that he would heap this level of responsibility on me. Or did I need to revise my self-image a bit?

Sarah chimed in. "Dad wouldn't have picked you if he didn't think you could handle it. You have less confidence in yourself than other people have in you." *I know. That's because I know the real me. You might not be so confident if you spent a little time back here behind the curtain.*

"Okay," I said. "If that's what Sam wanted, I'm in. What do we need to do?"

Lang paused before he spoke. He had been glib and confident so far, but now he looked like the dog ate his homework. He cleared his throat. "There's actually another issue we need to discuss."

I raised my eyebrows at Joan and Sarah but they didn't seem to know what was going on. I looked back at Lang. "All right."

"It's important that you all understand the law so you can understand why we are where we are. I apologize in advance, Bob, for telling you things you already know."

"Pretend I didn't go to law school. Use layman's terms so the ladies can understand." I hardly remember anything from law school. I was always just smart enough to get a good grade without actually learning anything. I was an expert in the nonfunctional accumulation of knowledge. I screwed around the entire semester and then crammed for the final. I knew the material for the three hours of the test and not before or after. Law school for me was like those temporary Internet files your computer creates when you surf the web. You have to clean them out after a while or they start to gum up the works. I would empty my legal knowledge cache once the class was over.

The dirty little secret of higher education is that it's hard to flunk out of law school. Or college, for that matter. And the better the school, the harder it is to flunk out. Hell, everybody at Harvard has at least a B average. They figure if you're smart enough to get in, you must be above average. Lots of people do well in school without learning a thing.

Lang continued. "Remember how I said you can pass an unlimited amount of property to your spouse? You don't necessarily want to do that. You want to give as much as you can straight to the kids so it won't be taxed when the spouse dies. That's why we created two trusts. The marital trust is completely controlled by Joan to do with as she pleases. The family trust is set up to provide income to Joan during her life and then pass tax-free to Sarah. The family trust is funded with whatever the current exemption amount is at the time of death. The marital trust gets the rest. You with me so far?"

I didn't really remember any of this from law school, but I was paying close attention. What new issue could make Lang more nervous than telling the grieving widow that her son-in-law was going to be in charge of her dead husband's considerable estate? "I think we're with you. What's the exemption amount?"

"That's the funny part," Lang said, but you could tell he didn't think it was funny at all. There was a layer of sweat across his upper lip. "Under the..." he put on his reading glasses and looked down at the document on his desk as if it was crucial to get this information exactly right. The glasses probably had plain glass in them. I'll bet he just used them to look lawyerly... "Economic Growth and Tax Relief Reconciliation Act, the estate tax was repealed completely. In other words, this year there is no exemption amount. Any amount can be transferred to anyone tax-free."

I was all over this. I felt like one of the gunners who used to raise their hand and answer every professor's question back in law school. "So there's no exemption to worry about, and all of the money would go into the marital trust."

Lang winced a little and gritted his teeth, like he was about to receive a shot from his doctor or down a particularly nasty shot of whiskey. "That's what you might expect to happen, Bob, but it's actually the opposite. In any other year, the marital trust would get the vast majority of the assets, but this year…"

"Because there's no estate tax," I interrupted, "Sam's entire estate goes in the family trust."

"That is correct, Bob," Lang said. "So as trustee, you, not Joan, will be in charge of all of Sam's money."

"I don't understand," Joan said. "What's the difference? Everything's in a trust either way, right?"

Lang got lawyerly again. "In a basic sense, the two trusts are very similar. Joan is the beneficiary during her lifetime and Sarah is the beneficiary upon Joan's death. But as a practical matter, the trusts are very different for the beneficiary. In the marital trust, it's all essentially Joan's money to do with as she pleases. She could request that every penny be distributed immediately and that request would be granted."

"But you just told us none of the estate was going in that trust," I said. "Why are we talking about the trust provisions of an empty trust?"

"I want everyone to understand the thinking that went into this. If Sam had died in any other year, Joan would have complete access to the vast majority of the assets in the estate."

I was beginning to understand. "So, ironically, because Sam died in a year with no estate tax, Joan will have limited access to her own money in order to avoid paying estate tax."

"I don't know if it's 'ironic,' but the substance of what you said is correct." *Ironically, no one really knows what "ironic" means.*

"Maybe it's not ironic, but what are the odds of Sam dying right before his estate was essentially going to be cut in half by the government?"

"It's not that unusual," Lang said. "There are reports of sick and elderly people who essentially willed themselves to die before the end of the year so their families would get all of the money they accumulated."

"Or got smothered with a pillow by those families." It just popped out. I looked at Sarah and Joan. "But certainly not this family." I'm sure some greedy adult children tried to beat the end of the year deadline by tripping over mom's ventilator cord, but in our case it would have been absurd to think saving some taxes would be a net financial benefit to the family, compared to having Sam still in charge.

Lang jumped in quickly. "No one is suggesting anything like that. It was just a coincidence."

"Right," I said. "So we know everything we need to know about the trust that doesn't exist. What about the trust with all the money in it? How does that work?"

"In order to avoid paying estate tax on those assets at Joan's death," Lang said, "the family trust has to be set up with limited right to the funds for the beneficiary."

"How 'limited' are we talking about?" I asked.

"Joan will receive all of the income from the trust during her lifetime." Lang placed his "reading" glasses back on his nose. "She will also have the right to distributions of principal 'as the trustee, in its sole and absolute discretion, determines to be necessary or advisable for her support, maintenance, health, and education.'"

"That sounds reasonable," Joan said. "Support, maintenance, health, education. That's pretty much everything isn't it?"

There was an elephant in the room, but I wasn't going to point him out as long as he just sat there silently munching hay. Unfortunately, my wife is a pretty sharp cookie and spotted him herself. "It sounds reasonable, but that means you have to get the trustee's permission any time you want to spend any of your money and it's in the trustee's absolute discretion whether to give it to you or not."

Now Joan was the one looking ill. "So I'll need to get Bob's permission if I want to use the principal?"

"That's right," Lang said. "You'll need to request a distribution in writing and explain to Bob what it will be used for so he can determine if it's an acceptable expense under the rules of the trust. Certain recurring expenses can be set up to be paid automatically by the trust. For example, Sam's own trust paid for his heart medicine every month."

"Joan, you don't have to worry about a thing," I said. "I'm honored Sam would entrust me with such great responsibility and I'll do my best to honor his wishes, which would first and foremost be that you are taken care of in the manner you deserve. You tell me anything you need and I'll see that you get it. I'll be a rubber stamp."

"Thank you, Bob."

I truly would do my best to keep Joan happy because she's a good woman and that's what Sam would have wanted. But like a lot of husbands, I felt that my mother-in-law thought her daughter could do better. I confess I couldn't help fantasizing about her being forced to come to me on bended knee for even the barest necessities.

"I think your current car is just fine, Joan, but when your odometer hits two hundred thousand miles, I'd be happy to readdress the situation with you. Good day."

"But—"

"I said good day!"

◇◇◇

"So what's the next step?" I asked Lang.

"The next step is for us—and you, Bob—to get busy administering this trust. Give us a couple of days to get everything together. Why don't you come here to our offices Monday morning, let's say eight o'clock?"

"I certainly want to do my best to carry out Sam's wishes, but you do understand I've already got a full-time job, right?"

Lang knew perfectly well I didn't exactly grind out ten-hour workdays all week. I was always available to take his call or go to lunch or do anything else I wanted during the day. But at least he had sense enough not to let the cat out of the bag in front of my wife and mother-in-law. Maybe he wasn't a crappy lawyer after all. Sarah obviously knew on some level I wasn't all that busy at work, but we had kind of an unspoken understanding that she wouldn't say anything about it because it allowed me to handle a lot of the traditionally female household duties like grocery shopping and picking up the kids after school. If I really did work a traditional nine-to-five job where I had to show up and work all day, she wouldn't have been free to concentrate on all the Sarah stuff she likes to do. And as far as I knew, her mother thought when I was at work I was hard at work. I don't think she could even imagine anything else.

"Don't worry about it," Lang said. "It's going to be pretty busy at first, but in a month or two it'll settle down. Trustee of this trust is not a full-time job."

I knew that by my standards it was far more than a full-time job, but what could I say? "Well, I'll have to make sure we've got everything covered at my business. We may have to move some meetings around, that kind of thing—"

"Sam didn't think it would be a problem for you."

"Well, I'm glad he had confidence in me." *But he didn't know me like I do.*

Lang started to gather up his papers. "Oh, one more thing. Sam and I also discussed the trustee's compensation for the exercise of his duties. I suggested a significant salary because the trustee would be responsible for quite a large estate, the administration of which would occupy a good portion of his time."

"Really?" I asked. Old Lang finally coming through. "What's a trustee pull down these days?"

"It can be in the high six figures for an estate of this size."

"It can be but isn't, I take it."

"That's correct."

"How much?"

"Nothing," Lang said with what I read to be a phony pained expression on his face. He was secretly enjoying this part. "I'm sorry. The trust specifically states that the trustee will receive no pay. Sam thought you'd be insulted if he even offered it."

I told you no one knew the real me.

◇◇◇

"What's wrong?" Sarah asked me on the drive home from Lang's office.

"What do you mean? Nothing's wrong."

"You haven't said a word since we got in the car." Sarah thinks she can tell my mood by how I'm acting. She's usually way off base but that doesn't stop her.

"I'm just thinking," I said. "I'm quiet in the car all the time. You always have your nose buried in your laptop so you don't notice."

She gave me one of those *It's cute that he thinks I can't read him like a book* female looks and said, "What are you thinking about?"

"I don't know if I can do it."

"Does it bother you that you won't be getting paid?"

"Not really. I'd like to be fairly compensated for my services, but since I don't know what I'm doing, a salary of nothing seems about right. Plus I'll be overseeing an estate that eventually will go to you, so it's not like I don't have a vested interest in helping in any way I can."

"Then what's the problem?"

"I can't understand why your father would pick me as trustee."

"I told you," Sarah said. "Dad respected you more than you think."

"I think he respected me to a degree," I said. "But it still doesn't make sense. I'd think you'd see it more than anyone."

"What do you mean?"

"I'm not the one he's been grooming since birth to take over his business. I'm not the one with all the Ivy League degrees or the features in magazines about the top young executives in the country. I'm not the one Sam would have trusted to run everything in his absence. He clearly didn't want to bring me into the family business."

"That doesn't mean he didn't have confidence in you."

"Maybe he did," I said. "And I'd be an excellent choice compared to ninety-nine percent of the population. But what I don't understand is how I'm a better choice than his only child, who, in addition to being his own flesh and blood, is more qualified in every way. If Sam didn't want Joan or the law firm to control the trust, why didn't he appoint you?"

"At first I thought, 'Is it because I'm a woman?'"

I shook my head. "That's not it. Your father has never treated you like he expected anything less from you because you were a girl. He's raised you to be a titan. Some good old boys may treat you differently because you're female, but your dad sure as hell never did."

"I know. I rejected that idea pretty quickly. I think I finally figured it out while listening to Dan drone on about your duties and all the meetings you were going to have."

"Okay, what's the answer?"

"The trustee job is really just administrative. You're going to have a bunch of advisors to help you make every decision. A lot of what you'll be doing will be a waste of time. My father wants me to keep doing what I'm doing, which is running the business that allowed him to generate such a large estate in the first place."

Of course Sarah was right. She needed to remain in a position that actually required brains and effort and know-how. I would handle the administrative bullshit so that Sarah could do the real work. Although it was a slight blow to my ego, it just confirmed what I already knew to be Sam's opinion of me. The idea that anyone would consider me the equal of his daughter would have been laughable to him.

"I guess that makes sense," I said. "I'm the best man for the job when you really don't want your best man on the job."

Chapter Six

This trustee gig was plainly going to be the hardest work I'd ever done. Admittedly, it wasn't work as a lumberjack knows it, or a farmer, or anyone else who physically *labors* in his job. But for a guy who has made his bones in the workaday world by *not* working, or really doing much of anything, this was going to be a real comeuppance.

It was only the first workday following our conference with Lang, but it felt like I'd been at it for months. The mere prospect of all those meetings was hanging over my head like a black cloud.

While spending the weekend worrying, I'd called Lang four different times at home. Generally, he's a lot more helpful out of his Brooks Brothers gear and I usually don't get billed. But the main things he kept emphasizing were "don't panic" and "don't fuck it up." With that sound legal framework under my belt, what could possibly go wrong?

Although I live in constant fear of them, business and/or social disasters rarely actually happen to me. Apparently from the outside looking in, I come off as a cool, competent professional. People assume I know what I'm doing and I've learned if I don't say too much, they'll keep thinking it. Fortunately for me, it takes a lot to move a person off his initial impression. From the outside, it may look like I'm listening to elevator music or cool jazz, but inside I'm hearing, *Incoming!* and *I can't find my legs!*

Lang was actually very helpful in setting up a couple of the key meetings for me already. In the morning I met with Sam's accountants. They assured me they would continue as they had been, except their quarterly reports would go to me instead of Sam. Maybe this wouldn't be so bad after all. A work group made up of me and two other people who not only know what they're doing but also do all the work? That's page one of my playbook.

My second meeting on Monday was with a guy named James ("Don't call me Jim!") Madison, another lawyer at Lang's firm. Someone faxed over a letter from Madison introducing himself and laying out how things were going to work. At the bottom it said *Dictated but not read,* which translated into non-legalese meant: *I'm so busy I don't even have time to read the letters I send and if there's anything in there you don't like, it's my secretary's fault.* I hadn't even met this guy and I already hated him.

From the letter—*Read but not fully comprehended*—I understood that Madison was to be my Sherpa as I scaled Trust Mountain. Without his expert guidance, I'd never make it to the top and would most likely freeze to death. I had no reason to doubt his trust-administering skill, but what was up with the James Madison thing? If you insist on being called James, you're probably an asshole no matter what your last name is, but to gravy train off one of America's founding fathers? I'll bet he was called Jimmy or something growing up but went to James when he became a lawyer. Well, I'm not calling him James Madison unless there's an original copy of the Federalist Papers on his desk.

Anyway, I was finished with the accountants by ten a.m. and I had to be downtown at the law office of Mr. Madison at two-thirty p.m., which gave me plenty of time to get my work done at the office before my second job began.

I went into my office and stared into my computer screen for the next hour, just like a regular workday. I still had a lot of time to kill before the meeting, so I caught up on the latest cultural headlines, news blogs, and sports analysis. You really need the discipline to do it every day or you get hopelessly behind. I couldn't quite enjoy my usual mindless morning activities, however, because my thoughts continually returned to Sam's death. I already missed him. He thought his daughter—my wife—could have done a lot better in the husband department, but he learned over time that she also could have done a lot worse. We had come to an unspoken truce over the last decade or so. He realized I was never going to ascend to the throne of "city father" as he had done so many years ago, and I realized he was never going to completely buy my act. It bothered him to think about our city and what would happen when the puppet masters all died off and the idiot politicians were set free to make important decisions on their own, but he could tell I wasn't the man for the job. He hoped Sarah was the woman for it.

But he also realized I was an excellent father, if not provider, to his grandchildren, whom he loved dearly. Over the years we had become friends. Not great friends, not drinking buddies—Sam didn't drink—but friends nonetheless. As only a father can, he understood the unique difficulties of being married to his daughter. He was always living a similar version of the same insanity over at his house, so we were able to bond over common ground.

Sam was always in control. He had the discipline of a monk. He exercised and ate right. I'm sure it annoyed him that his daughter would marry a man who was his opposite, but girls often do, and not necessarily to punish their fathers. In a way it's a compliment. They know they can never find Daddy's equal, so they go in a completely different direction.

I couldn't wrap my head around the idea that Sam was really dead. If he'd lived the life he did and still died younger than he should have, what chance did I have? I might as well start saying my goodbyes now because the likelihood of my seeing sixty seemed out of the question.

I grabbed a quick lunch and headed downtown to meet Madison. I don't mean to suggest I don't care about lunch. I'm not one of those masters of the universe who's so busy he only has time to grab a quick bite to eat every day between meetings. My pre-trustee workdays often revolved completely around lunch. An early lunch would make it pointless to get started on anything in the morning, and a late lunch would make it impossible to take on a new task in the afternoon before it was time to pick up the kids. A well-scheduled lunch could pretty effectively kill a whole day.

I once again entered the law offices of Whatever-the-hell-I-called-it and Langham. I'm not ashamed to admit I was looking forward to seeing the hot receptionist again. I was now in charge of a multi-multi-million-dollar estate being administered by the firm. Like Richard Gere at the dress shop in *Pretty Woman*, I figured I was going to need some major sucking up.

She was sitting at one of those high receptionist's areas that's more like a bar than a desk. So I treated it like one and leaned against it and said "Hello again" in what I thought was a friendly, if not flirty, manner.

She looked up and smiled back at me. "Hello. What can I do for you today?"

"Today, I'm seeing James Madison to go over some of these trust matters. It's good to see that he managed to get work after he left the presidency."

She giggled. If she hadn't had to answer the phones, she probably would have loved to meet me at a downtown hotel. "Your name, sir?" *Or maybe not.*

"Patterson? I was here Friday meeting with Dan Langham?"

She looked up in the universal sign of "I'm searching my brain," especially popular among attractive women because it makes their eyes look even bigger. "Doesn't ring a bell."

"You served coffee to my wife, mother-in-law, and me in the conference room."

"Oh, right. Mr. Bennett's daughter. I'm sorry, I guess I didn't see you. But I love your wife. She's a real role model for women in business."

I'm sure she is. I'll ask her if she has any tips for women in the receptionist business, like how to paint your nails with a telephone cradled on your shoulder. If this is the kind of sucking up I'm going to receive, maybe I should take my business to another boutique. "Could you tell Mr. Madison I'm here?"

◇◇◇

Madison made me wait in the conference room for the same reason he calls himself James Madison. And the same reason he was wearing a bow tie. He had the classic "look at me" personality. He probably had a 1936 Packard in the parking lot that he drove while wearing a scarf and goggles. Why can't he like whatever he likes without making sure the rest of us know about it?

Madison's hair was blond and thinning. A little too long for a lawyer, but just right for a quirky one. He looked like Philip Seymour Hoffman when he was playing a total prick.

It was a different conference room this time. The other one was for impressing important clients like Sarah and her mother. This one was for work. There was one of those white cardboard file boxes on the table.

He stuck out his hand. "Bob, James Madison." It was damp, as I knew it would be. "I'm the lawyer in this firm who handles the administration of large trust estates. It's basically all I do and I'm very good at it."

"That raises the obvious question," I said. "What do you need me for?"

We sat down and he continued. "True, I could handle everything myself, but one, you'd be violating your fiduciary duty as trustee if you failed to oversee the administration of the trust, and two, these are decisions that Mr. Bennett specifically wanted you to make. If he wanted me to make the decisions, he would have named the firm as trustee. But he didn't. He named you."

"Okay," I shrugged. "Where do we start?"

He gestured at the box on the table. "We need to go over all these files so you can familiarize yourself with Mr. Bennett's business interests." That didn't sound too bad. I could probably stand a week or two of dealing with him.

The door opened and a man came in pushing a dolly with five more white file boxes on it. "Where do you want these, Mr. Madison?"

"Just stack them in the corner."

"Okay. It's going to take me three or four trips to get the rest."

◇◇◇

I didn't get out of Madison's office the rest of the day. I smelled the unusual aroma of cooking food when I walked into the house at eight. Sarah was in the kitchen wearing an apron over a dress and pearls.

"Excuse me, Mrs. Cleaver," I said. "Is the Beaver home?"

"If you play your cards right, he might be," Sarah said. "I knew you'd probably be working late, so I thought I'd prepare you a home-cooked meal. The martini shaker is on the counter."

I poured myself a drink. "Home-cooked?"

"Well, home-heated. Costco lasagna. It's like regular lasagna except it serves forty-eight."

I came up behind her at the sink, put my arms around her, and kissed her neck. "It smells great. Where are the kids?"

"They already ate. They're doing their homework in their rooms and getting ready for bed."

"Are you sure this isn't the Cleavers'?"

"This is the performance you get when I'm in charge for the evening."

She was right. In every aspect of her life, Sarah gets shit done. I'm sure she'd turn into Martha Stewart if she ran the household on a daily basis. I finished my martini and poured another. That's the thing about martinis. You can drain that tiny little glass in one gulp and the entire shaker in about ten minutes.

We sat down to dinner, just the two of us. I took a bite of lasagna. Delicious. "This lasagna really is as good as any other lasagna. Why does anyone make their own food from scratch?"

"If they bought pre-made food, what would all the stay-at-home moms and housewives do with themselves all day?"

"I don't know," I said. "Screw the pool boy?"

Sarah's face lit up with excitement. "Can we get a pool boy? Or at least a pool?"

"I don't think people use pool boys anymore except in porno movies. Times are tough for lonely housewives."

Sarah sighed theatrically. "It wouldn't matter to me anyway

because I'm not one of those women with nothing to do. My day is already pretty full. Speaking of full days, how'd yours go?"

"It started off pretty well. I got some work done at my office in the morning." As much as I ever do anyway. "Then I met with the accountants and that's going to run smoothly, I think."

"Dad's accountants won't waste your time with a bunch of bullshit," Sarah said. "They'll just handle it."

"That's what I wanted to hear," I said. "The rest of it's not going to be so easy."

"What do you mean?"

"I met with James Madison for five hours today."

"Working on some rewrites to the Constitution?"

"I wish," I said. "I'd get this country straightened out. But unfortunately, it's a different James Madison."

"What kind of parents would name a child James Madison and what kind of asshole would *call* himself that?"

"Exactly the kind of asshole I have to spend at least the next month working with."

"A month? Are you kidding?"

"No, I'm not kidding," I said. "With everything going into the trust, I have to familiarize myself with Sam's business interests. I'll bet even you don't know about all of them."

"I'm sure I don't," Sarah said. "I only work for corporate. I don't have anything to do with the holding company. Dad was involved in a ton of deals I know nothing about."

"Well, there's an entire room full of files," I said. "I'll be spending more time with Mr. Madison than his wife Dolly."

"Is that really her name?"

"I wouldn't be surprised."

Sarah came around the table and put her arms around my neck. "Poor Ward Cleaver, working two jobs so that his beautiful wife can stay home with the kids."

"The trustee job doesn't actually pay anything."

"Still, I'm proud of you, Ward." Sarah used her best Barbara Billingsley voice. "Put on your cardigan sweater and slippers and come back into the bedroom and tell me all about it."

Chapter Seven

Despite the weeks of tedious trustee drudgery looming ahead of me, I woke up the next morning in a good mood, no doubt caused by the rare weeknight sex I'd experienced the night before. Who knew being one of those work-focused guys too busy to help out with his family would get me laid? If I'd realized that fact years ago, I'd probably be a titan of industry by now. But despite her brief little housewife fantasy, Sarah is no more suited to a life of taking care of home and hearth than I am to a life of boardrooms and power ties. This was a one-time turn-on for her. Women are "in the mood" for their own indecipherable reasons. You can't explain it and neither can they. You take what you can get, and last night I got some, so I was happy.

I got to Madison's office at eight a.m. sharp. Yesterday we had laid out a tentative plan that included more appointments and meetings over the next few weeks than I'd had in my entire life up to that point. I don't have a secretary who fills in every available time slot in my calendar because my days are so fucking full. Not only am I not that much in demand, I'm physically incapable of doing it. I could never meet with and talk to different people all day long. There is admittedly very little actual preparation *for* the meeting, but there is a lot of time spent *dreading* the meeting, hoping the meeting will be postponed, and thinking of reasons to cancel or reschedule the meeting myself. Afterward, I feel a tremendous sense of relief, like when your plane lands after a bumpy flight or you reach the end of a Catholic wedding: *Thank God that's over!*

The receptionist was already seated at her throne, but all the joy had gone out of our relationship, so I pointed down the hall toward the conference room and started walking. "Sir!" She shouted. "Sir!! You can't go back there!"

I had clearly made quite an impression on her. I stopped and turned so she could see my face. "Remember me?" I looked at my watch. "From, let's see, about fourteen hours ago? I'm using Madison's conference room."

"Oh, right. Mrs. Bennett's husband."

"Her name is Mrs. Patterson. I know it's hard to believe, but she actually took my name when we got married, instead of the other way around."

"Oh, sorry. I assumed she went by Bennett." *Who wouldn't?*

Madison was waiting for me in the conference room this time. We had meetings scheduled, so he didn't have time to be an asshole. "The first couple of days are meetings with the various charitable organizations with which Sam was involved. They're understandably nervous about the effect Sam's death might have on the continued beneficence of the Bennett Foundation toward their particular causes."

"Beneficence?" I asked. "Could you try to use simple English? You don't need to impress me. You've already got the job."

Madison smiled thinly, although his face remained fat. "Generosity, then."

"That's better," I said. "These people don't have anything to worry about. I'm not going to stroll in here and kick Sam's pet projects to the curb."

"They just want to be reassured. And they want a chance to show you all the good work they do and will continue to do with your support."

"So we're talking about two full days of listening to pitches from charities."

"Pretty much, yes."

"Maybe you could have a beggar accost me out front so I don't get rusty over lunch."

His smile was so thin it might have been a grimace. "We do not allow street people to loiter in front of the building." He was hiding it well, but I could tell he was warming up to me.

Suffice it to say that a pitch is a pitch is a pitch. Most organizations brought their leader and a community bigwig that sits on their board. The community types either knew me or didn't, but all saw this exercise as demeaning somehow. I'm sure I'd have felt the same way, going to solicit some son-in-law for a contribution you had already secured with the real man of the family, only to have him up and die on you. Bad break!

The droning voices in all unnecessary meetings blend into one for me, but it was literally true in this case: They were all saying the same thing. Each team of charitable solicitors could have picked a name out of a hat right before our meeting to learn what organization they'd be pitching for and there would have been no difference. The Boy Scouts guy might have had to pitch for the Special Olympics. The home for wayward girls would have had to convince me of the worth of the local crime stoppers organization. The end result would have been the same but it might have spiced things up for me.

I sat in that conference room for twenty hours over two days and had to endure the spiel of every kind of philanthropist, solicitor, bleeding heart, flimflammer, benefactor, charlatan, Good Samaritan, fairy godmother, and snake oil salesman you could imagine. They all had one thing in common: They wanted to preserve the gravy train that was paying them an exorbitant salary to suck up to people like me and justify it in their hearts as an altruistic act because they work for a 501(c). I wanted to tell every fucking one of them I'd double whatever Sam had been giving to the organization if they'd cut their own salary in half.

I know how these charitable organizations work. I know how inefficiently they use their money, partly due to the lack of effective oversight by boards of directors filled with people like me. Of course, unlike these professional money solicitors, I wasn't being paid a handsome salary to screw up your charitable donation. These guys had made a career out of it, but they were all members of that group of charity-mongers who are so busy patting themselves on the back for all their good works that they don't notice that what they're doing isn't really helping. It's a constant atmosphere of "aren't we superior to other people?" Their charitable efforts aren't about the particular disease du jour or protected class of the month. It's all about *them*. They don't really care about the genocide in Rwanda—they care about *caring*. It doesn't matter if their new Prius has no effect on the environment; the only thing that matters is it makes them feel good about themselves. It doesn't even matter if they neglect or treat their own families like shit in pursuit of their causes, because they're *good people, dammit*, and they prove it with all the charitable work they do. As long as they can look in the mirror and see a "good" person staring back, they're happy. Actually improving the world or helping people? Not really relevant.

While I listened, I couldn't help but think of the *Seinfeld* episode where Jerry butted into the life of a Pakistani restaurant owner named Babu in order to "help" him. Jerry patronizingly recommended that Babu make his restaurant into an authentic Pakistani restaurant. It turns out that's not the kind of restaurant New Yorkers want. It is, however, the kind of restaurant a do-gooder would want New Yorkers to want. Of course, Jerry's "help" eventually destroyed Babu's business, not to mention it was pretty condescending and possibly racist for Jerry to assume he knew more about the restaurant business than Babu did. But all in all, it was a successful do-gooder experience because it made Jerry feel better about himself. The rest is only background noise.

In the end, I just sat there. I didn't want to argue with these people about the merits of their particular organization or cause. I had no intention of changing anything Sam cared about. I felt like my job was to do what he would want, whatever that may be. I adopted my "seriously listening, though rarely making eye contact" face. I also added my "appearing to be taking notes on my laptop with the occasional head nod." Basically, I feigned interest in whatever they were saying.

When I got home Wednesday night, I was as exhausted as my wife always is. I was even reconsidering whether she in fact was legitimately tired all the time from hard work instead of my previous theory that she was a raving bitch.

Sarah was cooking dinner when I came into the kitchen and kissed her on the cheek, normal for everyone else but a role reversal for us. The difference is I didn't complain about my hectic day or how tired I was like she would have. Not because I'm a better person than she is. I wanted to bitch about it, but I didn't want her to think actually working all day was a new thing for me. Plus, did this even count as "working" or just enduring something incredibly boring? People frequently confuse these concepts.

"How was your day, honey?" Sarah asked.

"Fine," I said. "I learned a lot about the amazing work people are doing in the community."

"I'm sure you're doing a great job. Daddy always knew what he was doing."

If Sam's plan was to torture me from beyond the grave, then he knew exactly what he was doing. It was the worst kind of day for someone like me, an unusual combination of moments of nervous tension caused by having to make small talk with these people, followed by the mind-numbing boredom of listening to their rehearsed pleas for money. It was similar to attending one of their crappy benefits, only if it lasted twenty hours and there was no booze.

The rest of the week was a blur, a steady parade of introductions and updates for each of Sam's business interests. I don't know how he could have possibly kept track of it all, but Madison assured me that Sam was no passive investor. He was involved in everything. I didn't have the passion or the intellectual capacity for it, but I was starting to realize how a hard-working person gets through the day. If you're that busy, there's no time for your mind to wander and think about what you'd rather be doing.

Because you never stop, the day actually flies by. The totality of the experience isn't awful because you have no time to think. At the end of the day, you're beat. I don't know how Sarah does that all day and then works on her laptop at night. Some people aren't happy when they're not doing something, I guess. I'm not one of those people. I love doing nothing. Nothing is my favorite thing to do.

Nobody told me to, but I'd even started wearing a suit every day. My office was business casual at best, but Sam always wore a suit and I knew he would have appreciated my effort to be professional. Personally, I hate to wear a suit, and the stupidest part is the tie. Who the hell thought it would be a good idea to cinch a colorful noose against your throat right before you go to work? I always feel like I'm being strangled. A tie is just a leftover vestige from an earlier age that now serves no purpose. In the old days, silk came from halfway around the world and it was important to show people you were a man of means and worthy of respect. Apparently this is still true in the 'hood, based on the dollar-sign necklaces the rappers wear, but for the rest of us there's no point. Billionaires wear tee-shirts now. There's a theory that a tie is really just a colorful arrow pointing at your crotch. A power tie says "My dick is bigger than yours." The tie may say it's bigger, but the Porsche parked outside says it's smaller, so let's just call it a wash.

On Friday I met Joan for lunch at one of those places that prides itself on being a bistro and not a restaurant, meaning, in my experience, it would be full of women eating salads. I got delayed by a guy who didn't realize you're supposed to leave immediately once the meeting is over. I finally walked out while he was still talking. Joan was already seated when I arrived at the restaurant.

"Well, don't you look nice?" Joan said as I sat down across from her. "I didn't know we were dressing for lunch." She gestured at her light blue pantsuit, which was casual for her but would be appropriate for most mothers of the bride. Well, maybe grandmothers of the bride.

"We're not," I said. "I'm trying to project a professional air when I'm representing Sam's estate as trustee."

"You're doing a fine job." Joan smiled. "If I didn't know any better, I'd think you were one of those high-priced lawyers who bill us hundreds of dollars for every e-mail and phone call."

"I'm working with those people all day. Speaking of which, feel free to order the lobster. This meal is on the Trust!"

Joan's eyes twinkled mischievously. "You mean I won't need to make a written request for a distribution?"

I laughed. Joan had always had a sly sense of humor underneath her grande dame persona. "Not this time. But seriously, it must be galling to have to ask someone like me for access to your own money."

"Someone like you?" Joan asked.

"You know, someone who's never really achieved anything."

"Now, Bob, that's not true," Joan said. "You have a business and a beautiful family."

"I know. But what I do is such small-change compared to Sam and Sarah."

"That's the way it has to work, Bob. You can't have two Type-A career-oriented spouses and raise a proper family. One of you has to sacrifice."

"I don't consider it a sacrifice." I thought I was just lazy.

"But it is. Who knows what you could have accomplished if you'd put all your energies into your career? You know, I was going to go to law school before I met Sam. Maybe right now I'd be Ruth Bader Ginsberg. But I did what was best for the family." She reached out and put her hand over mine. "Just like you do."

"Thanks for saying that, Joan, but I've always had the feeling you and Sam felt like Sarah could have done better."

"Are you kidding?" Joan widened her eyes in amazement. "We hated those Ivy League investment banker jerks she used to bring home, always sucking up to Sam. To you, we were your girlfriend's parents, not some potential shortcut to the top of the business world. The only thing you wanted from us was Sarah."

"You don't wish I was more ambitious?"

"We love you *because* you're focused on Sarah and your family, not in spite of it. Sam talks about it all the time." Joan's voice cracked and her eyes welled up. "Look at me, still referring to him in the present tense."

"I still do it, too." It got a little dusty on my side of the table too, but as a man I was obligated to block any actual drops of liquid from leaking from my tear ducts. "Maybe it will never stop. He was such a big presence in our lives, it will always feel like he's here." I squeezed her hand.

"I hope so." Joan squeezed back. "But in any event you and I will have a chance to spend more time together. So let's not make this a business lunch. For my first official disbursement request, I would like to order a bottle of Chardonnay."

"Although clearly a conflict of interest because the trustee will benefit personally from the disbursement, request granted."

Chapter Eight

On Monday morning, I walked right by the hot receptionist without so much as a glance. I wasn't going to give her a chance to snub me. I sat down in the conference room next to Madison.

"What's on for today?"

"As you would know if you read the detailed schedule I provided you on Friday, this week we're going to be meeting with people from the VC side of Sam's business."

"Look, I don't care what Sam did during the Vietnam War, but I think it would be inappropriate to have any business dealings with the Viet Cong."

Madison had stopped even favoring me with his fake smile. He sighed. "VC stands for venture capital. Sam invested money from Bennett Capital into various ventures he took an interest in. Hence the term 'venture capital.'"

"I get it. It was a joke, Madison."

"Sometimes it's hard to tell with you, Mr. Patterson."

I guess I have what you might call a dry sense of humor and sometimes the message doesn't come across. A few months ago, Emily had a particularly good soccer game, meaning she actually tried to kick the ball instead of politely allowing the other girls to take it from her. After the game was over and we'd had post-game snacks and the kids had run through a human tunnel of cheering parents, we got in the car. "Great game, honey!"

"Are you being sarcastic?" Emily asked.

"No, of course, not. Why would you think that?"

"It sounded like you didn't really mean it."

My own daughter thought I might be mocking her in a post-game pep talk.

I have the same problem with e-mail. I wish there were a sincerity font I could use for condolence letters and "congratulations on the new baby" e-mails and the like. I'd hate to have someone think I wasn't really sorry their mother died.

"So what's the purpose of these meetings?" I asked Madison.

"Well, each one is different. If we've already invested, it's more of a 'meet and greet' so you can familiarize yourself with the players and learn about the business. If we haven't invested, it's a pitch. They'll be trying to convince us—well, you—that they have an opportunity too good to pass up."

"So this is the for-profit version of last week."

"I wouldn't say that," Madison said. "If you make a philanthropic mistake, it may not be the optimal use of your funds, but the money is still theoretically going to a good cause. But if you make an investment mistake, it could cost the company millions of dollars. That's why I gave you that stack of prospectuses to review over the weekend."

"Right. I've got them with me." Still safely tucked away in my lawyer's briefcase, which prior to this trustee gig contained only magazines and snacks. I hadn't gotten around to reading the prospectuses.

Throughout the morning, we were treated to a bunch of presentations showing us what great investments we had made in the various ventures. If things were going well, we got Power-Points with graphs showing spectacular sales increases. If things weren't going so well, we got PowerPoints with graphs showing spectacular *future* sales increases. In each case, I wasn't required to do anything. They were really saying, "Leave us alone. Everything's fine. You'll get your return on investment."

And they were in luck. I was just the guy to leave them alone. I turned down Madison's obligatory invitation to go to lunch. We were spending too much time together as it was. I didn't want to eat with the man any more than he wanted to eat with me. Plus, it was the only time I had to myself anymore.

I grabbed some unhealthy food at a diner down the street. It was nothing special but delicious. Everything tasted sweeter when away from Madison, as if I were an ex-con appreciating everything more after getting out of prison. When I got back from lunch, Madison was already at the table going over one of the prospectuses I hadn't read.

"Who's next?"

"This one's a little different, Bob." After all this time together, we'd moved on to Bob. I still refused to call him James. "The company is called Sanitol Solutions. As I'm sure you recall from the prospectus, they're looking for a major cash investment. It would represent by far the biggest outlay in our portfolio but the projections seem almost too good to be true."

"Right," I said. "And they…make, uh…build…sell…"

"They make a sanitizing system they claim can clean anything," Madison said. "You *did* read the prospectuses."

"I read them. I didn't memorize them. What's the difference? They're all the same. Every prospectus is ninety percent disclaimers about how you shouldn't believe anything they say."

"The disclaimers are merely legal protection—"

"I don't care," I interrupted. "Let's just bring them in. They're going to tell us everything again anyway."

The receptionist ushered in three men in expensive, well-tailored suits. They had cuff links and monogrammed shirts and their ties weren't clip-ons, all signs pointing to men of wealth and substance. I was glad I had suited up for the meeting.

A sandy-haired man in his fifties stepped forward. He was dressed well but was otherwise nondescript. He could easily have been a dentist or an insurance salesman, except he exuded a slimy quality. He was the kind of guy you might find with his arms around your wife, showing her how to swing a golf club or shoot pool. I stuck out my hand.

"Bob Patterson. Good to see you." For all I knew, I could have met him somewhere before.

"Pleased to meet you, Bob. Tom Swanson, Sanitol Solutions. And these gentlemen are from the New York investment firm that's helping us raise financing."

"And this is James Madison." I waved my hand toward Madison like I was a model on *The Price is Right* and he was the world's worst showcase. "He loves jokes about his name." Everyone chuckled except Madison, who never learned how to laugh as a child. We all shook hands and sat down around the conference table.

Swanson spoke first. "Before we start, I want to express my condolences for the loss of your father-in-law. He was a great man. We were really looking forward to working with him on this project."

"Oh, did you already meet with Sam about this?"

Swanson smiled. "Yes, several times. He had a lot of ideas and was very excited about our process. We were going to finalize the deal after the first of the year, but then...you know."

"Well, if Sam was interested, it must be good. Let's hear about this process."

Swanson smiled at me and made too much eye contact for my tastes. Fortunately, he pushed a button on his laptop to start the PowerPoint presentation, which gave me somewhere else to look. "Sanitol Solutions provides an environmentally friendly, one hundred percent green, easy-to-use sanitation system that is more effective and affordable than traditional sanitation chemicals and products. Because our system doesn't use chemicals to clean up chemicals, there's no waste."

I'd had to do my share of cleaning up messes on the farm, so I was on fairly firm ground. "If you don't use chemicals, how does it work?"

Swanson smiled again. He was a happy guy. Or more likely just a good salesman. "That's the billion-dollar question. And yes, that's billion with a B. We can't give away trade secrets in this meeting, but I can assure you it works and we are in the process of getting it patented. If you commit to invest, we'll give you the grand tour."

"Why would I commit if I don't know how it works?"

"You could agree to invest, subject to independent verification of our cleaning claims or something similar. Don't worry. We'll work all that out. I can assure you it works."

"Okay," I said. "Tell me more about the effects. You said it was green. This is crucially important. I wouldn't want to invest in anything that would sully the Bennett name. If there's any chance this thing is a pollutant, we want nothing to do with it." I'm no environmental activist, but Sarah would kill me if I turned her father into a posthumous polluter.

"Our process is the most environmentally safe cleaning system out there," Swanson said. "Because there's no waste, it reduces pollution. It completely eliminates the environmental impact of producing, packaging, transporting, using, and disposing of harsh chemicals. And it's also been proven to destroy odors, salmonella, E. coli, MRSA, campylobacter, and many other harmful pathogens. Our process doesn't hurt people. On the contrary, it saves lives."

"Wow," I said. "Have you tried it on cancer yet?"

"Ha ha, not yet," Swanson laughed. "But maybe we should. It can do everything else. And the best part is it's completely portable. This isn't just for huge factories. It could be used in schools, garages, basements, even your own kitchen. It's completely safe and it will literally clean up anything."

"You haven't seen my wife's cooking." Everyone laughed a little too hard at that, especially since if they knew who my wife was, and dollars to donuts they did, they knew she was a ball-busting executive who rarely cooked a meal. But they laughed just the same.

"I guarantee it could even handle that," Swanson said with yet another grin. You normally have to go to a children's cancer ward to see so many phony smiles.

"So what do the projections look like?" I asked.

"I was lying when I said portability was the best part," Swanson said. "The best part is it's cheap to make and easy to sell. We expect immediate and dramatic growth." He punched another laptop key.

The numbers were staggering. Not only were they looking at hundreds of millions of dollars in sales within five years, but it was almost all profit. Being the expert poker player I am, my jaw dropped on the table. "Jesus Christ!"

Swanson couldn't stop smiling, just like I can't stop mentioning that he was smiling. He was a living ad for teeth whitener. "I know. Can you believe it?" he said.

"Not really, no. But I'm no expert. Maybe Sam could have made a call like this by himself, but I sure can't. We need to get all this stuff over to our financial analysts at Bennett Capital."

Swanson nodded at his New York compatriots, who had done nothing during the meeting except sit there and try to look smart and rich. I recognized the strategy. It was my signature move. "My financial guys here can get your people whatever numbers they need," Swanson said.

"Great," I said. "Once they have a chance to go over everything, I'll meet with them next week and get back to you."

Swanson stood up and once again gave me his politician's smile. *I'm from the government and I'm here to help you.* A guy like Swanson could piss on you and tell you it's raining and most people would say, "That's good news. We've had a really dry summer." A guy like Swanson could sell girls' baby clothes in China or condoms in NBA locker rooms. He could, in fact, sell a product to people who have no need or desire for that product.

"Bob, it was truly a pleasure meeting you," Swanson said. "I only wish the necessity of our meeting wasn't caused by such unfortunate circumstances."

"Me, too, Tom. The best thing we can do to honor Sam is just try to run things the way he would have."

We shook hands. Swanson's were soft and smooth. I'll bet he gets manicures. "That's exactly what I would do in your place. And it's very good news for this project. Sam was very excited about it."

◇◇◇

I sat there for the rest of the week listening to presentations. Most of them were for investments we were already involved in and all of them combined didn't amount to the possible windfall from the Sanitol deal. Once I determined that no action by me was necessary, I went into meeting-autopilot. I have to actually sit there at the table, but my mind can wander all over the place without affecting my performance at the meeting. If you asked the other participants, they would say I was engaged and knowledgeable, but my meaningful contributions and retention of the subject matter would be functionally zero.

I was settling into a rhythm and becoming confident enough to sail through this trustee gig like every other job I've had. But since my physical presence seemed to actually be required, it was still wearing me out. I don't think I could handle the job year after year, but I felt like I'd be able to get through these initial stages and then turn most of the actual work over to the law firm.

I do admit the Sanitol deal kept popping into my mind. I held no illusions that I was in Sam's league as a businessman—or a man or a husband or a community leader or a golfer or a card player or a friend—but I felt like if I made the call on this deal and it made a bunch of money for the company and the family, I'd finally be pulling my weight. I wouldn't only be a guy who married well, I'd be a guy who did well himself. At the country club, I'd still avert my gaze and pretend to be busy with my iPhone when I passed any of those arrogant pricks, but I could hold my head high.

Chapter Nine

I'm not one of those gung-ho guys who throws off the covers in the morning and leaps out of bed ready to carpe diem. But I was actually feeling energized on my way to meet with the financial guys at Bennett Capital.

Harriet was sitting at the desk outside Sam's office like she always had, even though the office itself was obviously unoccupied. She saw me coming and came around her desk and gave me a big hug.

"I see at least one thing hasn't changed," I said. "You're still running the company."

She smiled at me but she had tears in her eyes. "I miss the old bastard so much."

"We all do."

"I know," Harriet said. "And I don't want to compare what I feel to the grief felt by Sarah and Joan. But I'm the one who spent nearly every hour of every day with him. They loved him more. He's not my father and not my husband. But I miss him more in the sense that he's *missing* from my life. He was here right next to me literally all the time. And now he's not."

"I've been meaning to come by, but I've been over at the law firm every goddamn day for the past two weeks on this trustee bullshit. It's usually crap when someone says they've been really busy, especially someone like me. A guy's so busy he can't even return an e-mail and then you find out he played eighteen holes yesterday. But I've been in meetings nonstop since the funeral."

Harriet rolled her eyes. "The busiest week of your life would have been a vacation for Sam."

"I know," I said. "I'm like a fat guy trying to run a marathon. But I'm not making the schedule."

"Who is?"

"James Madison."

"Oh, too bad," Harriet said. "I hate that prick."

"Why?" I asked. "I mean, it's obvious he's a prick, but do I have anything to be worried about?"

Harriet shook her head. "He's a good lawyer. In fact, to be a good lawyer, you almost have to be a prick. He's just got no sense of humor."

"I noticed. Listen, Harriet. Once everything settles down, I want to talk to you about helping me out on this trustee stuff."

"What do you mean by 'helping you out'?"

"I mean 'doing all the work.'"

"That's what I thought. I'm not sure what anyone else has in mind for me, but I'd say you're pretty much the boss now, so it's going to be your call."

"I don't want you to do anything you don't want to do, so think about it and let me know."

"I will. Did you come all the way over here to tell me that? Especially when you're *sooooo busy*?"

"I'm far too busy for the likes of you. I'm here to talk to a couple of your analysts about an investment possibility Sam was working on."

"Which one?" Harriet asked.

"A company called Sanitol," I said. "They've developed some kind of cleaning process."

"I remember it. Sam spent a lot of time looking into that one. It was a huge investment, if I recall."

"The biggest deal by far," I said. "Could you see if Sam had a file or some notes on it? If I knew what he was thinking, it would be a hell of a lot easier for me to make the call. Sam has forgotten more about business than I'll ever know."

"A kid with a lemonade stand has forgotten more about business than *you'll* ever know."

"Tell me about it. When Nick and Emily had one, I paid for the supplies and did all the work, and they kept the money."

"You're a good dad." Harriet smiled. "I'll look around and see what I can find."

"Thanks. You're the best."

The Bennett Capital financial analysts were housed in a room divided up into half a dozen small cubicles. The analysts themselves were all young, nerdy types who wore ironic tee-shirts, jeans, and crocs. Sam ordinarily required his employees to wear suits, but he made an exception in this case because, one, these guys were brilliant and, two, they would never be allowed anywhere near a client. They weren't even supposed to use the front door.

In a movie, there would be at least one black kid and one woman. But here in real life, the true demographics held. They all appeared to be Asian, Indian, or Jewish young men, although they could have passed for boys. They looked like the student section at a Duke basketball game. I took this as a good sign. Unlike the permissive American society under which I was raised, these guys' cultures valued intelligence, education, and hard work. There's a reason they're all doctors and technological geniuses.

Investing in the modern era was effectively controlled by young computer jockeys like these. It wasn't a people business anymore; it was a numbers game. The sheer volume of information available was too immense to be processed by the human mind, at least in the time needed to make an informed decision. So the "experts" had to rely on these young kids who knew nothing about dividend yields and price-to-earnings ratio but everything about crunching numbers and analyzing data.

I like young computer geeks. They think nobody knows anything and I truly don't know anything, so we get along great. I walked into the room, which was riddled with empty cans of Mountain Dew and Red Bull, plastic cups full of discarded sunflower seed shells, and five-pound bags of gummy bears.

"Hi, guys. This place always reminds me of my fraternity days. Except there's no booze or drugs."

"We keep the good stuff hidden," answered a thin Asian-American man shooting a Nerf ball at a hoop hanging over the edge of his cubicle. "To find out the secret location, you'd have to survive a series of quests." His tee-shirt read *There are only 10 types of people in the world—those who understand binary, and those who don't.* I didn't get it, but I think that was the point.

"That won't be necessary," I said. "Since I got out of college, I've been able to obtain my own booze and drugs. The only difference is now I hide them from my wife instead of the house mom."

I looked around the roomful of ironic messages in tee-shirt form.

She's dead so get over it with a photo of Princess Diana.
If we aren't supposed to eat animals, why are they made of meat?
Strangers have the best candy.
I support single moms with a silhouette of a stripper on a pole.
I bring nothing to the table.
Voted Most Likely to Travel Back in Time—Class of 2057

"What, do you guys have some kind of a hipster tee-shirt contest every day?" I asked.

"Nah, man," said the Asian guy. "We just like to express ourselves."

"Well, you're doing a better job than a guy in a suit would. Which one of you is working on the Sanitol financials?"

A pale young man with frizzy brown hair stood up and looked over the top of his cubicle. "That would be me. I'm Eric Jacobs."

I walked around to the entrance to his cubicle. There was enough room for me to sit down across from his desk, but barely. It was like a kid's room, filled with toys and posters and games, anything that might waste time during the day. I figured if the higher-ups didn't hassle him about his unprofessional office space, he must be very good at what he did. I was surprised to see that he wore a plain white tee-shirt. "Yours is ironically blank, right?"

"Mine is just a tee-shirt."

"Oh."

He broke into a grin. "I'm kidding. Isn't it cool? I went to every tee-shirt shop in town trying to find one."

"Good thinking," I said. "Or you could have gone straight to Walmart and bought a six-pack of them for five bucks."

"Eventually I figured that out," Jacobs said. "So what do you want to know?"

"Give me your analysis on the Sanitol prospectus."

"I looked it all over again to be sure, but I'll tell you the same thing I told Mr. Bennett. The numbers foot."

"Foot?"

"They balance," Jacobs said, "meaning that if their assumptions are correct, the numbers are computed correctly. It doesn't mean they'll come true, but the math is good. Those enormous profits aren't the result of somebody adding two and two and getting five."

"But are they realistic?" I asked.

"Nobody ever comes in here with pessimistic projections. Nobody says, 'Invest in our company because sales are going to suck over the next five years, as you can see on this graph I prepared.'" The kid was smart. If he was a bigger asshole, he could have been Mark Zuckerberg.

"Okay. So how likely are the projections?"

"It's impossible to say without knowing how well the process really works. If their environmental claims are true and if their cleaning effectiveness claims are true and if their cost estimates are accurate and if their patent holds up…"

"That's a lot of ifs."

"Yes, it is. But if all those ifs come true, I'd say the projections are conservative. My analysis shows they would absolutely dominate the commercial sanitation market. They can sell this process to every business on the planet."

I stopped by to see Harriet on my way out. She was gone, but there was a thick manila envelope on her desk with my name on it.

I returned to what was now becoming the normal domestic tranquility of my homelife. Martha Stewart was in the kitchen, the kids were studying quietly in their rooms, and the dogs were outside. It would almost be worth working hard all day if it meant coming home to this. Except I wasn't getting paid.

After dinner, I stuck my head into the family room. Sarah was sitting on the couch typing on her laptop in front of the TV. "I'll be in my office," I said. "I've got a few things to go over before my meetings tomorrow."

"What do you have to do?"

I didn't want to discuss the Sanitol deal with Sarah. If I told her about it, she would try to take over. She can't help it. She'd ask a bunch of questions and start calling contacts and having meetings and the next thing you know it would be her deal. I wanted it to be my deal. Plus I wanted to find out what Sam thought before I went any further. "Nothing interesting. Just speed-read some financial crap so I can pretend to know what I'm talking about."

She didn't look up from her laptop. "You don't need to prepare to pretend you know what you're doing. You've been doing that for years."

"Maybe this time I want to actually be prepared."

◇◇◇

I went into my office and shut the door. When I use my office in the evenings, it's generally to catch up on any Internet reading I didn't get to during the day and watch TV in peace. Sarah doesn't like the kids to be exposed to inappropriate material, which includes just about everything I like to watch.

I sat down at my desk and opened the envelope Harriet left me. It contained a single file folder. I could tell by the handwriting that Sam had personally written "Sanitol" on the tab. The bulk of the folder contained copies of Sanitol's financial projections and printouts of e-mails back and forth between Sam and Eric. Eric had told Sam essentially what he had told me. If the assumptions were correct, Sanitol was a gold mine.

There were also a number of sheets of yellow, lined paper torn from a legal pad. Sam's notes. I recognized his old-fashioned fountain pen scrawl. I'd seen it for years on birthday cards and thank-you notes. Sam still believed in the personal touch of a handwritten note. He could have handled that kind of thing easier with an e-mail, but he always said, "How can they tell it's really from me if I don't write it myself?" He was right, they couldn't, which is exactly why most people of his stature don't handwrite them. You can't farm the job out to an underling if it's ink on a piece of paper.

Seeing his handwriting sent a little pang of sadness, with a tinge of survivor guilt, into my heart. The penmanship was virtually indecipherable, but it was pure Sam. The more powerful the person, the worse the handwriting. I'd decoded enough of his missives to the family that I figured I could get the gist of it without asking Sarah.

I could tell from the notes that Sam was struggling with the numbers. There were a lot of columns of numbers added up by hand with question marks next to the results. It looked like he thought there must be some sort of math error. But even my rudimentary arithmetic skills could tell that everything added up. There were other notes to himself, like "Have E analyze competition" and "industry contacts." Finally on the last page he had written "TOO GOOD?" in block letters.

According to his notes, it sure looked like Sam had reservations about Sanitol, despite the possible financial boon. Selfishly, of course, I wanted this deal to be solid as a rock. A lot of people might say I already got a seat on the gravy train when I married my wife, but I needed something that was mine. This could be my chance to show everybody that I'm not an empty suit riding my wife's family's coattails. Like when George W. Bush decided to run for President. Whatever you think of W, he was the *President of the United States* for eight fucking years.

I don't know what the hell I thought I'd find in those notes. I hoped somewhere in there it would say something definitive. *Green light special!* or *Well worth the risk!* or *You'd have to be an idiot not to jump on this deal!* Unfortunately, as a heterosexual man of nearly seventy, Sam wasn't much of an exclamation point guy. There were no bold declarations and what *was* there seemed to be negative.

So what to do? Throughout my life, I've been quick to give up at the slightest resistance. But I wanted to see this one through. If I was going to turn this deal down, I needed more evidence than the barely legible, enigmatic chicken-scratchings of my dead father-in-law.

◇◇◇

I thought things through logically. Swanson had said Sam was excited about the deal. Of course Swanson is full of shit, but suppose Sam really did tell him that? If so, there could be an e-mail or a letter or something on Sam's computer. Therefore, I needed to go down to Sam's office and check it out.

I was too excited to go to sleep, but I didn't want to discuss it with Sarah, so I decided I would only go to Sam's office right now if she was already asleep. I opened the bedroom door and peered in. Sarah thinks she doesn't snore but she does. I heard the telltale sawing sounds and knew it was safe.

I took Sarah's keys from the hook by the garage door. She didn't spend a lot of her time at Bennett Capital, but she had a key. Sarah's had to stop by that office a bunch of times after hours and I've gone with her, so I knew the key worked. I also knew the alarm code. Daddy's daughter's birthday. 4973. No master criminal is ever going to crack that code unless he has five spare minutes and an Internet connection. Sam's computer password is probably "password" or "guest."

There were no cars in the parking lot and I knew there was no security. All they had in there were computers, and even junkies know computers have no resale value. They're obsolete as soon as you walk out the door with them. The people working with sensitive material at Bennett Capital were expected to encrypt all their files to keep them safe and they no doubt did. I'm sure I couldn't break into Eric Jacobs' computer if I had the black character with glasses in every action movie with me. But I was counting on Sam's e-mail, at least, to be unprotected. There was no way he typed in a password every time he wanted to forward an Obama joke to his buddies.

After about nine false starts, I found the right key. I managed to get the alarm stopped in just under the thirty seconds. There's a lot of pressure entering those numbers when you're somewhere you're not supposed to be. I left the lights off. For all I knew somebody checked on the place periodically throughout the night. I probably wouldn't be in any real trouble, but I didn't want to explain myself to anyone, especially my wife, who would no doubt be their first phone call.

The emergency lights provided plenty of illumination as I made my way down the hall. Sam's computer was already on when I sat down at his desk. There was a photo in a frame of Sarah and the kids standing on a mountain. I was conspicuously absent, but someone had to take the picture.

The only computer icons on his desktop were the worthless ones that show up the first time you power on the machine. This was not the computer of a man who was downloading a lot of crap from the Internet. Sam knew how to use e-mail and that was about it.

I clicked on Outlook and it slowly opened. Just as I thought: no password. Also just as I thought: a multi-multi-millionaire uses an ancient computer. The Texas Instruments calculator I had in high school had more memory. I'm sure Sam thought "I don't need all those fancy bells and whistles like having two windows open at the same time. I only do e-mail." And since he never turned it off, he didn't know how slow it was. It's a cliché when you find out a rich guy is cheap to say that's how he got rich in the first place—by watching every penny. But nobody ever got rich by wasting time on a shitty old computer. Maybe being stubborn helped him get rich.

I searched Sam's Sent box for the word "Sanitol." There were only two results. The first one was an e-mail to Eric Jacobs from a few months ago: *Get me everything on Sanitol and Tom Swanson. Use all resources.*

The second one was an e-mail directly to Swanson from about three weeks ago:

Dear Mr. Swanson:

Thank you for presenting your proposal to Bennett Capital. After careful consideration, we have decided not to make an investment at this time. Best of luck with your venture.

Sincerely,

Samuel E. Bennett
Principal, Bennett Capital

So Swanson was lying about Sam being excited about the project. Not exactly a shock. Swanson probably figured he might as well take a shot at the new guy. Maybe I'd have a different opinion than Sam. This was worse than normal sales bullshit. It was a flat-out lie right to my face, and one he had to figure I could check out. Did he think I was an idiot? Of course he did.

I wanted copies of these e-mails, so I started to forward them to myself. Then it occurred to me I really didn't want any record of an e-mail sent to me from Sam's computer in the middle of the night. I don't know who would ever look at it, but if anyone did, it might look a little fishy, what with Sam being dead and all. I decided to print the e-mails instead. Sam had one of those old inkjet printers that take forever to warm up. Christ, for a guy with a million-dollar house, four vacation homes, and his own jet, Sam had office equipment that would embarrass an Amish family. The professor on *Gilligan's Island* could have made something better out of bamboo and coconuts.

I hit *Print* on both e-mails and the printer came to life. In the quiet office, it sounded like a jet engine when the pilot flips that switch right before you're ready to take off. There was a series of whirrs and buzzes and clicks as the old girl adjusted herself to prepare to spread ink slowly back and forth across the page. After completing its warm-up calisthenics, the printer started to print the first e-mail. I could barely see the print, but it seemed to be working. Back and forth, back and forth.

After the first page was done, I heard a noise that sounded like the front door was opening. I wasn't sure whether I was more afraid of getting caught or murdered. Caught probably, but either way, I needed to hide. I closed Outlook and grabbed a letter opener off Sam's desk as a weapon. If I got a free stab and threw all my weight into it, I thought I might be able to break the skin.

I didn't really think I was in any physical danger. I was more concerned that someone would find me. I cursed Sam's ancient printer. Gutenberg printed his first Bible faster than this thing could print an e-mail.

Mercifully, the printer stopped right as a shadow appeared in the doorway. I held my breath behind the door. We've all imagined these moments. What would I do if confronted with an intruder? Would I spring into action and gain the upper hand? Now I knew the answer: no. I stayed silent and hoped the person would think the office was empty and leave. No such luck. The figure continued into the room and slowly pulled the door away from my cowering form.

◇◇◇

"I thought I heard the printer," Harriet said.

No, that was just an armored tank division going by outside. "I turned the printer on because I was going to type you a note. It makes a lot of noise when it's warming up."

Harriet glanced at my hand and saw the letter opener. "Did you drop a letter behind the door? Or were you planning to poke me to death with that thing?"

I sheepishly lowered my hand and let out a long breath. "Jesus, Harriet. I could have killed you."

She brushed me aside. "Please. You don't have it in you."

"What are you doing here?" I asked.

"What am *I* doing here?" she asked. "I work here."

I walked over and leaned against the edge of Sam's desk,

hoping to block her view of my freshly printed e-mails. "Why are you here in the middle of the night?"

"The alarm company called me."

"But the alarm didn't go off."

"There's a ten-second grace period where a silent alarm goes off if the person hasn't been able to hit the right buttons in thirty seconds. The real alarm doesn't go off for ten more seconds."

"But why would you come down here if the alarm went off? Why didn't you call the police?"

"Since the alarm got turned off before the siren went off, we usually assume it's someone too inept to push the right buttons in time. Sam wouldn't have wanted people to see the police here for no good reason, so I decided to drive by and see what it looked like. I saw your car and here I am."

Harriet sat down in one of Sam's guest chairs and looked me up and down. "The question isn't what am I doing here. The question is, what are *you* doing here?"

That was indeed the question I'd hoped to avoid by the hackneyed ploy of asking the other person what the hell *she* was doing there. Unfortunately, that kind of tactic only works on someone like me, who becomes so defensive I forget what we were even talking about. I considered telling Harriet what I'd found out, but I still wasn't sure what I was going to do. Just because Sam turned Swanson down didn't mean I should. Maybe he was just being conservative. Either way, I didn't want Harriet to know. She'd side with Sam, no matter what. I needed to make this call on my own.

So I lied. I'm a good liar. "I told Sarah I was in Sam's office today and she asked me to bring some of his personal stuff home." I walked around and grabbed items at random. "This photo. This plaque. His George Brett autographed baseball."

"And this was an emergency that required a trip to Sam's office in the middle of the night?"

Even for a good actor, there's only so much you can do when you have shitty material "I'm so fucking busy with this trustee bullshit, I don't have time to do anything else during the day."

Harriet laughed. "Well, now you know how the rest of us feel."

"Do you have a box?" I asked.

"There's probably one in the file room." She got up and left the room. I grabbed the e-mails from the printer, folded them and put them in my jacket pocket. When Harriet came back with the box, I piled the mementos I'd collected into it.

"Is that it?" she asked. "You came all the way down here for just those things?"

"Sam really did love that baseball," I said. "He wanted Nick to have it." Nick's a huge fan of baseball players who retired years before he was born.

"Did you get that file of Sam's I left you?" Harriet asked.

"Yes, I did," I said. "Thank you. I'll let you know if I need anything else."

"All right," Harriet said. "Then let's get out of here. It's late and I need my beauty sleep."

"If you got any more sleep, the men wouldn't be able to get any work done around here."

She smiled. "Does that line of bullshit actually work on women?"

I picked up the box. "I don't know. I've never tried it on anyone I was actually trying to sleep with."

"That's probably wise," Harriet said. "Let's go. And stay away from the alarm. I'm afraid it'll go off if you get near it."

I got home without incident and climbed into bed. Unless I'm tripping over ottomans and falling down trying to take off my pants, I can easily slip into bed without waking Sarah.

I lay in bed trying to decide what to do about the Sanitol deal. Sam was dead and he put me in charge for a reason, so I figured I'd handle this myself. It was time for me to do something, one way or the other.

Chapter Ten

My endless series of meetings continued unabated. I don't know how Sam could possibly keep it all straight. Subsidiaries, subsidiaries of subsidiaries, limited partnerships, limited liability corporations, IPOs, LBOs, EBITA, cash flow, sale and leaseback. In every case, I pretended to mull things over. "Let's just keep things going the way they are for the time being. If there are any new developments, be sure to let me know."

Concerning Sanitol, I reasoned that by doing nothing, you often force the other guy's hand, like a girl playing hard to get.

Midway through the week, I received a call on my cell phone. Normally I would never answer a call from a number I didn't recognize, but I'd been stuck in a conference room all morning and I wanted an excuse to get away. I never give anyone my cell number who I wouldn't want to call me, but I looked down at the display and mouthed "I've got to take this" to Madison. I went out into the hall and said "Hello."

"Bob? Tom Swanson, Sanitol Solutions."

"Hello, Swanson. Where'd you get this number?"

I could hear him smiling through the phone. "You gave it to me at our last meeting. Said to call you if I needed anything."

No way that happened. "That doesn't sound like me."

He laughed harder than necessary. He doesn't have a sincere bone in his body. "Well, the guy sure looked a lot like you. Ruggedly handsome, nice suit, trustee of a nine-figure trust estate."

"Okay, that does sound like me," I said. "What can I do for you, Tom?"

"I wanted to help you with your decision. I'd like to take you to lunch today," Swanson said. "Talk a little more about this tremendous opportunity we're offering."

"Okay." I did need to hear more about the company, but was it worth enduring lunch with Swanson? "When?"

"I'll pick you up in thirty minutes," Swanson said.

I didn't like business lunches. I preferred to enjoy my meals. But I knew I was going to have to meet with Swanson sooner or later, and I was pretty sure we wouldn't be going to Burger King.

Swanson had reservations at Mann's Steak House, where the movers and shakers in town have been having two-hour lunches and billing the time to their clients for over fifty years. This was one of those places where the waiters don't write anything down. I don't know why that's supposed to impress us. I just want my waiter to hustle back and forth with the food and drinks. The waiter in this case showed up promptly to ask what we wanted to drink, so I liked him already, even if it turned out he couldn't memorize π out to a hundred digits. He was a very polite young man in his early twenties named something I can't recall. I'm not one of those guys who uses the waiter's name all night like we're old friends.

I ordered a Ciroc martini. After all, it was on Swanson. A couple of these and I might almost actually enjoy this lunch.

The waiter brought the drinks and asked, "Would you gentlemen like to hear the specials?"

"Only if you've got them memorized," I said. Polite laughter from the waiter. The customer is always right, especially when you make your living on tips.

"Indeed, I do." He proceeded to recite them in great detail. He reminded me of one of those Indian kids forced by their parents to learn every word in the dictionary so they can win spelling bees.

Swanson decided to big-time me by ignoring the menu and telling the waiter exactly what he wanted. "I don't need the menu. Bring me a porterhouse steak, seared on the outside, pink in the middle. Tell the chef to slice some potatoes and fry them in butter, just short of crispy. I'll start with a salad, iceberg lettuce only, none of that mixed greens crap, with chopped tomatoes and cheddar cheese. Have the chef mix some olive oil with a tablespoon of mayonnaise and bring it on the side." Like I'm supposed to be impressed.

I would never go off-menu. These people are experts. The chef has relied on his experience and expertise to decide on a combination of ingredients that go together in a pleasing way. That's why you go to a nice restaurant in the first place.

So I ordered one of the specials, steak, and told the waiter whatever came with it was fine. "You pick whatever sides would go best."

He beamed. "I'll treat you right, sir."

I took a sip of my martini and waited for Swanson to start. This was his show, after all.

"Bob, I appreciate you making time to have lunch with me. I know you're very busy these days."

"No problem. I needed a break anyway." This wasn't a break. This was more of the same, only worse, because it was one-on-one.

"Glad I could help," Swanson said. "I wanted to get together and make sure you have all the information you need to make your decision to invest in Sanitol."

"I think we do," I said. "I'm not really the numbers guy. More data wouldn't really change anything for me."

"Okay, forget about the numbers," Swanson said. "What can I tell you about the company?"

I mulled that over as I sipped my drink. If I was going to sign off on this deal, what did *I* really want to know? "How'd you come up with this cleaning process? You don't seem like the scientist type. More like the game show host type."

Swanson laughed. "Oh, I'm no scientist. I'm the sales guy. The inventor is a guy named Hans Becker. He used to work for Dow Chemical. He was fooling around trying to come up with a solution to clean up a stain on his garage floor and he stumbled across the greatest sanitation innovation since the discovery of soap."

I pictured an über-nerd pouring a bubbling liquid from one test tube to another. "And the Nutty Professor is running the company?"

"Of course not," Swanson scoffed. "You never put the inventor in charge. What the hell does he know about business?"

"Bill Gates did okay," I offered, just to be contradictory.

"There are exceptions to every rule," Swanson said dismissively. "Becker's on the board of directors, but basically the company purchased the patent."

"There's no question about ownership of the patent?"

"None whatsoever," Swanson said. "There's an opinion letter in the materials we provided you from the top intellectual property law firm in the country. Becker owned the patent free and clear and now we own it."

"So everything looks good then," I said and then let out a little rope for Swanson. "I figured it would or Sam wouldn't have been interested in the first place."

Swanson grabbed the rope and wrapped it around his own neck. "That's exactly right. Sam knew business, and once he did his due diligence, he was on board."

"So how much did he plan to invest?"

"He wanted in for the entire forty mil. He was in the process of getting the funds together when he had the heart attack."

"Unfortunate timing."

"It was just unfortunate, period." Swanson adopted a somber tone. "Obviously all of his business interests were affected, but Sam was a husband and father first. His loss is a tragedy. It can't be measured in dollars and cents." Swanson was good. I wanted to hire him to walk around with me and make appropriate condolence conversation at funerals.

"It's been a tough time for our family."

"I realize that." As if Swanson would graciously put a giant business deal on hold out of respect for a personal tragedy. "And I understand that you're going to want to get with your people and complete your own due diligence before you sign off on the deal."

I didn't need to get with my people, even if I had people to get with. Sam didn't trust Swanson and neither did I. As much as I wanted to stake my own claim and prove my worth as a shrewd businessman in my own right, I was no Sam and I never would be. If Sam rejected Sanitol, who was I to overrule him?

"I appreciate that, Tom. I'll let you know as soon as I can." I had another martini and we spent the rest of the meal just conversing like normal people, if one of the people is completely full of shit. Swanson has a salesman's gift for keeping a conversation going, which was helpful because I have an introvert's knack for running out of things to say. He asked a lot of questions about my family and I asked none about his. Looking back, I should have found it strange that he already knew so much about my personal life, but a couple of martinis have a way of dulling your senses.

As I got out of the car back at Madison's office, Swanson stuck out his hand. "I'll be in touch. What's the best way to contact you?"

I pretended I didn't see his hand and shouted "Friend me on Facebook!" back over my shoulder.

By the time I got out of the elevator on Madison's floor, my phone beeped. I already had a friend request from Swanson. I hit *Decline* because there wasn't anything stronger. I was hoping there'd be a *Fuck Off* button.

I spent the rest of the day thinking about Swanson while pretending to pay attention to PowerPoints and prospectuses. I had already decided to turn him down, but I wanted Swanson to know I knew he was lying about Sam. Who knew how long he'd keep on the full-court press if he thought I was waffling on the deal or afraid to pull the trigger? I didn't want to spend the next six months ducking his phone calls.

When I got home that night, I went into my office and reread Sam's e-mail. Then I sent an identical e-mail to Swanson:

> Dear Mr. Swanson:
>
> Thank you for presenting your proposal to Bennett Capital. After careful consideration, we have decided not to make an investment at this time. Best of luck with your venture.
>
> Sincerely,
>
> Robert Patterson
> Trustee, Samuel E. Bennett Irrevocable Trust

I thought Swanson would be smart enough to recognize the language and decide to let the matter drop. I was half right.

Chapter Eleven

"Don't forget," Sarah reminded me over dinner the next evening. "The kids and I are going to the mountains with Carol next week."

"Better you than me." I can't go anyway. For once, I'm legitimately too busy at work.

"You spend a lot of home time with the kids. It's fun for me to do something special with them."

"Okay. You make all the 'special' memories and I'll just be happy to be remembered for laundry and bologna sandwiches."

Sarah and a friend took the kids on a memorably "fun" trip to someplace exciting every year. *Mom's Amazingly Spectacular Vacation, sponsored by Dr. Pepper!* I'm happy not to be included. The week provides me with a wonderful opportunity to do whatever I want, which most of the time means absolutely nothing. Sarah leaves me with a list of Honey Dos, but it's a pretty short list because my past efforts have given her the impression that household tasks take a lot longer than they actually do. So I get those done and then spend the rest of the time productively watching what I want to watch, and eating and drinking what I want to eat and drink. That may not seem exciting to you, but good husbands and fathers *never* get to do what they want, so there could be no better use of my time.

"I'm sorry you're too busy to come," Sarah said. "I hate to think of you here all alone."

"Don't worry about me. I think Corny's going to be in town for a night."

"What does that asshole want?"

"Remember when I saw him at the gala? He said he had something I'd be interested in. He said he was already working with Sam."

"Even if that were true, which I doubt, it doesn't matter now. The guy is nothing but trouble. Everybody sees it except you and your immature friends trying to relive your fraternity days."

"I don't like certain things about him either, but he's forty-something years old now. He's not screwing sorority girls in the laundry room anymore." I may have forgotten to mention earlier that the girl who unwittingly starred in Corny's sex show was a close friend and sorority sister of Sarah's. So Sarah had a pretty good reason for not liking him.

"Just knowing he would ever do something like that, how can you even stand to be around him?"

"He *is* entertaining. For men, that's all that matters."

"It's not all that matters to me," Sarah said.

"I know," I said. "That's why I'm waiting to wheel him in until after you're gone."

"I don't want him in our house."

"You're overreacting."

Truth be told, I hadn't had any real contact with the guy since college. I was on a huge distribution list of guys who received almost daily doses of Internet porn from him and we occasionally exchanged alma mater sports-related e-mails, but nothing substantial. I didn't see him at Sam's funeral, but they apparently had some business dealings that were bringing him to town again. It seemed serendipitous when his offered dates fell during my family-free independence. I was actually looking forward to reliving our college days for a night or two.

"Well, get him and any traces of his DNA out of here before we get back," Sarah said, presciently, as it turned out. The next morning, she was still pissed and rebuffed my attempt at departure sex.

Your friends from college often turn out completely different from what you would expect. One of my buddies who used to love to get high and sit around watching TV and listening to music became a Mennonite. He used to be too lazy to get off the couch. He ordered a pizza every single night. Now he drives a horse and buggy and churns his own butter. Another guy was so shy around girls we had to set him up with a date for every fraternity party. Now he fucks around on his wife constantly. The point is, people change. But not Corny. I didn't notice when I saw him at the gala because he was wearing a tuxedo. But when I picked him up at the airport Tuesday evening, he looked exactly like he did in college.

Same ball-hugging jeans, same boots, same navy blue sportcoat, and same thick head of hair. The only difference was he had shaved his 1990s porn 'stache.

"Look at you!" I exclaimed when he got in the car. "You could pass for a college student. I'd screw you myself if I wasn't aware of your numerous anonymous sexual partners."

"And you could pass for…" Corny looked me over, "…the father of a college student. We can hit the college bars and tell the girls it's Dad's weekend."

Once I'd managed to maneuver us out of the typical airport traffic clusterfuck, Corny put a serious expression on his face. "Hey, I just want to say how sorry I am about Sam."

"Thanks, Corny. It's been pretty rough."

"Is Sarah taking it hard?"

"She is," I said. "They were very close."

"If there's anything I can do for either of you, let me know."

"I will. But for now let's head back to the house, shower up, and have a couple of cool ones. I wouldn't expect much since it's a Tuesday, but Nellie and Lang managed to secure a couple of limited weeknight passes."

"Every night's a Saturday night if you play it right."

"My Saturday nights are probably like your Sunday nights."

"Sunday's one of the best nights. The bars are filled with hairdressers and dental hygienists because they don't work Mondays."

"How do you know this stuff? No wonder I never got laid in college. Who goes out on Tuesday nights?"

"Doesn't matter," Corny said, with what in hindsight must have been a devious smile. "I'm sure we'll run into some fun people. Fun always finds me."

When we walked in the front door, my mongrel mutt Max trotted up happily and then suddenly stopped. He lowered his head to the ground and bared his teeth. The fur on his back was standing up. I don't think I'd ever seen Max growl at anyone like that before.

"I guess it's true what they say, Corny," I joked. "Animals can sense evil."

"As long as women can't sense it, I'll be okay," Corny said. "And I have a lot of experience that says they can't."

"Seriously, animals can sense things. I once read if you ever see a turtle climbing a tree, run for high ground. There's a flood coming."

"Thanks, Bob. That's a helpful safety tip."

"Do me a favor and don't go anywhere near our horses. We don't want a stampede."

Corny held out his hand and Max cautiously approached. "I'll win him over. I'm impossible to resist." Max sniffed the hand and it apparently passed his admission test because he allowed Corny to scratch his ears and come into the house. It took Corny all of five seconds to turn him. Max is quite a watchdog.

"Can I get you a drink, Scarface?" I walked into my kitchen after showering. Corny was sitting at the kitchen table right where my children eat their breakfast, gesturing toward an enormous pile of white powder. You didn't have to be Lindsay Lohan to figure out it was probably cocaine.

"Come on, jump on in," Corny said. "The water's fine."

"I'll pass this round," I said. "And clean that shit up before one of my kids accidentally puts it on their cornflakes."

"They'd probably be a lot more focused in class."

"Good point," I said. "But we'd like them to live at least through high school."

Corny threw a couple Bud Lights on top of his cocaine dinner and I threw a couple on top of my ham sandwich and we headed out to meet the guys. We took a cab to avoid any possible trouble. A sound plan in principle.

When we arrived at the bar, the boys already had a table. We'd all been friends in college, if by "friends" you mean people who got drunk together frequently. Nowadays we rarely see Corny, but Kevin Nelson and Dan Langham are closer friends of mine now than they were then. Our wives are friends, too, so we even vacation as a group. Corny was an indispensable ingredient for a wild time in college, but he wasn't the guy you forged a life-long friendship with, unless you planned to stay single and nail twenty-five-year-olds until you were fifty.

"Corny!" Nellie shouted. "You made it! I thought Bob might have fabricated your visit just to get me out of the house on a weeknight."

The cocaine made Corny's eyes sparkle. "I've come to town to wake you pussies out of your doldrums. For this one night, you're going to forget you're old, fat, and married."

"There's not enough alcohol in this bar to make me forget that," Nellie said.

"Goddamn," Lang said. "You look the same as you did in college. Maybe married life is killing us."

"Boys, lemme tell ya," Corny said. "It's all about clean livin'. Work, church, home is my daily schedule and moderation is my middle name."

"Says the guy who just did a kilo of cocaine on my kitchen table," I said.

I thought I saw Nellie's ears perk up at the word cocaine, but Lang headed him off. "You don't want to go down that rabbit hole, Nellie. Karen wants you home by ten. Once again, everyone, it's a *Tuesday.*"

"You're right, she'd kill me," Nellie said. "So Corny, what are you up to these days?"

"Let's call it high finance," Corny said. "I do a little M&A work for an East Coast firm. That's one of the reasons I'm in town. I can't talk about it but you'll be able to read about it in the funny pages eventually."

We all probably thought the same thing. Mergers and acquisitions? *Pure. Unadulterated. Bullshit.* Corny always talked a big game. It's one of the reasons he got laid so much in college. His sales pitch was relentless. He wouldn't take no for an answer.

"What do you mean you can't tell us?" Nellie asked. "If you tell us, you'll have to kill us?"

"Something like that." Corny winked at me. I hate when people wink. I never know if it was intentional or even if it was, what it was supposed to mean. I guessed Corny was telling me he was here to follow up on the deal with Sam he mentioned at the gala, if it really existed.

"Something in your eye, Corny?" I asked.

"You idiot," Corny said. "That wink wasn't directed at you. I was winking at that MILF over there."

I turned around. Sitting at a table against the wall was a fairly attractive woman of an indeterminate age due to years of drinking and smoking.

"That's not a MILF," I said. "A MILF is the mother of one of your kid's friends or the attractive woman you see in an SUV in the school parking lot. That woman is a barfly."

"Okay, call her a BILF," Corny said. "But I'd still L to F her."

"You'd L to F almost anyone," I said.

Corny played along. The same confidence that allowed him to pick up strange women also made him impervious to mockery. "Well, excluding children and men."

"Let's get a few more drinks in you before we make that call," I said. "Hopefully there won't be any children in here."

"Nice, Bob," Corny admonished me. "Nothing funnier than a good pedophile joke." He paused and then went on. "Like this one: This guy and his girlfriend are fighting. She says, 'I'm breaking up with you.' He asks why and she says 'Because you're a pedophile.' The guy says 'Pedophile? That's an awfully big word for a ten-year-old.'"

Corny burst into laughter. The rest of us didn't laugh but that didn't bother Corny. It made him laugh harder.

When we were on our third round of beers, Corny turned to me. "So, Bob, how's the trustee work going?"

Had I even told Corny about my new job?

"Very well, thanks. I'm still not entirely sure why Sam put me in charge, but I think I've got everything under control."

"How the hell did that happen?" Nellie asked, looking at Lang. "Bob in charge of a giant trust. Shouldn't your firm have advised against that?"

Lang wouldn't comment—client confidentiality—but Corny had no such issue. "What are you talking about? Bob's perfect for that gig."

"How so?" I asked.

"You're a coaster, Bob."

"What's a coaster?" Nellie asked.

"Let me explain to you guys how American society operates at the highest levels," Corny continued. "Let this be a primer on the various species you'll see on a safari to big swinging dick country."

Nellie looked at me. "Big swinging dick country?"

"Forget it, he's rolling," I replied.

Corny held court. "At the top of the heap are the engines. These are the bigger-than-big swingers, the CEOs, the chairmen of the board, the men who make the big deals and create all the jobs. These are the guys who would have found the top of the heap in almost any era or set of circumstances. They deserve the highest status in our hierarchy of rich people living well."

"Okay," Lang said. "We're with you so far."

"So then one level down, though almost as rich and equally admirable, are the propellers. The propellers are the lieutenants for the engines or top dogs in lesser companies or industries. The distinction here is minor. Both engines and propellers are the people who truly make the world go 'round." Corny stopped talking, chugged his beer, and signaled the waitress for another round. The rest of us had barely taken a sip of ours.

Nellie raised an eyebrow at me. "Yeah, we definitely need another one," he said. "Good call, Corny."

I tried to get Corny back on track. "Engines and propellers. Those are pretty self-explanatory. What's next?"

"The next group exists because these engines and propellers need friends to hang out with. They really don't want to spend time with other engines and propellers because they are so accustomed to being the alphas, they can't share a stage. Thus the need for a new class of people. These are Bob's people!" Corny looked at me with a huge smile. "Bob is a coaster."

"I'm not sure if I should be insulted or not," I said.

"I wouldn't feel too bad," Nellie said. "He hasn't even gotten to us yet."

"I'm getting there," Corny said. "Coaster status is not necessarily difficult to achieve. Anyone can do it, really. But only a select few have the talent to do it well. The coaster's gift is the ability to socialize with the powerful people and make them laugh or think or whatever might be needed."

"But I'm not good at hobnobbing with those people," I said.

"You think you're not, but you are," Corny said. "You may not be comfortable around them, but they're comfortable around you. Maybe because you're non-threatening. Who knows?"

"So, how does one get to be a coaster?" Lang asked.

"A coaster connects to a higher level person directly by birthright or indirectly through marriage or friendship."

"It can't be that simple," Nellie said.

"Sure it is," Corny said. "Look at Bob's family. Sam was the engine, Sarah is the propeller and Bob is the coaster. And that's where you clowns come in. You guys are drafters. Basically, any friend of a coaster is a drafter. If Bob has access to the incredible trip or fantastic golf course, you and Lang will be the guys he invites to share it all with. You're in the same social strata, but Bob is just better connected."

"Okay," I said, "Maybe it *kind of* works for my family, but not every group."

"It works for anybody." Corny said. "Further down are the barnacles, the people nobody likes but who get to hang around because they make beer runs or do the driving."

"So how can you tell what you are?" Nellie asked.

"If you don't know for sure, then you're a barnacle. Of course, even a barnacle is a step up from your everyday working stiff, who's not even in the picture at all, unless he's serving drinks to these people or parking their cars. Which is why the barnacle is willing to take the shit he does. It's worth it."

"That's an incredible theory, Corny," I said. "You've really outdone yourself this time. But there's one thing I haven't figured out. What are you?"

"I'm a shark, Bobby. I take what I want from everybody else."

Chapter Twelve

At about ten, the ribaldry began to slow down, but Nellie had had enough beers to rethink his plan to go home early. "Come on, Lang, let's stay out a while. How often is Corny in town?"

"Don't you have to go to work in the morning?" Lang asked.

"Hell, no, I own the place," Nellie said. "I can do whatever I want."

"Well, I can't," Lang said. "Unlike you two, I have to show up at work. I have to meet with clients. I can't be all hungover, with alcohol seeping out of my pores. Maybe if I could steam it all out in the sauna, like the one Bob's father-in-law had. That thing was awesome."

I was puzzled. "When did you ever see that sauna? It was in the master bathroom."

Lang shrugged. "Sam must have told me about it. I was his lawyer, you know. Anyway, I can't stay."

"Okay, you go," Nellie said. "I'll stay out with the fun people."

"I'm your ride," Lang said. "Plus, your hall pass expires at ten. Your wife told me herself."

"You better go, Nellie," I said. "I don't want her blaming me when you're too 'sick' to go to work tomorrow."

Corny was strangely quiet during this exchange. In college, he would have called Nellie a pussy and forced a couple of shots down his throat. Instead, he said, "I understand you guys have family obligations. I appreciate you making the effort to come out at all. Don't worry, I'll be back in town soon."

Nellie grudgingly acquiesced. "All right, let's go. But try to remember what happens if it gets crazy so you can tell me later."

"If it gets crazy, we'll be calling you in a couple hours to bail us out." I hoped Corny knew I was joking. I was a little nervous about my ability to keep things under control by myself. Corny was fearless even in the sober light of day, but get a few drinks in him and he thought he was bulletproof.

Nellie and Lang each threw the obligatory inadequate twenty down on the table and headed out. "I must not have seen that sign that said beers were three for one tonight," I called after them.

Corny grinned at me. "Don't worry, Bobby. I got it. This night's a business expense for me." He handed me one of the twenties and winked. "We just made twenty apiece off book. It may come in handy later."

"See, you *were* winking at me earlier."

"When someone winks at you, it's a secret between you and them," Corny said. "You don't point it out to everyone else. I didn't want to talk about the deal I was working on with Sam in front of those guys. Obviously now that Sam's dead, everything's up in the air."

"So do you want to run it by me?"

"Sure, sometime. But not tonight. We're here to have fun. All work and no play makes Jack a dull boy. So what *do* people do for fun in this town?"

"Old people like me go home and get a good night's sleep and go to work in the morning with a clear head."

"*Or*, we could stay out late and you could not worry about work. You're your own boss. And how often does your old buddy Corny come to town?"

"That's exactly what Nellie said and you let him go home."

"Nellie's wife and kids aren't out of town," Corny said. "Let's go to Club Paradise."

"That's where the hip twentysomethings hang out," I said. "I'm sure they'll be thrilled to have a couple of middle-aged guys join the party."

"I've got some people we can meet."

"You have some people?" I asked. "Why do you have people here?"

"I have people everywhere."

Corny was one of those annoying out-of-towners who knew your city better than you did. In the cab on the way to the bar I asked him, "Why Club Paradise?"

"It's Two for Tuesday."

"How the hell do you know that?"

"The question isn't how I know it, it's how do you not know it?"

"I'm like a retired golfer," I said. "You don't ask Jack Nicklaus about the new courses on tour."

"God, Sarah keeps you on a tight leash, doesn't she? I remember how she can be."

"She was pretty cool back when you knew her in college. She didn't really care what I did."

"Maybe not," Corny said. "But I'm talking about when I went out with her."

I must have had a shocked expression on my face. "We went out for a while in college," Corny said. "You knew that, didn't you?"

Corny had to be full of shit. He usually was. "Are you joking?"

"We just went on a couple dates," Corny said. "Well, not really dates, just late night booty calls. Maybe that's why no one knew."

Sarah wouldn't cheat on me, would she? I know she doesn't know the real me. What makes me think I know the real her? *Nobody knows anybody.* "We pretty much dated throughout college, except for a few brief breaks. What year was that, again?"

"How the hell should I know? I'm pretty sure you were broken up, though. Don't worry. It was no big deal. Just sex. She was chasing danger and a little wild fun. I was just the boy toy."

"That makes me feel a lot better, Corny."

Club Paradise was hopping. I'd forgotten what two-for-one nights were like. At my age I prefer my bars empty and quiet.

On the rare occasions I go out with my friends, I like to have a conversation with them without shouting, so Club Paradise is not high on my list. Although the name made it sound like a strip joint, it was actually a typical dive bar for young professionals. Which meant it was a pretend dive bar designed to appeal to hipsters who thought they were cool when they were slumming it. It was kind of dirty and there were initials carved into the tables and they had dancing, shots, and cheap drinks, but the place wasn't full of alcoholics and barflies like a real dive bar would be. Whatever it was, it was packed. Two for Tuesday was alive and well.

We sat at the bar and I ordered two Bud Lights. "Fuck that!" Corny shouted. "Bring us the house special. Two hurricanes." The bartender set four hurricanes in front of us. For some reason, when it's two for one, everybody orders the normal amount and then gets twice as many drinks as they want. You'd think we'd be smart enough to just order one and get two. Maybe it's more fun to get a bonus than a discount.

Corny turned his stool around and surveyed the bar. "Not bad for a Tuesday. Lots of possibilities."

"Yeah, for somebody looking for a father figure."

"Fortunately, most of them are."

Corny turned and slid a hurricane in front of me. "Since we got two, let's chug the first one." Maybe that's why people go four for two instead of two for one. To force their friends to drink.

Corny raised his glass in toast. It's easy to say this now, but it felt like a significant moment, like my life was changing and would never be the same again. "To old friends, new possibilities and ham-handed foreshadowing!" he said. Or at least that's how I remember it.

By the time I managed to choke my hurricane down, Corny was gone from the bar, I assumed to "powder his nose" for the fiftieth time that evening. Corny's hurricane was gone in an eye blink, but mine took thirty-seven tiny gulps, each one more bile-inducing than the last. A hurricane was not a shot, we just drank it that way. I had no idea what was in it, but it's almost all liquor and it was in a plastic keg cup with four measly ice cubes floating on top. Not an easy chug for me. I spent the next few minutes swallowing saliva in an effort not to throw up all over the bar. The evening was taking a bad turn.

When I finally regained my equilibrium, Corny returned and he was not alone. He had two friends with him and by "friends" I mean "hot chicks."

"Bobby, this is Natalie and Alexis. Girls, this is my best buddy, Bob." A bit of an overstatement since we've seen each other maybe three times in twenty years and he just confessed to sleeping with my wife in college, but I didn't contradict him. What difference did it make?

These women were late twenties, attractive, and dressed sexy casual in jeans and sandals with higher heels than anything in my wife's closet. My first thought was apprehension. Hot women intimidate me. Whatever limited game I ever had has been long lost to the ravages of marriage and time. I had nothing to say, but it appeared the floor was mine. Fortunately, I was still on the upward track of the roller coaster that is my conversational skill when drinking.

Glancing at Corny, I said, "So are you all old friends or new friends?"

Natalie, or maybe Alexis, smiled sweetly. "Well, both. We've known Dave a long time but we just met you."

Corny barked out an order for four (read: eight) tequila shots. I'm a fairly seasoned drinker (just ask my wife!), but the dam in my throat was already backing up at the mere thought of a tequila shot. Corny and his "friends" made me feel like a fourteen-year-old girl with a bottle of Boone's Farm.

During one of the girls' frequent trips to the restroom together, I believe I turned to Corny. "So who are these chicks?"

"Well, I guess you could say they're coworkers of mine," Corny probably said with a grin. "They help me at the office."

"Help with what?" I asked. "Is there a staff fluffer position at your office? Are you running an escort service on the side? These gals don't look like any financial people I've ever seen."

"Right," Corny said. "Not the kind *you've* ever seen. But that's not saying much. Don't sweat it, Bobby. They're with me. And they're also with *you*. You know what I mean?" Big smile, possibly leering.

I'm not a guy who goes out looking to score. I'm too self-aware to think there wouldn't be guilt or other negative ramifications. But I also normally don't have the temptation. I'm not out trolling and nobody is seeking me out, but tonight for some reason they seemed to be. And I was still rattled from that Corny firebomb about him and Sarah. No wonder she didn't want him to come to the house.

Add in Sarah rejecting my bid for pre-trip sex, and I may have been a little more susceptible than usual to the charms of an attractive and seemingly interested woman. It's not an excuse for cheating but it's more understandable when your own wife acts like it's a chore to have sex with you. You think to yourself, "She doesn't want to. Maybe I should find someone who does."

I thought about the logistics of a possible hookup with Alexis/Natalie. If I had sex with a hot young girl, it wouldn't look right. My flabby old man body pressed up against her taut, glistening, young flesh—well, maybe I could give it a shot. "Look, I'm as horny as the next guy," I said to Corny. If the next guy is so drunk he can't feel his legs. "But I'm not looking for action."

"Bob, we're just partying. Don't get your panties in a bunch."

The girls came back from the bathroom, noses "powdered" and spirits high. At some point it became clear that we had paired up. I was with Natalie, Corny with Alexis. It made no difference to me since I could barely tell them apart and I wasn't going to do anything anyway.

Corny and Alexis were getting pretty cozy when a very large young man approached our table. He apparently had also taken a shine to Alexis and asked her to dance. He was in his early twenties and ridiculously muscular. He had bulked up everything you could bulk up to the point that his unalterable parts were now too small for his body. Beady little eyes inside a massive block of a head. A tiny soul patch under his lip that looked like his Hitler mustache had slipped down an inch. Surprisingly small hands and feet and ears. But the guy was strong, no doubt about that, and probably full of 'roid rage. I wouldn't have messed with him.

Nobody needed to jump in anyway. Alexis could handle guys like this in her sleep. "No, thanks, Junior. I'm having a quiet drink with my friends."

The guy looked slowly back and forth between me and Corny and then turned his attention back to Alexis. "Come on, a beautiful girl like you can do better than a couple of old guys." A minor insult, no harm, no foul in my mind, we'd ignore him and he'd go away. Corny leapt out of his chair, grabbed the guy's wrist, twisted it violently behind his back and shoved his face down on our table, scattering hurricanes everywhere. Corny used the guy's face like a bar rag to mop up the rapidly spreading pool of red liquid. It looked like cough syrup—maybe that's the secret ingredient. I kept waiting for the guy to shrug Corny off, but he couldn't do a thing. He was completely helpless.

"Apologize to the lady," Corny said.

The guy was able to squeeze a sound that might have been the word "sorry" out of the corner of his mouth, so Corny let him up. He was furious. "You got the jump on me there, but this isn't over. Let's take this outside and I'll mop up the parking lot with *your* face."

"Okay." Corny pulled out his cell phone and dialed three numbers. "But before we go outside, I'm going to call you a ride."

"What are you talking about? I don't need a ride."

Corny waived him off and spoke into the phone. "Hello, 911? Please send an ambulance to Club Paradise. A man has been seriously injured. Specifically? I'm not sure yet, but I'm guessing at least one dislocated elbow, a broken jaw, and definitely a concussion. Maybe even a fractured skull. Thank you."

The guy's eyes darted around the room at all the people watching. "We'll see who needs the ambulance." He stormed out the door.

Corny sat back down and signaled our waitress. "Four more hurricanes and sorry for the mess."

"What about your friend outside?" I asked.

"Are you kidding? He's long gone. He'll say I never showed up outside to fight him. Which is technically true, but he practically ran to his car."

"Did you really call an ambulance?"

"Hell, no," Corny said. "I would have left that motherfucker in a ditch. You fuck with me, Bobby, you get what you get."

Corny was a maniac. I'd forgotten after all these years. One time in college a few of us were in line at a late night deli where people would try to sop up the liquor in their belly with a sandwich or a donut. A couple of townies were hassling me and another guy. We were too drunk to engage in any kind of verbal exchange, but there was a decent chance we were going to get our asses pounded anyway. Without warning, Corny took out both guys with roundhouse kicks. We called him Chuck Norris for a while. Kids today would probably go with some vampire or werewolf.

Corny wasn't the biggest guy around, but he had that rare combination of crazy confidence and extreme ruthlessness that's essential in a street fight. Was he smarter or tougher than everyone else? No, but he would go the extra mile, do horrible things other people wouldn't do, ratchet up the stakes until it wasn't worth it to the other guy. But it was always worth it to him.

The rest of my recollections are an out-of-order kaleidoscope of Fellini-esque images. I would feel comfortable testifying to the fact that the following events transpired in one form or another:

Shots.

Spelling YMCA with my body on the dance floor.

More shots.

Pantomiming throwing a lasso over Natalie's head on the dance floor.

Shots.

Vomiting in a trash can.

Shots.

Belting out the words to "Dancing Queen," "Sweet Caroline" and "Brandy (You're a Fine Girl)." The songs I like are so old they've come all the way around to being popular with young people. Mostly as a joke, but still.

Shots.

Being lifted into a cab.

Chapter Thirteen

I woke up hard. No, not in a good way. Hard in that it was difficult to attain consciousness. I struggled to open one eye. I felt like my entire circulatory system was too dry. My organs were dried-up and shriveled like raisins. A visitor would have seen a glassy stare out of my one open eye and a completely motionless body. My skin felt like it was made out of light bulbs. It was secreting alcohol like a tree in the rain forest releases oxygen. I felt pain in individual hair follicles that had been misdirected by the pillow during the night. I could feel other follicles reaching for water like thirsty tree roots. My head throbbed like a cartoon character's thumb when he hits it with a hammer. My stomach couldn't decide whether it wanted to shit or puke, but for the moment the battle was being fought to a draw. It was early rounds Leonard-Durán but eventually one of them was going to say *"No más."* To call this a hangover would not be doing it justice. People come out of a twenty-year coma fresher than I was.

To say I felt "bad" would be like saying Evel Knievel felt "bad" after he broke every bone in his body on the Snake River Canyon jump. This was the hangover to end all hangovers. If I was up to it, in a week or so we'd have a ceremony retiring the trophy.

My bedroom shades were wide open. The light of day was pouring in. It was as bright as the sun because it was in fact the sun, but I had no idea why it was hovering right outside my bedroom window. I closed my one open eye and pulled a pillow over my head. I may have lost consciousness for a few more hours. Or days. Time had no meaning. A native girl sat by my side dipping a damp cloth in a wooden bowl and pressing it against my forehead as I rambled deliriously about jungle fever.

Later I opened my eye again. The same one. It scouted the surroundings and found no immediate danger, so I gave the second one a try. Two working eyeballs enabled me to focus my vision to "blurry," an improvement from the earlier "legally blind."

People who drink in moderation have no conception of how terrible a killer hangover can be. They see a bloodshot-eyed guy in sunglasses, ice bag on his head, *shhh, no loud noises, ha ha*, it's all very comical. But the real thing is no laughing matter.

Despite possessing a body that appeared to be totally devoid of liquid, I had to pee. I steadied myself and swung my feet out of bed and to the floor. I sat up. I could see the clock said 11:38. I hadn't slept this late since before Nick was born. I still had my clothes on from the night before. Everything, including my shoes. I staggered to the bathroom. Despite both arms outstretched and hands flat against the wall, I wobbled to the point that I had to sit down. As I finished up, I felt my organs returning to their original positions that had been usurped the previous evening by my engorged bladder.

I made the decision that, despite the supernova going on in my bedroom, staying awake was not an option. I stumbled out of the bathroom, took off my clothes, and climbed back under the covers. Before I could drift back into blissful unconsciousness, I felt some movement on the other side of the bed. Did Sarah come back late last night? Was she already in bed when I got home? I had the typical hangover horniness, so I decided to see if she might be willing. I sidled over and whispered through morning-after liquor breath, "Are you awake?" It hadn't occurred to my addled brain that my wife hasn't slept past seven in twenty years. And if Sarah was in town, she'd be at work.

As I lay there trying to focus my bloodshot eyes on the form next to me, it became apparent that my wife was not only inexplicably sleeping but she had also colored and cut her hair. It should have been obvious to me by now, and it's surely obvious to you, that the sleeping form in my bed was not in fact my wife.

I scrambled away from her. The figure remained motionless. I climbed out and crept around the bed using the same gait I would use to exit a sleeping baby's room. I reached down and carefully peeled back the comforter to reveal a still unconscious, mouth-breathing Natalie from last night, her makeup smeared all over my wife's pillowcase.

For several minutes I stood there and watched her sleep. I was in no condition to handle this. I needed a morning-after expert. Fortunately, I had one in Corny. He'd sent more girls home in the morning than a school nurse.

I heard some commotion downstairs so I headed to the kitchen. Corny stood there in American Flag bikini briefs whipping up some eggs in a bowl. "Morning, sunshine! You look like shit."

"Why is that woman in my bed?" I asked. "There's makeup and saliva and probably nosebleed on my wife's pillow."

"What happened to 'good morning,' Bobby? Lexi and I were in the guest room bed. Where was Natalie supposed to sleep? On the floor?"

"I don't know, but not in my bed. Sarah will be able to tell. Women have a sixth sense for that kind of thing."

"You're such a fucking pussy," Corny said. "It's no big deal. I'm a pro at this. And anyway, we've got bigger fish to fry today."

He returned to making his eggs and I sat in a stupor. Nausea washed in and out of my gut like the tide. It still felt like there were hurricanes sloshing around in there. I sat there hating people like Corny who never worry about anything but also never have anything to lose.

Corny scraped some eggs out of the skillet and onto a plate and slid it in front of me. The mere sight of the egg film on the pan almost made me gag. "Just have some breakfast," he said. "Nothing cures a hangover like some bacon and eggs."

"The only thing that would cure this hangover is a morphine drip."

"Are you serious? I've probably got some Vicodins if you need them."

We ate our eggs in relative silence, Corny conceivably because he was enjoying his meal, me because I was trying not to puke. This wasn't an "Oh, my God, I'm starving" kind of hangover. Corny made a few references to the night out that rekindled some fuzzy memories, none of them good. I was more interested in the future than the past anyway.

"Corny, go get those gals up and let's get them the fuck out of here."

He headed toward the master bedroom and returned a minute later. I heard the shower kick on. He walked by me in silence and returned to the guest bedroom and shut the door.

I thought about checking in with the office, but why? They weren't expecting me and if they really needed my help, I was in no condition to give it. I went into the family room and collapsed on the couch. I must have dozed off for a few minutes because when I looked up, Corny was standing in front of me.

"Get up, Bobby. We've got a big day ahead of us."

I stared at him out of my good eye. I kept the other one closed. If I didn't, there were two of him. "What do you mean 'we'?"

"I mean you and me," Corny said. "I've got a meeting set up with one of my business associates."

"I don't go to meetings when I feel good, Corny. There's no way in hell I'm going to a meeting when I feel like I just spent a week in Tijuana."

Corny leveled his gaze at me and spoke softly but with gritted teeth, like he'd been practicing *Dirty Harry* lines in the mirror. "You're going to that meeting with me, Bobby."

I covered my face with a throw pillow to protect myself from the blinding light. "The fuck I am. I'm going back to bed as soon as we get these girls out of here."

"I'm going to have to insist."

Then silence. I thought maybe he'd given up, so after a minute or so, I slid the pillow off and opened my eyes. There was a gun in my face.

◇◇◇

When someone suddenly points a gun at you, the most important thing is to remain calm.

"Holy fucking shit, Corny!! Are you out of your mind?" I flung myself off the couch and sprinted down the hall toward the bedroom. "Girls, run for your lives!! Corny's gone crazy! He's got a gun!"

Natalie stepped out of the bedroom, holding a tiny, hot-chick-appropriate gun. I'll bet she posed with it in front of one of those trifold full-length mirrors they have in ladies' dressing rooms to see how it looked before she bought it.

"Jesus Christ," I screamed. "What are you doing? You can't fight him with that thing! He has a real gun!!"

Natalie sighed and shook her head disgustedly. If she was tweeting what was happening, she would have typed "smh." It was a gesture I've seen a thousand times from my wife. "Jesus, Bob. Dave said you weren't the sharpest tool in the shed but he didn't put near enough emphasis on the tool part. Are you a complete dumbass?"

Natalie marched me back into the living room at gunpoint. Lexi came out of the other bedroom and followed us. They were both dressed businesswoman-sexy, tailored suits with hose and black pumps. I was dumbfounded at how clean, professional and, well, normal they looked. Do they do this every night and wake up looking like they were home in bed before *The Tonight Show*? I was dying and they were raring to go.

I sat back down on the couch. I looked back and forth among these three individuals towering over me in their expensive suits as I sat shirtless in my underwear. I held the pillow on my lap. Corny still held the gun loosely in his hand. "So how about someone telling me what the fuck is going on?" I said.

Corny nodded at Lexi and she brought over a laptop. Corny sat it down on the coffee table and punched a few keystrokes. He had put the gun away somewhere, but what was I going to do, hit him over the head with the laptop and run out the front door in my boxers, dodging bullets from Natalie all the way down the drive? When he turned the laptop toward me, the eggs I'd eaten decided to make a run for it. I stumbled over to the kitchen and vomited in the sink. I drank some water right out of the tap and went back to the couch.

The laptop images themselves didn't make me lose my breakfast. They weren't gruesome crime scene photos like a cop uses to shock a witness or anything. In fact two of the three participants in the photo montage were quite attractive. The third was me.

Chapter Fourteen

The first photo showed Natalie and Lexi totally naked crouching over my similarly nude body. Corny hit a button and the next picture appeared and another and another, all showing me getting expertly worked over by two beautiful women in my marital bed. These were the kind of high-quality sex scenes Corny would have forwarded to all of us on his e-mail distribution list. He had a talent for staging.

I shouldn't have been so surprised. In college, Corny was notorious for messing with unconscious guys. Even though he drank more than anyone, Corny never passed out. When his drinking partner for the night inevitably succumbed, Corny would go to work. We didn't have digital cameras back then, thank God, so he couldn't record the incident for posterity, but he would strip the guy naked and lock him on the fire escape or draw cocks all over him with a permanent marker. One of our pledge brothers had to go to a job interview senior year with the faint outline of an impossible-to-scrub-off dick right in the middle of his forehead. He didn't get the job.

I scrolled through all the pictures. No Corny, just me, Natalie and Lexi. My first three-way and I wasn't even awake for it. "I'm just glad you weren't in the photos, Corny. I've seen what you do to unconscious people."

Corny grinned at that. Unfortunately, he was born without the shame gene. "I saved all the teabagging photos to another disk. I'm having them made into an album."

"Does all this have a point?"

"The point is, I don't imagine your wife would approve of what you've been doing in her bed."

"I wasn't even awake."

"But Mr. Happy was, as you can plainly see," Natalie said with a giggle. "Well, if you zoom in real close."

"You can also see a couple lines of coke on your wedding photo on the bedside table," Corny said. "Photo glass is a good chopping surface."

Lexi laughed. "The wedding photo was my idea."

"Good work, Lexi," I said. "You're showing some real initiative."

"Enough chitchat," Corny said. "Bob, go take a shower and get yourself cleaned up. We have a meeting to go to. This is one your wife would definitely want you to attend."

I stood in the shower and tried to assess the situation and by assessing the situation I mean I threw up. I sat down on the shower bench and told myself I was a fucking idiot. How could I let myself get in this situation? I don't look for trouble and trouble doesn't look for me. But here I was.

I thought about Sarah. I thought about my kids. I even thought about my father-in-law, who would never have let himself get in a situation like this. For all I know, he had a mistress in every town, powerful men often do, but he would never humiliate Sarah's mother by letting anyone find out about it. None of this was explainable. None of it. I was guilty. I got shitfaced and out of control with a beautiful young woman who was not my wife. Whatever happened after that is my fault. I didn't know what Corny wanted me to do, but my quick hungover shower-analysis led me to the inescapable conclusion that whatever it was, I was going to have to do it.

I got out of the shower and dressed in a daze. As I was pulling on my normal business-casual khakis, Corny shouted from the family room. "And put a suit on. You need to show some respect."

◇◇◇

I put on my suit and joined the group in the family room. Corny said, "Let's go."

A new problem entered my mind. What was one more? "We can't just leave the house with two strange women in the car."

"Why not?"

"Because Sarah's horse trainer is probably out there."

"So what? He's your employee. He does what you tell him."

"He's Sarah's employee. He'd love to tell her about this.'

"Okay, girls, you'll have to lie down in the backseat. I'm guessing it won't be your first time."

We got into my car in the garage and the girls assumed their positions, making lewd noises and giggling. "It's not the same without you, Bob," Natalie purred. Ah, the simple pleasures of the party slut. You probably wouldn't want to marry one, but they definitely had their charms.

I peered out the garage door before opening it and all was quiet. As we backed out, I glanced anxiously toward the barn. When I needed the trainer's help, I could never find him, but of course this time he was walking across the grass toward us, shouting "Bob!"

I pretended not to hear him, gave a perfunctory wave and sped off down the driveway. When he eventually told Sarah, and he would, I would just say Corny and I were late for a meeting, which was true. Include as much truth in your lies as possible, I always say.

As I drove, I realized I was still probably over the legal limit for blood alcohol content from last night's drinking. Adding a DUI to my resume would be a nice topper to the day. Corny directed me to one of the nice hotels downtown. Think Ritz-Carlton, but that wasn't it. "A hotel?" I asked. "Don't you have enough blackmail material?"

"Lots of meetings are in hotels," Corny said, shaking his head. "You really don't know anything about business, do you?"

"No, I don't, so I'm sure I won't be any help to you. Why don't I just drop you off somewhere and we'll forget this ever happened?"

"Afraid not, Bobby. You're the right man for the job."

We valet parked and approached the revolving glass doors. I stopped and bent down to tie my shoelace. It wouldn't look good to be seen walking into a hotel in the middle of the day with two attractive young females. If I was *lucky*, people would think they were just hookers.

"What are you doing?" Corny asked.

"What's it look like? I'm tying my shoe."

"You're wearing loafers."

"So I am." I stood back up and followed the girls inside, where they were thoughtfully waiting for us. I tried to act inconspicuous and avoid eye contact with the staff, but almost immediately, I heard my name shouted. I turned the opposite way, hoping whoever it was would think they were mistaken.

"Bob!" If I saw someone I knew in a strange place, the last thing I'd want to do is talk to them, suspicious women in tow or not, but this person wouldn't be denied.

I turned around as if I just heard him and there was Ned Kruppen, a harmless but overly friendly fellow I knew from the country club. We golfed occasionally and tennised if I got roped into it. We weren't great friends, but I knew him. The only time I would ever call out to *him* would be if my tee shot was about to hit his golf cart. And maybe not even then.

"Ned." I said and shook his hand.

Ned eyeballed each of my compatriots as he spoke. "What brings you downtown, buddy? You normally don't cross the mid-town line."

I had wasted the drive here *not* concocting a cover story, so I couldn't think of anything to say. Anxiety flushed my face, I'm sure, and liquor-fueled perspiration began to flow. Obviously, I should introduce these people to Ned, but as what? As I fumbled for a response, Corny spoke up.

"Hi, there. Scott Van Pelt. These are my associates Linda Cohn and Hannah Storm. We're treating Bob here to a late lunch trying to convince him to switch his company's Internet and phone service. We knew since Sarah and the kids were out of town, Bob couldn't claim he had to have lunch with the missus."

"That's right, Ned," I said. "And we're actually running late, so I'll talk to you later. When it gets warmer, we'll knock the pill around."

"Sure, Bob, looking forward to it." Ned looked a little puzzled, but by then we were walking away. I doubt it was lost on him that we were headed not for the restaurant but toward the room elevator banks.

"That was smooth, *Scott*," I said. "Let's hope he doesn't watch SportsCenter."

"He doesn't," Corny replied. "Look at him, for Christ's sake."

Corny hit the elevator button for one of the top floors, although not all that high in a mid-sized city like ours. We followed Corny down the hallway. There weren't very many rooms on the floor, so I assumed they were all expensive suites. Corny stopped in front of one of them and knocked. A nondescript smiling man, who could easily have been a dentist or a pet shop owner, opened the door, smiled and said, "Bob, Tom Swanson. Good to see you again."

I know what you're thinking. Who else would it be? But I was a hungover, frightened husband who didn't know what to expect and it shocked the shit out of me to see Swanson open that door. He was an overly aggressive salesman, but I never would have pegged him for a ruthless blackmailer. On the surface, he was a virtual stereotype of the successful, middle-aged white guy. *Nobody knows anybody.*

We all took seats in the sitting area, like normal people in a normal conversation. "Bob, I've tried to do this the easy way. You make money, we make money, everybody wins. Apparently, you're not smart enough to recognize this for the opportunity it is."

"It doesn't matter what I think. It's not what Sam wanted."

"Look, about that," Swanson said. "It's true Sam sent me that e-mail, but that wasn't the end of it. He had some legitimate concerns and we answered them. We continued to work on the deal and he was reconsidering. You can't tell what Sam would have wanted from one tiny form letter of an e-mail. And even if you could, Sam's dead. I'm sorry to be so blunt, but it's a fact. You've got to make the decisions now and the sooner you realize it the better."

"I do realize it and this is my decision."

"You understand this deal could also be lucrative for you personally?"

I sat up a little at that. "How so?"

"I understand you're not even being paid for all the work you're doing."

How the hell did he know that? "I'm happy to do it." I think I even meant it.

"Maybe so," Swanson said, "but we could put you on the board at Sanitol and pay you a couple of hundred thousand dollars a year for going to four board meetings."

"Isn't that unethical or a violation of my fiduciary duty or something?"

Swanson snorted in derision. "Hell, no. Every powerful person is on a bunch of boards and gets paid for essentially doing nothing." *I'll admit I liked the sound of that.* "If you couldn't invest in any company that the Bennett Trust is involved with," Swanson continued, "you'd have to start keeping your money in a coffee can in your backyard."

"The answer is still no."

"I understand your family is still grieving and you're new to the job," Swanson said. "The last thing I want to do is push you. But we're running out of time here."

"I don't see how ruining my marriage is going to help you, Swanson."

"Nobody's trying to ruin your marriage, Bob. You're just an impossible man to convince using traditional business methods, which you seem to be largely unfamiliar with."

It was at about this time in the meeting that I released a silent but excruciatingly deadly fart. I note this only because under normal circumstances, I would have been completely embarrassed. In this case, I found it interesting that even criminal enterprise types, in a business setting, politely pretend they don't smell it. Even Corny couldn't mention it in case it was Swanson who'd dealt it.

I moved on. "You guys have crossed a pretty serious line. It's one thing to try to convince me, but another to commit felonious extortion."

Swanson leaned forward. "Bob, business *is* extortion. When people buy up the shares of a company to threaten a takeover, they call it greenmail, not blackmail. If somebody pays me to drop a lawsuit, how is that different from extortion? I threaten to do something unless they pay me to stop. It's exactly the same. I know you're not a very sophisticated businessman, Bob, but grow up. This is how things work. You use whatever leverage you can get to make the best deal for yourself."

"That leverage doesn't usually involve incriminating photos."

"Sure it does. It happens all the time. But whatever. The bottom line is you have until Friday to agree to this deal or we'll have a DVD of last night's festivities delivered to your wife."

Corny leaned in and winked at me. "I might even throw in some old Polaroids I took in college."

I left the three of them in the lobby to check in. "Remember," Corny said as I walked away. "We're going to be watching you. I may even stop by to check on you once everyone's back in town. I'm sure Sarah would love to see me."

I turned around and pointed my finger at him. "Stay away from me and my family, Corny!" I shouted.

Corny was as rattled by that pathetic outburst as you'd imagine. "Take it easy, Tiger. Just do the deal and you have nothing to worry about."

I made my way to my car. My hangover was still operating at about fifty percent power, so it was down to the level of a normal, run-of-the-mill, "I swear I'll never drink again" hangover. Unfortunately, I was faced with a situation that required more than I could give on my best day.

I went home and sat down on the couch to think. Remember how I said everything is relative? A week ago I was unhappy with my unfulfilling life. Now I'd give anything for that boring existence. Because of the anxiety of the day combined with my already jittery hangover nerves, I was suddenly bone-tired. I felt like my entire nervous system had been on high alert all day and now it crashed. I fell fast asleep sitting up on the couch.

At around eight-thirty, the house phone began to ring. Normally I can't fall into a deep sleep sitting up, but there was nothing normal about today. I practiced a couple of hellos to see if my voice would work and picked up the phone.

"Bob?" My wife's voice on the other end. "Why do you sound like that? Did I wake you up?"

"Yeah, you did, but I'm glad." My entire body filled with guilt and dread just from hearing the sound of her voice. "How's your trip going?"

"The usual deal. The kids are having a blast and Carol and I are enjoying our time and our wine together. But as always happens after a few days, I'm ready to come home."

I jumped on that a little quicker than I would have normally. "True, but you promised the kids four days. You always say you feel guilty that you don't get to spend enough time with them."

"This is true. But I wish we hadn't gone so rustic. This place is really roughing it and I hate that I have to drive fifteen miles of mountain roads to make a phone call. But that means the office can't reach me either, which I'm always grateful for. So how'd it go with Corny? Is that why you're asleep at eight-thirty? Please tell me he didn't nail some bar skank in my guest bedroom."

I forced a chuckle. "Nothing like that." Actually, exactly like that. And you'll never guess what happened in *your* bed. I made a note to myself—wash the sheets and walk every square inch of the house for evidence collection. "But we did stay out drinking pretty late and I'm just beat from that. He left this morning. Are the kids with you?"

"No, they send their love, but they stayed back to play games at the ranch."

"Well, tell them I love them. Tell them I love them a lot. And I love you, too." I realized this was completely out of character as soon as it left my mouth, but guilt conjures strange feelings, and I couldn't help myself.

Fortunately, Sarah's a woman, so she wasn't suspicious, just pleased. She misconstrued it as romantic. "Gee, I should wake you up more often. I love you, too, and I'll see you tomorrow."

With newfound energy, I stripped the sheets from the guest room bed and threw them in the laundry room. I walked back to the master bedroom and entered the chamber of horrors for the first time since this morning. I stood there and viewed my boudoir like a cop at a crime scene. The makeup on the pillow, Corny's footprints everywhere in the carpet where he filmed "the action." Our wedding picture still lying down but wiped clean. It all made me want to puke again. I'd dug my own grave in this very room and wasn't even conscious when it happened.

I pulled the comforter off the bed and stripped the sheets and pillowcases and threw them in a pile by the door. I picked up the comforter and gave it a sniff. Yep, there was Lexi. The perfume smell hit my male nose and I knew it would knock Sarah's female nose into next week. Since it was not something I could buy a covert replacement for, I took it outside and hung it over the deck railing, hoping it would air out. I carried the sheets down to the laundry room and, along with the guest room sheets, shoved it all into the washer. This was not something I'm very experienced at, so I hoped I was doing it right. The last thing I needed was some kind of *Mr. Mom* laundry disaster to call attention to the fact I was washing the sheets.

I did one more once-around the house, cleaned up all the dishes, and got the towels out of the bathrooms and threw them in the laundry room. I checked the showers for telltale Lexi and Natalie signs and opened the windows to air out the master bedroom. I lay down on the family room couch. Somehow, I didn't feel worthy to sleep in my own bed. I was putting myself in the penalty box for the night.

I examined my options. (1) Bring the wife under the tent and hope she understood. Not ideal, but the cover-up's often worse than the crime. Every veteran sitcom-watcher knows it would be easier to explain that you accidentally made two dates for Halloween than to run back and forth changing your costume every five minutes. But this was a little more serious than that. I'm pretty sure I didn't really do anything wrong, but none of it would have happened if Corny hadn't told me about him and Sarah. My heart was hardly pure. And the pictures were really horrible. I was passed out, but you couldn't tell.

(2) Sign off on the damn deal and hope Corny would do the right thing and give me all of the copies of the photos once I'd done what he asked me to do. Possible, but unlikely, because blackmail doesn't work that way. They just keep bleeding you and bleeding you.

I didn't have a (3). What I needed was a (3). (3) should have been *Fight back. Make these bastards pay and come out a winner.*

It wasn't just the specifics of this particular nightmare situation that I couldn't handle. I was at that stage in life where men often start to feel a kind of existential angst. You begin to realize that this is it, you're doing whatever you're going to do and you're not going to achieve any of your dreams. You feel like you've wasted your life and squandered whatever talent you might have had. This is the point when men get sports cars, wear toupees, and have affairs.

I knew I wasn't that kind of guy. For one thing, I didn't have the initiative. For another, a long-term affair seemed crazy to me, like having two wives, but with the added hassle of keeping one of them completely secret.

My mind continued to wander. I was semi-dozing and thinking of all the things I wished I could do over. But what I could have or should have done didn't matter anymore. What was I going to do now? The next play is the only one that matters. Control what you can control. Don't let one bad shot affect the next shot. Don't look back except to learn something. No regrets. Clean slate. What steps could I take?

Chapter Fifteen

I spent the morning double- and triple-checking my cleaning efforts and as far as I could tell, nothing was amiss. Sarah and the kids arrived home without incident, and we spent a normal evening together as a family, although I had my head on a swivel like an NHL defenseman anytime they entered a room that might contain incriminating evidence in spite of my forensic sweep of the house.

Even though the horses we keep are Sarah's, I often do the night check, which mostly involves going down to the barn and feeding them. Just a couple flakes of hay per horse. Sarah is usually feverishly working on her laptop every night, trying to get a few more things done before she goes to bed. So I do the horses. Someone familiar with my schedule would know exactly where to find me at ten at night.

The truth is I volunteer for night check duty because I enjoy it. We have a beautiful barn. It probably cost more than our house. I know it's better cared for.

I like to survey my property like a land baron. The clear sky and fresh air, the smell and sounds of the animals. It feels substantial, like I really have accomplished something, and haven't been just wasting my time, treading water while everyone else swims past.

It was a nice night for winter. Crisp, but not cold. I walked into the barn and was tossing hay over the gates into the stalls when I heard a noise outside in the darkness. It was a male voice singing softly.

> *You can't hide your lyin' eyes*
> *And your smile is a thin disguise*
> *I thought by now you'd realize*
> *There ain't no way to hide your lyin' eyes*

I walked over to the barn door. "You're a riot, Corny. Come on in." When he stepped into the light, I could see that he was holding a DVD. He was dressed all in black—watch cap, turtleneck, jeans, gloves.

Despite Corny's recent transition from friend to foe, the only way I knew how to relate to him was the way we all did in college: giving each other a bunch of shit. "O.J. called, Corny. He wants his stalking clothes back."

"Hey, it worked for him. He got away with murder."

"Why are you here?"

"Just like Glenn Frey said, Bobby. You can't hide your lyin' eyes."

"I disagree. I hide my lyin' eyes all the time. Constantly, in fact. My eyes are way more likely to be lyin' than tellin' the truth. Even when I haven't really done anything."

He tossed the disk up in the air like he was flipping a coin. "Well, in this case, you *have* done something and it's all right here in vivid Technicolor in the new DVD format. In the old days, a blackmailer had to carry around a bulky videotape cassette. Nowadays we have CDs, DVDs, flash drives, mpegs, jpegs, mwavs, there's been a real technological revolution in the extortion industry."

"I'm happy for you, Corny. It would be a shame to see technological advancements wasted on upstanding citizens. Maybe we can divert some of that R&D money from cancer research to illegal spy gadgets."

"We can always hope. But I'm here, Bob, because you haven't kept up your end of the bargain."

"Bargain? What bargain? A bargain is 'buy one get one free.' A bargain is not 'you do something for us or we'll tell your wife you cheated on her.'"

"Okay, you haven't lived up to your end of the coercion. Is that better?"

"Yes, because I didn't agree to do anything. I said I'd think about it."

"And have you?"

"Have I what?"

"Thought about it?"

"Yes."

"Did you come to some kind of a decision?"

"Some kind, yes." I was stalling, but Corny didn't seem to notice. He loved to banter. I'd really been doing nothing but stall for the last couple of days. I was basically running the old North Carolina four corners offense for the whole game, a tactic that made college basketball so boring they added a shot clock. Dean Smith used to do it even with superior talent, but that's because he thought he was smarter than everyone else. When other coaches do it, it's a desperation ploy by a team that's hopelessly overmatched. In this case, me.

But this time I was stalling for a reason. After Corny entered the barn, I thought I heard the back door to the house open followed by the running footsteps of my beloved dog Max. So I was biding my time until the moment when Max would burst into the barn and rip Corny's throat out.

"Well, what was it?"

"What was what?" Max was just outside the door.

"Your decision?"

"It's complicated." Max leapt at Corny.

"How can it be complic—hey, it's my old buddy, Max. Come here, boy, there's a good boy." Max curled up in Corny's arms like a baby. Like an evil, traitorous baby. He was licking the face of my worst enemy while staring at me across the barn. I decided Max just didn't know any better. He thought Corny was my friend.

"I think you're a prick but my dog likes you," I said.

He nuzzled the top of Max's head and scratched his belly as he held him. "He does, doesn't he?"

"It's not surprising. Max has always had terrible judgment." Max obligingly licked Corny's face.

Corny snorted and set Max down. "All right, I've had enough of your bullshit." He started toward me in what I would describe as a menacing manner. I had never actually been menaced before and this didn't look like something Dennis would do to Mr. Wilson until he was a tattooed and pierced teenager, but I was being menaced. "I need to know if you're going to play ball."

Corny's tough guy act was legitimately scaring me but this made me laugh out loud. "Play ball?"

"What's wrong with 'play ball'?"

"Nothing, if you're a gangster in an old black and white movie."

"What do people say now?"

"You tell me. You're the bad guy."

He stepped in close again. "How about this? Any more fucking around and I am going to beat the living shit out of you."

"Much more effective."

"Thank you. I meant it. So let's hear it. What's the verdict?"

"I'm not going to do it."

He waved the DVD in my face. "Okay, then I hope you've got some popcorn because I'm just going to head on up to the house and invite Mrs. Patterson to a special midnight screening of *SpongeBob NoPants*."

"Nice title."

"Thanks. I've watched a lot of porn. They always take a real movie title and make it dirty, like *On Golden Blonde* or *Good Will Humping*."

"Whatever. Go ahead and show it to her."

Corny was at a loss for words. No pithy comeback for once. He probably looked a lot like I looked when called on at a business meeting when I didn't even know what the discussion was about. But unlike me, he was frustrated and angry instead of charmingly self-deprecating. He started toward me with what looked like intent. Max, as ever attuned to the mood of the room, trotted alongside him, panting and wagging his tail. Corny turned and kicked him. Violently. He booted him like Adam Vinatieri trying a fifty-yard field goal. He kicked *my dog* as hard as he possibly could.

We all have our limits. Unfortunately, kicking the crap out of my dog is apparently below mine, because I stood there like I was one of Cruella de Vil's henchmen. Max yelped and hurriedly limped away down the long barn aisle. Now we were alone.

"You don't get it, Bobby," Corny said and backhanded me across the face like he was Roger Federer. It reminded me of one of Federer's backhands because you could admire the power and grace even as you were getting your brains beaten in. In my case, literally. I think he'd done this before.

Okay, now I was scared. I hadn't been in a fight since I got my ass kicked on the playground in third grade. I spat blood out of my mouth. I ejected the snot out of my nostrils one at a time, a method we used to call the "coach's handkerchief" in high school. My cheek was numb, which made talking more challenging than usual. "You're wasting your time with this show of force, Corny. I already know you're tougher than me. Everybody's tougher than me."

"You're right about that, Bobby. But you're wrong about a couple other things. First, you may have been drunk, but those pictures are real. That scene wasn't staged. You brought that girl home with you. And second, you don't realize it, but I'm the best fucking friend you have in this deal."

"With friends like you, who needs enemies?"

"You think the people I work for wanted to try this shitty blackmail scheme?" Corny asked. "I talked them into it because I said I knew you and further escalations were unnecessary. I told them you'd cave, Bob, and now you're making me look bad in front of my employers."

"What do I care?"

"You do *not* want to fuck with these people, Bobby. After this little project, I'm getting out. Even I'm afraid to work with them."

He was standing directly over me. His eyes were bulging from their sockets and the vein in his neck was throbbing. I was beginning to get the idea that Corny didn't just coke up for fun on blackmail nights. "Now you're going to do what I tell you or I'm going to cut off your head and put it on that shelf so you can watch your body run around like the chickens you butcher on this farm."

"It's a horse farm, Dave," Sarah said from the barn doorway. "We don't raise chickens."

◇◇◇

Corny whirled around to face the voice. "Well, if it isn't the lovely Mrs. Patterson!" Corny singsonged. "What brings you to our party tonight?"

"I started to think Bob ran into trouble feeding the horses, and then I heard you talking and started listening from the tack room door." She wasn't intimidated by Corny. Women are often braver than they should be in the face of physical violence, to their own detriment as well as that of the husbands whose asses get kicked in bars because they won't shut up. Attractive women are so used to men ogling them that they lose their fear. They're like lion tamers. They're accustomed to bossing around powerful animals.

"I'm glad you're here." Corny held up the DVD. "I've got something to show you."

I interrupted him. "There's no need to show her the DVD, Corny."

Corny turned back to me and smiled. "So now you're ready to 'play ball'?"

"No. You don't have to show it to her because I already told her."

◇◇◇

"Bullshit," Corny said. It was true, though. I did tell Sarah, after dinner when the kids went to watch TV. There were quite a few tears, but eventually she calmed me down.

"It's true, Dave," Sarah said. "Bob told me and I believe him. My issue was more related to his being a fucking moron for getting together with you in the first place."

"That's right," I said. "I told her and it was easier than you'd think. I couldn't start doing whatever you wanted me to. Trying to keep the incriminating material secret by doing what the blackmailer says is a temporary solution to an ongoing problem. Blackmail doesn't stop."

"With all due respect, Bob," Corny said. "What the fuck do you know about blackmail?"

"I know that it doesn't work if the blackmailee doesn't care if the 'evidence' comes out. You don't really want to show my wife the video. Once you do, your leverage is gone. So if I tell her myself, game over." I smiled at Corny and continued. "I realized living in constant fear of Sarah finding out was much worse than what would happen if she actually found out. So I told her. It was like ripping off a band-aid."

"And Sarah forgave you," Corny said derisively. "Just like that."

"Come on, Corny. Sure, you had some mildly incriminating photos, but there was no dead hooker, no real sex act."

Sarah jumped in to help. "Plus, I know he couldn't pick up a pretty young woman and get her to have sex with him if his life depended on it."

I glared at Sarah. "Unnecessarily cruel, but true." I turned to Corny. "It was an obvious setup. You must have slipped something in my drink at the bar. No wonder my hangover was such a killer."

"We were prepared to do that if we had to, but there was no need. You drank yourself into a stupor on your own."

"Glad I was able to help," I said. "Now you won't have to go back to Walgreen's before your next date-rape."

Corny paced back and forth in frustration. "Look," he said. "You two think you've cleverly defused this blackmail thing, but you have vastly underestimated my employer. That little video was not their normal MO for getting people to do what they want. I came up with that so as not to cause my old pal Bobby any undue pain and suffering."

"So you blackmailed me for my own good."

"I wouldn't put it exactly like that, but in effect, yes. I did it to help you." Corny lifted up his stalking sweater and pulled out a document in one of those clear report covers you used in high school. He had it tucked into the front of his pants like an NFL offensive coordinator. "Now that the blackmail ship has sailed, you're going to need to sign this Letter of Intent to Invest right now or pain and suffering is definitely back on the table."

"A document signed under duress doesn't mean anything."

"Oh, yes it does. It will stand unless you say it shouldn't and if you say anything, I'm going to make 'under duress' seem like a walk in the park for you. You're going to lie awake at night dreaming of the days when you were 'under duress.'"

I shuffled a few steps to my left. Corny began to ease the space between us so he could keep one eye on Sarah. His brain told him we were a benign threat, but his criminal experience made him act like all three of us were pointing guns at each other in a Mexican standoff. Our stance had backed him up against the opening of the new horse's stall and the stallion was interested in him. The horse was pushing his nose into Corny's back, trying to decide if he was friend or foe. Like most stallions, Rex was suspicious of any male he considered a potential rival for the affections of the females in the herd. Corny kept pushing the horse's head away but he kept coming back: sniff, jerk away, sniff, jerk away.

After a final push away, it occurred to Corny that being taunted by a horse wasn't helping his command presence. "Get this fucking animal away from me!" he shouted at Sarah.

"You move," Sarah countered with steely calm. "*You're* bothering *him*." It would have been easy for Corny to move away and that's exactly what he would have done if Sarah hadn't told him to. No way was he doing her bidding.

"Oh, that's right. You're the horse expert. You gals love your horses," Corny leered. "Rubbing against the saddle gets you off, doesn't it?"

"What do you know about getting a woman off, Dave?" Thankfully, Sarah left me out of this line of inquiry.

But Corny didn't. "If you'd like to know what your husband knows about it, I'd be happy to show you the DVD."

"I don't need to see it," Sarah said. "I'm all too familiar with Bob's sexual performance when he's drunk."

I gave Sarah a hurt look. She ignored it and continued. "I also told Bob your little story about the two of us in college was complete bullshit. I wouldn't let you touch me if you were wearing a full-body condom."

Corny looked sheepish. "I actually felt kind of bad about that, but I wanted him in the right frame of mind to meet the girls." He mimed a sad clown face at me. "Forgive me, Bobby?"

"Of course not."

"Well, it's water under the bridge now. You've got bigger problems. Do you think we'll go away because you've defused the blackmail threat? Blackmail was the easy way for *you*, not for *us*. I was doing you a favor because we're old friends."

I wiped a fake tear from my eye. "Your concern is touching, Corny."

"I promised my employers the blackmail would work because I know you."

"I guess you don't know me as well as you thought."

"I'm serious. You may not like being blackmailed, Bobby, but believe me, the alternatives are far worse. What do you think happened to your father-in-law?"

Chapter Sixteen

"What are you talking about, Dave?" Sarah asked through gritted teeth.

"Swanson wasn't lying about your father being interested in Sanitol," Corny said. "He really was."

Finally, my chance to enlighten everyone. "That's true. But you may not know that shortly before he died, Sam sent an e-mail to Swanson declining the deal."

"Of course I know that," Corny sneered. "After Swanson got that e-mail, he tried everything to change Sam's mind, even bribes and veiled threats. But Sam had seen something in the deal he didn't like. He wouldn't be persuaded."

"That was Dad," Sarah said. "Even I couldn't get him to change his mind once it was made up."

I smiled at her. "And you had him wrapped around your little finger."

"So Swanson knew he was screwed," Corny said. "He wasn't the better man in this negotiation. As long as Sam was in charge, the deal wouldn't go through."

"But Swanson couldn't have known the deal would go through if something happened to Sam," I said. "Sarah's just as smart and tough as her father."

"Exactly. They needed someone like you in charge of the trust."

"How could they know my father would name Bob trustee?"

Corny shrugged. "They have ways of getting what they want."

"And you're one of those ways," I said.

"That's right, I am. But they have others. Even if they had something to do with you becoming trustee, who would question it? You're Sam's son-in-law. You're a lawyer. You're a respected member of the community, for some reason. Why do you think they picked you?"

How ironic. Hoisted on my own petard. I should have kept my petard locked in my petard safe. But the only way they'll get my petard now is to pry it from my cold, dead hands.

Sarah came to my defense. "Swanson and his roving band of Cornies had nothing to do with it. My father chose Bob as trustee because he thought he was the best man for the job."

"Have it your way," Corny shrugged. "It doesn't matter. The bottom line is we're all in the same boat. And it is rapidly filling up with water and alligators and piranhas and nasty shit. When that boat goes down, we don't want to be on it." Corny tucked the Letter of Intent back into his pants. "Now let's go up to the house and figure out what we're going to do."

Sarah said, "All right," and started out the barn door. I followed. Corny gave a little bow and said "Age before beauty." I walked past him toward the door. I was beginning to see that Corny was a complicated man. Deep down, he was actually a pretty good guy, I thought, as he hit me in the back of the head with a shovel.

◇◇◇

When I came to, Corny was dragging me by my ankles along the dirt floor of the barn while Sarah pounded on his back with her fists and screamed obscenities. I don't think I was ever truly unconscious, more stunned than knocked out. Corny had delivered a glancing blow, like a pool player trying to make a shot at a difficult angle by hitting the outer edge of the ball. He was trying to briefly disable me, not hurt me seriously. Or maybe he just missed.

Corny leaned me up against the trough we use to water the horses and grabbed a chair out of the office and told Sarah to sit on it. Surprisingly, I felt okay. The hangover had been worse.

Corny walked over, lifted me up by the front of the shirt and let the back of my head hang over the water in the trough. "Bobby, I'm just going to give you a little taste of what you can expect if you don't cooperate." He lowered my head in the water for a few seconds. The water was cool and actually felt pretty good on my wounded head. I didn't choke, although I was a little grossed out because I'm sure the water was full of horse spit. Before it got any worse, Corny pulled me back out. I opened my eyes and saw the reason why. Sarah was yanking his head back by the hair.

Corny turned, picked Sarah up, and slammed her back in the chair. "Once I get your wife under control, I'll continue with Corny's CIA-approved waterboard torture. It's so torturous, they won't even use it on terrorists anymore. But I'm going to use it on you, Bob."

Corny's first effort didn't count as waterboarding. It was more like fraternity pledge hazing, without the homoerotic under-tones. At least in my case. I can't speak for Corny.

But I sure as hell didn't want him to take another crack at it. When Corny said he was going to torture me, he meant it. And if that didn't work, he'd move on to something that would, like hurting my family. He was a true psychopath, willing to do anything to get what he wanted, with no empathy for his victims.

"We're all going to have a nice long chat. But first I need to immobilize the two of you." Corny started walking around the barn.

"What are you looking for?" Sarah asked.

"Rope. I'm going to tie you to that chair so you don't butt in while I make sure Bobby here has a clear understanding of the situation."

"You don't need to do that," Sarah said. "Bob can barely sit up and I'm just a woman." Yeah, right. And a shark is just a fish. Even I wasn't buying that one.

"*What we have here is a failure to communicate,*" Corny drawled. "This isn't a negotiation. I'm either going to tie you to the chair or shoot you in the kneecap. Your choice."

"You don't even have a gun," Sarah scoffed.

Corny reached behind him and pulled a small black handgun from his waistband. I'd seen it before, pointed at my hungover face.

"Corny, put the gun away," I said. "There's rope in the stall."

Corny pointed a finger at Sarah. "You stay right where you are. Don't even think about making a run for the house or I'll make a surprise bedcheck on the kiddies."

Sarah sprang out of the chair "If you so much as go near any of my children, I will kill you."

I reacted too but could only raise my head a few inches before a wave of nausea hit me and puke came out of my mouth instead of the vicious threats I'd intended. I mentally added vomiting to my concussion checklist. Dizziness, check, headache, check, cartoon birds circling my head, check, vomiting, check.

Corny ignored me and pointed the gun at Sarah. "Sit down. Stay put and you have nothing to worry about."

Sarah sank back down. Corny tucked the gun in the back of his black jeans, unlatched the stall door, and went in. Rex snorted and shuffled around nervously.

"That's a good boy," Corny whispered. He eased behind the horse and looked at the wall. "I can't see anything. Where's the rope?"

"Do you have a flashlight?"

"Of course I do. I'm a professional."

The second Corny switched on his flashlight, Rex went absolutely batshit. He snorted and whinnied and made whatever the hell noises horses make when they're pissed. He smashed the stall door apart with his front legs and kicked back toward the light with his hind legs. A sickening thud rang as hoof met flesh. I heard Corny's body hit the ground. So did Rex. Like an experienced street fighter, he knew the fight wasn't over when the other man went down. You finish him off with your boots. That's what Rex did. He backed up and stomped twice, burst through the splintered door, and pounded out into the night.

Chapter Seventeen

Like most grazing animals, horses are generally not aggressive. They're prey, not predators. Because they don't have to hunt and kill their food, their first instinct is flight, not fight. Their response to danger is to run away. Thank God for that because if they knew what they were capable of, they would never serve their human masters again. Fortunately, horses don't know they're practically superheroes. They can run forty miles an hour. They're three-quarters of a ton of pure muscle. They have steel shoes nailed to their feet. Yet they allow little girls to order them around like slaves. For a treat they get a measly sugar cube. As Corny found out, an angry stallion in a confined area can really do some damage.

Sarah rushed over and helped me to my feet. Corny had to be at least unconscious, but we were careful in our approach to the stall. I find it ridiculous when the potential victim in a book or movie gains the upper hand and immediately blows it by being too cocky. In real life, fear doesn't go away. You don't suddenly turn into James Bond after a minor victory.

We peered around the corner of the stall. It was immediately clear that Corny was not lying in wait to dupe us. The elbow and hand of his right arm were absolutely crushed. If he survived this, no way that arm would ever work again. He also had a hoofprint right in the middle of his forehead. His head was caved in. His gun was lying in the dirt. He wouldn't be using it anytime soon, but just in case, I grabbed it and threw it out of reach.

Rex's initial kick must have killed Corny instantly. The stomping destroyed his arm, but he wouldn't have felt that, not when his forehead could now be used as a cupholder.

I retched my guts out next to the stall. I don't think this one was due to the concussion because Sarah joined me and no one had hit her in the head with a shovel. After the purge, I felt better, relieved that the danger was over. Maybe horses *can* sense evil.

Max came over and started lapping up my pile of vomit, which is reason number 5,762 to never let a dog lick your face. The worse something smells, the more a dog wants to put it in his mouth.

Sarah looked at me. "Should we call an ambulance?"

"No." I spat to get the taste of bile out of my mouth. "No point. He's dead."

"Call the police?"

"Let's think this through before we do anything."

"Bob, a man is dead," Sarah said. "It's some kind of crime if we don't call the police. Obstructing justice or something."

"You're probably right. But—"

"Probably? Didn't you go to law school?"

"I was twenty-three years old. I wasn't planning to be a criminal defense attorney. I was more concerned with whether the cops could legally search my car for dope at a traffic stop."

"Can they?"

"Only if they have probable cause. Why?"

"I wanted to see if you learned *anything*."

"Look, the legalities here are the least of our worries. We're in a shitload of trouble. We've got to do whatever's best for us."

"But isn't that the police? Tell them everything, Bob. They'll protect us."

"Will they? What can we tell them? Corny's been blackmailing me and now he's dead?"

"They won't think you killed him. Rex did. Obviously."

"Even if they believe our story, we'll be tied up with bullshit for days."

Sarah considered that. "But what can we do with him?"

"I'll bury him somewhere on the farm."

"But what if somebody finds the body? Nobody will believe us then."

"It'll be me at risk. I won't even tell you where I put him. I didn't kill him, so all I'm guilty of is hiding the body. If the cops ever dig him up, the hoofprint in his skull is pretty convincing evidence in my defense."

"But how will you explain hiding the body?" Sarah asked.

"The guy tried to kill me, he has friends who might want revenge, I was scared, not thinking clearly. Whatever, I might be guilty of something, but I won't go to jail."

"Good point about his friends. Won't they come looking for him?"

"I doubt it. From the way Corny talked, he was off-mission tonight. The last thing he wanted was Swanson to know he was having trouble with me. Corny assured Swanson he could handle me. He came over tonight to do just that. He wouldn't have told anybody."

"But what if he did?"

"He didn't. I know Corny. He would never have shown any weakness. That means Swanson didn't know he was coming here and won't know why he's missing."

"How does that help us?"

"I don't know. But it's the one advantage we have. We need to figure something out before Swanson gives up on Corny and moves on to plan B, whatever that is."

We keep an old pickup outside the barn for hauling firewood and hay and bags of feed and the constant sloppy work that comes with owning a horse farm. It's a mess, but I didn't think Corny would mind. It sits out in the elements and we never clean it out or wash it, but I thought I might have to make an exception later tonight.

I backed the truck into the barn and parked it with the tailgate flush to the opening of Rex's stall. The door was splintered—Rex had busted right through it—but Sarah had managed to prop it open so we wouldn't have to lift Corny over the wooden plank that was still intact along the bottom. I put his watch cap back on his head. With his forehead covered, Corny looked like he could have been sleeping. Sleeping after a horrible industrial accident that mangled his arm beyond recognition. I dragged him by his feet and angled him so he was perpendicular to the length of the truck and then I lowered the tailgate. He was wearing an all-black high-performance athletic shoe. *The new Nike Nightstalker. Make sure your approach to her bedroom window is perfectly silent.*

I didn't really expect fingerprints to be an issue, but neither one of us wanted to touch him with our bare hands anyway, so we were wearing work gloves. I guess they could get Corny's DNA on them, so I should probably dispose of them afterwards. As you might guess, I had no plan for that. Can you burn work gloves? Would they leave an obvious glove-shaped skeleton in the ashes? Should I toss them in a dumpster on the way to work? I could see every option blowing up in my face. A bloody glove would fall out of the trash when the garbage men picked it up or I'd be spotted prowling suspiciously around the dumpster behind McDonald's. I was a nervous wreck and I didn't even kill the guy. It was surprising, given my level of competence in other areas of my life, but it was beginning to appear that I was not a world-class criminal.

I could hardly bear to touch Corny's mangled limb. If I tried to lift him by his arms, it might come off entirely. So I folded his arms across his chest like a woman covering her naked breasts when you accidentally walk into the wrong locker room at the country club, and tried to lift him by his shoulders. I'll admit I dropped him a few times. I was finally able to wrestle him into the bed of the truck by lifting him by the turtleneck. My body was now a virtual forest of incriminating fibers, but as far as I could tell I avoided direct contact with any blood.

I shut the tailgate and tossed Corny's black-ops flashlight in there with him. I decided to keep the gun. There was a chance we were going to be receiving some more visitors in the very near future and even though I was more likely to shoot myself in the foot than shoot a bad guy, I might be glad I had it. I was the exact guy the gun nuts always talked about who didn't have time for any goddamn five-day waiting period. In five days, I might as well have my neighborhood Guns-R-Us store FedEx my new gun right to my gravesite.

I jumped back down out of the truck. Sarah was already hosing off the area where Corny's body had been. "Clean up the blood as well as you can," I said. "Use bleach if we have it. That seems to stymie the techs on TV. But leave the damage to the stall for now. If someone does find blood later, we can say it's from the horse when he broke through."

"Some of it may be his blood. We should probably look for him. He could be hurt."

"I don't want you involved in any of this. You shouldn't be out wandering around the property in the middle of the night. If any of this ever comes out, you need to be able to say you were asleep the whole time."

"I'm not afraid to take the rap right along with you."

"I know. But for now, let's keep one of us out of jail to raise the children." Truthfully, I'd be the better parent to take care of the kids. And Sarah would probably do better in prison.

"You're probably right," Sarah said.

"Once you've got the blood cleaned up, just put everything in a trash bag, turn off all the lights, and go to bed. I'll dispose of the body and then I'll find Rex. Okay?"

Sarah came over and kissed me. She was holding a bloody rag and wearing rubber gloves. It was like making out with Hannibal Lecter.

Chapter Eighteen

Max and I got in the truck and we bounced down the long gravel road that leads to the main entrance to the farm. Max loves the truck. He slides around like he's on skates but he never loses his footing.

I was scanning the fields out both sides of the truck, keeping an eye out for Rex. Nothing but darkness. When I turned back to the road, it took me a second in my flustered, adrenaline-sapped state to realize my headlights were reflecting off some creature's eyeballs right back at me. My reflexes were slow and shaky, but there are a ton of animals roaming the farm and they generally get out of the way. Not this time. I slammed on the brakes and Max flew snout-first into the dashboard. We skidded to a stop about ten feet short of what I realized was a doe. She stood there staring and then sprinted away.

"I know how she feels, boy," I said to Max, as he clambered groggily back onto the seat.

I planned to drive down and shut the main gate so we wouldn't have any more unwanted visitors tonight. We were about halfway there when, to my horror, I saw a pair of headlights turning into our drive. Whoever it was, it was bad news. In my neighborhood, nobody drives over in the middle of the night to borrow a cup of sugar. There were really only two possibilities. It was either the cops or Corny's ride, and whoever it was, I couldn't just turn and run because they'd seen my headlights. If it was the cops, I didn't want them to think I had anything to hide. If it was Corny's friends, I didn't want to lead them back to the house where my kids were sleeping. The gun was in the glove compartment and if it came to it, I could probably reach across to get it just in time to get shot in the back of the head. I decided my only choice was to continue on down the road like a confident man driving on his own property. As long as nobody got out of the car, I might be okay.

As the lights got closer, I could see the car was a police cruiser. It wasn't the old black-and-white Crown Victoria sedan we all grew up with. It was an all white Dodge Charger or Camaro or something. It looked like the cop's police car was in the shop so he had to borrow his sixteen-year-old daughter's car. It probably had a unicorn hanging from the rearview mirror and was full of lip gloss, tampons, and empty Diet Coke cans. Still, a police car was definitely better news than the alternative. At least the cop most likely wouldn't try to kill me. That would have to wait for my first day in prison.

I popped a mint to cover my vomit-breath, stopped the truck, and rolled down the window. I was hoping he'd pull up alongside me, driver's side to driver's side, so we could talk while he was still in the car. No such luck. The cruiser stopped directly in front of me and a young policeman got out. He had closely cropped blond hair and the obligatory cop mustache. He hadn't pulled his gun, which was a good sign. He approached my window.

"Mr. Patterson? It's Officer Tate. I've been out here a time or two when your burglar alarm went off by mistake."

Almost every cop in the county has been to our house for that reason. We finally had to stop turning the damn thing on, although we would have to change that policy starting tonight. "Sure, Officer, I remember you. Is there a problem?"

"I'm not sure," Tate said. "What are you doing driving around out here in the middle of the night?"

When you're lying, they say to stick as closely to the truth as you can. And I had a fair amount of experience with lying. "Something spooked our stallion and he busted out of his stall and ran off. We don't know if he's hurt or what. I'm trying to find him."

"Did it make a lot of noise?"

"Oh yeah, a hell of a racket," I said. "It woke me out of a sound sleep. I went down to the barn and he had kicked clean through the stall door and was gone."

"We got a call from your neighbor. She said there was a bunch of commotion over at your place. It sounded like someone was being killed."

"It did sound like that," I said. "The horse was screaming and whinnying like he was being attacked. Maybe a snake got in the barn or something."

"To tell you the truth, your neighbor calls the station with a lot of wild stories. I think she's seen *Rear Window* one too many times."

I smiled. "We've had quite a few dealings with her ourselves. She's not a big fan of my wife. She thinks a mother should stay home with her children."

"Well, I'll let her know it was just a horse. Can I do anything to help you find him?"

FOR THE LOVE OF GOD, NO!

"I'm happy to help. That's what we're here for." He pointed at his badge. "To serve and protect. Do you have a flashlight back here?" Tate started to walk back toward the bed of the pickup.

I couldn't think of anything to say, so I just sat there, waiting for the inevitable.

"Mr. Patterson?" Tate called from behind the truck. "Could you come back here, please?"

I got out of the truck and trudged slowly back toward the pickup bed. "Officer, I can explain."

"I'm sure you can. Are you aware your tags are expired?" Tate was shining Corny's flashlight on the license plate. How could he not see—nothing. I searched the bed of the truck with my eyes and there was nothing but an assortment of junk. The tailgate was open and Corny was gone. I tried to regain my composure.

"What was that?" I asked.

"Your tags," Tate said. "They're expired. The last sticker on here is a couple of years old."

I breathed a huge sigh of relief. "Oh, right. We only use the truck here on the farm. We never take it out on the street."

"You still have to register it and pay the fees. It's a personal property tax you owe just by owning the vehicle. It doesn't matter if you drive it. Like the property taxes on your house. You have to pay them whether you live there or not."

"I understand."

"On a piece of crap like this—no offense—it probably won't amount to much at all. It's a percentage of the value of the vehicle, which is practically nothing."

"No offense taken." We had the "vehicle" precisely *because* it was a piece of crap. We didn't want to ruin our other cars with all the dirty work on the farm.

Tate reached down and tried to shut the tailgate but it wouldn't latch. He handed me a bottle of Stallion Spray that we use to get the horses ready to breed. "This was just rolling around in the bed. You should probably get the tailgate fixed or you're going to have your haul sliding out of the back of the truck."

"You're right." I looked back in the direction we'd come to see if I could spot my current cargo. It was too dark to see anything. "I'll take care of the tags and the tailgate first thing tomorrow."

"See that you do. Since you don't drive it on the street, I'm going to let it go this time, but if I see it again without new tags, I'll have to give you a ticket."

"I appreciate that, Officer."

Tate held up Corny's flashlight. "I did find a torch. Man, this thing is high tech. What is it, some kind of military issue?"

"I had Q make it for me," I said. "Just don't punch the wrong button and accidentally shoot me."

"Who's Q?"

Cops are very literal people. You would be too if you spent your day hearing nothing but bullshit from everyone you talked to.

"Should we go try to find your horse?" Tate asked.

"Sure." I had no choice now but to carry out the play fake. The key would be not stumbling over Corny's corpse, which had to have fallen out of the back of the pickup. So we definitely didn't want to go back toward the barn. I hoped we could find the horse in the other direction.

But what if Corny's body didn't fall out of the truck? What if he somehow managed to climb down on his own? I wasn't truly certain he was dead. My only experience with dead bodies comes from TV and movies. I know to touch the victim's neck with my first two fingers and then immediately turn to my partner and say "He's dead." But I didn't feel Corny's neck and I don't think I would have learned anything if I had. I already knew he had a giant hoofprint in his forehead.

Tate handed me the flashlight. "Here, you take this. I've got another one in the cruiser."

Of course you do, you conniving bastard, I thought. Cops always carry big, heavy flashlights and Officer Tate was looking for an excuse to snoop around in my truck. Apparently he took the neighbor's complaint a little more seriously than he let on. At any rate, it was now clear I was not above suspicion, and I was going to have to be careful.

"Follow me!" I called as I got back in the truck. I drove down toward the gate and Tate turned around and followed. He must not have seen anything as his lights swept across the darkness because he kept coming.

I drove straight to the front gate. The odds of Rex finding this twenty-foot opening in the miles of perimeter fence were pretty slim, but I still wanted to discourage additional visitors as well as reinforce to Officer Tate that he was on my property and I controlled who came and went. It was also as far away as possible from where I thought Corny must be.

I shut the gate and then got back in and headed west along the south fence. A lot of times a horse that runs out of the barn will stop after a few hundred yards. Once they feel safe, they quit running and stand there eating grass. That's not very smart but they're so fast it doesn't matter. If the danger follows them, they'll run off again. In this case, though, I thought Rex might have been spooked enough to keep running until he got to the fence, then he would stop.

We drove slowly along the fence line for a half-mile or so and suddenly there he was, calmly eating grass and staring at the lights without blinking. I got out of the car and approached him cautiously. I wasn't kidding when I said he hated me. Stallions hate all other males. It must be our masculine scent or the lack of a female odor. Whatever, he considers me a rival and his sworn enemy.

Rex seemed to be fine. I shone the flashlight over his body from a safe distance and couldn't find any injuries. He wasn't bleeding or limping, so there was really nothing to do.

I walked back to the police cruiser. Tate rolled down the window. "Do you want me to help you corral him so we can get him back to the barn?"

I shook my head. "There's no point. His stall is broken, so there's no place to put him."

"You're just going to leave him out here?" Tate asked.

"He'll be fine. The gate's closed and he could never find it anyway. Plus, there's no way you and I could handle him. Sarah could probably do it by herself, but he'd beat the crap out of us. We'll have the trainer round him up in the morning."

"Then what was the point of driving around looking for him?" Jesus Christ! What is this, the Spanish Inquisition? I'm not saying another word until I speak to my lawyer!

"I wasn't concerned about him making it off the property. I had to make sure he wasn't hurt so my wife would stop worrying about him."

"I'm glad everything's all right," Tate said. "You never know what you're going to find when you get called out to a private residence in the middle of the night."

"Well, it's not exactly Charlie Sheen's house around here," I said. "I've only got the one goddess and she's usually asleep by ten o'clock."

He chuckled a little. Or at least his mustache moved up and down. "Well, I'll be on my way. Let us know if you ever need anything."

"I'll follow you down and shut the gate behind you." So you can't snoop around my property any more than you already have, you justifiably suspicious prick with what appear to be decent instincts for a career in law enforcement.

After Officer Tate drove away, I stood there watching for a good five minutes to make sure he wasn't planning to double back and spy on me with night-vision goggles or something. When I was satisfied, I got back in the truck and drove back up the driveway. I didn't know where I'd lost Corny, but I figured the place to start looking was where I'd stopped to talk to Officer Tate earlier. I found what I thought was the spot, give or take half a mile—it was dark and everything looked the same. I grabbed Corny's flashlight and got out of the truck. Just in case, I went back and got the gun out of the glove compartment. I was way more likely to accidentally kill Max than successfully defend myself, but it made me feel better nonetheless. I didn't ask Max what he thought.

It was overcast, so there wasn't much moonlight. I turned on the flashlight and followed Max back toward the house. The flashlight only illuminated the ground about ten feet in front of me, but Max has found every other rotting carcass ever deposited on the farm and tried to give it to me as a present, so I thought he could pilot this expedition successfully.

Max trotted happily ahead of me, occasionally dashing off the road to investigate a sound or smell or to pee in specific areas chosen for reasons known only to him.

Watching Max made me realize I had to pee myself, so I made my way to the weeds along the side of the driveway. I was about midway through when I heard a sound behind me. I stopped mid-stream—it's not like I'm shutting off a fire hose— and stood perfectly still, listening. Maybe Corny *wasn't* dead. I felt something touch the back of my neck, then my shoulder. I grabbed the gun out of the back of my pants and whirled around in the classic shooter's pose. Two hands on the gun, straight out from my body. The safety was probably on, but I *looked* ready to shoot. My target had brown hair and a long face. An extremely long face. Somehow I'd allowed a fifteen-hundred pound beast wearing steel shoes to sneak up on me. I thought about shooting the bastard and claiming self-defense, but I didn't think Sarah would buy it.

"Go on!" I whispered. "Get out of here." Rex just stood there and stared at me, which is one of only two behaviors he exhibits toward me. The other is open hostility. This was better, but not by much. He sure as hell wouldn't do anything I said.

I left him standing there and trotted to catch up with Max. About fifty yards ahead, he had stopped dead in the middle of the driveway. He wasn't growling, he was sniffing around cautiously. I aimed the flashlight where he was looking and there was Corny, lying facedown in the gravel. This time I went up and did the two fingers against the neck thing. Nothing. I nudged him with my foot and said, "Corny, wake up." Nothing. Time of death: about an hour ago. But it felt like a month.

I left Max to keep an eye on the body and jogged back to the truck. I was fairly certain Corny must have just bounced out of the truck because of the broken tailgate, but I didn't want him out of my sight any longer than necessary. When I drove back to the body, I saw Corny ripping Max's throat out with his bare teeth. Corny stood up, raised Max over his head and threw him through the windshield of the truck. I shook the safety glass and dog hair out of my eyes, and there was Max once again waiting patiently next to Corny's body. The windshield was intact. I was losing my mind.

I got out of the truck and dragged Corny out of the bright lights in front around to the darkness in back. The broken tailgate was still down. You may recall that Sarah and I could barely get Corny in the truck together, and now it was just me and Max. People in books usually carry dead bodies around like they're rag dolls. I'm telling you, Corny was fucking heavy. You know how much harder it is to lift your kid when he lets his body go limp? Dead is nothing but limp. Sure, I don't get to the gym as often as I should, but I'm not a small guy and I could barely get him off the ground.

I got down on my knees, slid both arms under him and lifted him up. I staggered around but managed to toss Corny into the bed of the truck. His head slammed against the metal bed. I winced involuntarily.

I got up in the truck and pushed and dragged Corny's body all the way to the back of the bed. Even that was harder than it sounds. It was a cool night but I was pouring sweat. I wedged him in with bags of grass seed and fertilizer and two-by-fours and all the other crap that had accumulated in the back of the truck. I set the Stallion Spray aside to return to the barn.

I figured all that stuff would hold him, but I still drove cautiously across our property to the east, the opposite direction from where Officer Tate and I found Rex, headed for the one place on the farm where I thought I could safely dispose of the body.

Chapter Nineteen

Once one of Sarah's horses died and she decided to bury the mare on the property. The hole, dug by the Equine Burial Company, and more expensively than you could imagine, was massive. It looked like a swimming pool. When they filled it in, there was a nice little dirt grave mound there. For years. It took me forever to get grass to grow on it, but to this day, it's a hump in the ground.

Obviously, Corny was a lot smaller than a horse, but the principle's the same. You need a much bigger hole than you'd think. Digging by myself, it would take me all night, if I could even do it at all. And when I was finished, you might as well put a sign there that said *Freshly Dug Grave*. It would be that obvious.

So I headed for the pond. If I could get Corny in our little rowboat, I could weigh him down with rocks or chains or something and then dump him in the middle of the pond. It's so murky you can't see your hand if you stick it under the water and it's a good twenty feet deep in the middle. There's no current, so unless the cops decided to dredge the pond, the body should stay there for a long time.

So my plan was to put Corny in the rowboat we use for fishing, row it out to the middle of the pond, and toss him overboard with something heavy to sink him. But as the philosopher/boxer Mike Tyson once said, "Everybody has a plan until they get punched in the face."

◇◇◇

I backed the truck up to the little wooden pier we use to dock the boat. I climbed in the back and rolled Corny over and over until he fell off the tailgate. I had ceased worrying about whether I was doing more damage to the body or leaving evidence all over the place. We were outside. I figured the evidence would get erased pretty quickly out in the elements.

I dragged Corny by his feet to the end of the pier. The boat was a twelve-foot fir rowboat that Nick and I put together from a kit one summer. It sounded like a fun father-son project, or in our case it sounded to Sarah like a fun father-son project. This rowboat was supposed to take one decent weekend of work for a reasonably handy adult male and his non-special needs child. It took us a month. At one point when we had about half a boat, Nick said to me, "We can't forget how bad this is or it could happen again." He was like a holocaust survivor. Eventually the craft was pond-worthy, but it took thirty terrible days of frustrating and difficult work and cost more than a brand new one, already built and delivered right to the water, would have. I guess you could say Nick and I bonded the way a military platoon or a fraternity pledge class bonds—through shared misery—but we didn't need to. We were already close.

We eventually ended up with a boat and Sarah arranged an elaborate ceremony where we lowered it into the water and Nick was supposed to break a bottle of champagne over it. Apparently Sarah believed we had been building a yacht instead of a few pieces of wood indiscriminately hammered together that would be easily demolished by a heavy blow from a champagne bottle.

When I shoved Corny off the pier into the boat, his head smacked hard against wooden planks that had been haphazardly secured by a man and his boy just trying to finish the job. The planks gave way just enough for water to begin seeping into the boat. The fucker was going to sink right here, two feet from shore. I could stand here saluting as the ship went down, or I could try to get the son of a bitch out to the middle of the pond. I jumped in with Corny and started to row. The water was up to my ankles, but we were moving. It's not a big pond, maybe fifty yards to the middle. I was freezing from the icy water but sweating with the exertion and the fear. If the boat went under in shallow water, I was screwed. Hell, I was probably screwed anyway, but when Nick inevitably asked me where the boat was, it would be a hell of a lot easier to say "I don't know" if you couldn't see the damn thing from shore.

As the boat filled with water, the going got slower and slower but eventually I got to what I estimated was roughly the center of the pond. I crammed Corny's body underneath the middle seat until it was wedged tight. I tugged on him from each direction and couldn't budge him. He wasn't going anywhere unless his body was eaten away by something. And I knew the fish don't bite since I fished here all the time.

I waited for the boat to fill and start to settle toward the bottom. I stood on it as it went down to keep it from drifting closer to shore, but it wasn't really necessary. It went straight down. Treading water right above it, I couldn't see a thing. Of course, it was pitch black and the middle of the night, but I thought it would be invisible in daylight too. I'd have to wait and see.

I swam the fifty yards to shore, expecting something to grab my leg at any moment like in a bad horror movie. I dragged myself out of the water, thanked Max for all of his generous help, got in the truck and drove back to the house. The truck was covered in mud and who knows what else, so I washed it down with the garden hose. I figured the weather would take care of anything I missed. I cleaned myself the best I could with the hose and then stripped naked. I carried my wet clothes inside, tossed them in the washer, poured in detergent and half a bottle of Clorox, and started it up. No problem, thanks to my recent practice with the sheets.

When I got upstairs, I took the hottest shower I could stand. I was so cold the water felt like needles against my skin, but my body temperature eventually got back to normal. As I dried off, I stared at myself in the mirror and thought: *You have no idea what you're capable of. You thought you did, but you don't. You better be ready for anything. The next few days may make tonight look like a walk in the park.* In the bedroom, Sarah was snoring gently. I crawled under the covers and went to sleep, imagining Corny's dead eyes staring up at me out of the water.

There's an old episode of *The Simpsons* where Homer takes a second job at the Kwik-E-Mart. The instant he gets home from his grueling night shift and lays his head down on the pillow, the alarm goes off and he gets right back out of bed to go to his day job. That's what I felt like when my alarm went off the morning after Corny's death. Eyes closed, just starting to drift off, followed immediately by *beep beep beep beep beep beep*. I hate that sound even after a full night's sleep and that morning I wanted to throw the clock through the window.

But I also knew it was important to act natural. The last thing we wanted was to let the kids think there was anything wrong. I reached over and touched Sarah on the shoulder. She mumbled "Not today" and turned her back to me.

"Not that," I whispered. "We need to talk."

She rolled back over and opened her eyes. I could see her recollections of last night gradually come into focus. "Did you—?"

"Yes. Everything's taken care of."

"What did you do?" We were both whispering. I don't know why, the kids couldn't hear us in the bedroom. At least that's the operating principle that allows us to have sex while they're awake, although it's not exactly a Roman orgy in here. Even Christian missionaries would have suggested we try a different position once in a while. We kept whispering nonetheless, like the conspirators we were.

"I took care of it. That's all you need to know. And I found Rex. He's fine. You'll need to get some of your guys to fix the stall and go round him up, but otherwise we need to treat this like any other morning."

Sarah pulled me close to her in a ferocious embrace. We're not big huggers around our house. I still hug Emily sometimes, but Nick's made it clear he wants no part of it. I hugged her back just as hard. "Everything's going to be okay. In a few days, we'll be back to our old boring lives."

"I hope you're right. I act all tough and I can handle myself in a boardroom fight, but I am not equipped to deal with real-life violence. And, no offense, but you're not exactly Chuck Norris yourself."

I nodded. "We are definitely fucked if I have to play hero."

"*Guitar Hero*, maybe." She kissed me and got out of the bed. "No, actually, you suck at that too."

"These kids today and their rock music. Give me an old acoustic camp song and I'll 'Kumbaya' the crap out of that game."

I went downstairs and started the coffee. I usually fill the coffee-maker the night before and program it to start brewing in the morning, but I'd been a little distracted.

I switched my wet laundry to the dryer and went upstairs to wake the kids while Sarah was in the shower. I kept things as normal as possible on the way to school. The kids both had iPods or iTouches or iPortabletelevisions with earbuds, so no one said a word. A typical morning. They didn't even notice that after all I went through last night, I must have looked like I was in the middle of a week-long bender. I stopped the car and the helpful volunteer students opened the car door and let the kids out. Our kids don't volunteer for that duty because it would require their father to "volunteer" to get them to school a half-hour early. Do these other parents get up every morning at five?

"I'll pick you up right here at three-thirty!" I yelled. They didn't hear me (earbuds), but something sort of tugged at my brain when I said it. I stopped and thought for a second but was angrily waved forward by the eleven-year-old early-morning drill sergeant who was directing traffic. I almost had it but the fear of being yelled at by a little girl knocked all cognitive ability from my brain.

I decided to go to the office. I was off trustee-duty for the week so I really didn't have much to do, but I didn't want there to be any visible interruption of my routine, anything that could lead someone to think anything was amiss. *Bob never has a second cup of coffee at work. I'll bet he killed a guy and dumped him in the pond.*

My routine when I'm in my office is to make a few phone calls and surf the Internet, and I thought I could probably pull that off. For the second time in a row, an evening with Corny had left me dead tired the next day. I really couldn't complain this time because it left him just plain dead, but I didn't want to give anyone in the office the impression that I was less than a hundred percent. An obviously sleep-deprived Bob could elicit embarrassing questions, as well as general mockery, so I fueled up on coffee and tried to look alive.

I spent an hour catching up on my e-mails, which in my case meant sifting through 789 offers to increase the size of my penis or refinance my home, just to find the three non-spam e-mails I got all weekend. My assistant, Pauline, appeared at my door, which is unusual. Normally I can't find her unless I've just farted in my office. Then she's certain to walk in.

Pauline was a pretty brunette about forty years old. She was the kind of woman who…hell, I don't know what kind of woman she was. She was the kind of woman who was frequently late and often had to miss work because one of her kids was sick. Fortunately, I had virtually no secretarial work that needed doing.

"Can you give me a ride to pick up my car over lunch?" Pauline asked.

"Sure. Eleven-thirty?"

"Great." She shut the door and left. The niggling thought was back in my brain. Whatever it was, I just couldn't reach it. It felt like the name of a song that's on the tip of your tongue but you can't think of it.

Although it clearly violated my "try to act normal" policy, I decided to use my time productively, so I made a few business calls I'd been putting off. On the last one, before I set the receiver down, I thought I heard another click. Was it possible these phones were tapped?

There was a good chance I was being paranoid. I've seen a few too many fictional scenarios where the bad guys know every move you make. In real life, why would they even bother? They're not worried about what I'm doing. Plus, it's risky. Even with all the other illegal activity Nixon was up to, it was the decision to wiretap the Democratic National Committee's offices that brought him down.

At eleven-thirty on the dot, Pauline knocked on my door. She is extremely prompt when it concerns lunch. We went down to the garage and got in my car. "Where to?" I asked.

"Lube shop on Tenth. I'm just getting my oil changed."

When I pulled in, I said, "Do you want to get your car and then go to lunch or something?"

She opened the car door and stepped out. "No, I'm not even sure it's done. I don't want you to have to wait around for me." That's the good thing about Pauline. She doesn't want to go to lunch with me any more than I want to go to lunch with her. Like me, she wants to get away from the people she works with… Then it hit me. *I don't want you to have to wait around for me.*

Now I knew what I was trying to remember. Corny had to get to my place somehow last night. It's a farm out in the middle of nowhere. He couldn't have been dropped off because he wouldn't want someone waiting around for him. He couldn't have known in advance how long it would take—he seemed to be prepared to work on me all night—so there couldn't have been a prearranged pickup time. Surely somebody would have come looking for him when he didn't show up. So he must have had his own vehicle. But where was it?

I was tempted to rush home and search our entire property, but I reminded myself of my own advice to treat this as a normal day. I take plenty of afternoons off, but I don't just disappear. I tell somebody where I'm going to be. So I'd have to make up a lie and then there might be follow-up questions.

I grabbed a quick bite and then went back to the office. I didn't have any trouble keeping busy until it was time to pick up the kids. My trustee work had kept me from keeping up on the celebrity gossip, so I didn't know whether Charlie Sheen was currently in rehab (no) or whether Lindsay Lohan was currently in jail (yes). I skimmed through the political sites I frequent and learned that a congressman sent dick pics to his mistress, and Donald Trump was considering a run for President (he's kidding, right?). I perused some angry sports columns and found out local sports team A's quarterback sucks and local sports team B's coach is an idiot. Good to know nothing changed during the weeks I had spent actually working during the day.

I was all up-to-date on current events by the time I had to leave to pick up the kids. As the line of parents' luxury SUVs moved slowly forward, I thought about Corny's missing vehicle. Normally I enjoy watching the rich young MILFs embracing their children after a long day of Pilates and yoga, but today I was too distracted for that. Somebody was going to come looking for Corny at some point and I had to find his transportation before they did.

Nick got to the car first and slipped in the backseat. "Hey, Nick. How was school?" Keeping it normal. Nothing to see here.

"Fine." The answer he always gives. "Dad, can we go fishing when we get home?"

Fishing? We hadn't fished in a month and he wants to fish today? I think he has some kind of sixth sense that makes him want to do whatever I would want to do the least, like fly a kite when I have a particularly evil hangover.

Obviously, I didn't want Nick anywhere near the pond. I pictured him reeling in a succession of Corny's personal belongings. *That's weird. A stocking cap and a watch? And this looks like a human ear.* "Not today, Buddy. I have some things to do on the farm."

"What kind of things?"

"Oh, you know. Maintenance. Upkeep."

I didn't really think he would buy it and he didn't. "Isn't that what we pay all those guys to do?"

"You'd think so, wouldn't you? But sometimes I have to help out when there's a lot to do. It's nothing fun, believe me."

I think Nick was going to keep interrogating me but thankfully Emily opened the door and slid in next to him. I tried again and this time I knew I'd get a different response. "How was school, honey?"

"Oh, my gosh, Dad. We're doing an experiment on these two rats at school? To see what kind of food makes them grow better?" Emily speaks in a series of questions. "We're giving one rat junk food and the other one good food?"

I was happy to avoid any more questions from Nick. I figured an Emily story could last the whole ride home. "You mean good food for rats? Like Purina Rat Chow?"

Emily gave me "the look" and rolled her eyes. "No, Dad. Why would they even make that? Like healthy people food. Meat and vegetables and stuff. The junk food rat gets chips and Twinkies and stuff."

"So is the healthy-food rat doing better?" I was pretty sure rats could eat anything and do just fine. We had a barn rat so big once I didn't want to shoot him because I was afraid it would just piss him off.

"That's what I'm trying to tell you if you'd quit interrupting."

"Sorry. Go ahead with your story, honey."

"Mrs. Wilson got the healthy-food rat out and to show us how he was growing more, she turned him over and showed us his big *testicles*. It was disgusting!" Emily fell over on the seat giggling. "I screamed and my friend Caitlin S almost passed out and had to go to the nurse."

"Caitlin S?"

"There's like four Caitlins in our class."

"Of course there are."

As I expected, Emily's rat story occupied us until we got home. She even had Nick and me laughing through most of it, although Nick kept shaking his head in a "girls are crazy" kind of way that I knew he'd be using for the rest of his life.

I told Nick and Emily to go in the house and do their homework because I had some things to do. Then I got on one of our

ATVs to go search for Corny's wheels. Nick and I have ridden these machines dozens of times but I never quite remember the procedures for getting the damn things started. I knew I had to push some kind of button or move the lever to the on position. It's pathetic, but I usually have to have Nick come over to do it for me. I tried a few things but nothing worked. I finally gave up and yelled for Nick to come outside.

"Oh, man," Nick said, "you're taking the ATV? Can I come?"

"No, you need to stay here and watch your sister. Just come over here to start it for me."

"Jeez, Dad. I've only shown you about a million times."

"I know. I'm old and clueless. Just show me one more time."

"You just move this thing up here to 'on' and then push that button. It's not that hard. Emily can do it."

It started right up. "Okay, thanks. I've got it now. Go inside. I'll be back in a little bit."

"Careful, the throttle sticks sometimes. Remember? You told Mom you were going to fix it."

"I do remember, thank you." Which meant "call someone to fix it," but I hadn't done it yet.

Fortunately, if the throttle didn't stick, the ATV rode like a piece of cake. Corny had to have come in through the front gate but not up the driveway or I would have heard him. He must have driven along the fence line and then ditched the car before he got too close, so I headed down to the gate to try to follow his tracks. I stopped the ATV at the edge of the driveway. I dismounted and lay down on the ground, examining the grass closely for clues like I was tracking an escaped prisoner. There was nothing to indicate where he might have left the driveway or what direction he might have gone.

There are really not that many places on our property to hide a car. There are some hills and hollows, but the land is mostly flat grassland, like a prairie. All of the buildings are too close to the barn. The only place I could think of with any cover at all was what we called a "copse" of trees maybe a half-mile south-west of the barn. Dictionary.com tells me a copse is "a thicket of small trees or bushes; a small wood." Did you know that to look up the definition of a word you used to have to manually flip through the pages of an enormous book with tiny print that was outdated the second you bought it? Life was so different five years ago.

That definition sounds about right, but it's a weird word. I was always afraid I'd be shot by an intruder and manage to croak out, "Go to the cops," and Emily would run as fast as she could to a small group of trees. Sarah and I have been making corny jokes about it since we moved here.

I wasn't sure the copse was big enough to hide a car, but Corny was planning to be gone before daybreak, so maybe he didn't really even hide it. He just needed a landmark so he could find it again in the dark. The copse was as good a place as any.

I parked the ATV and walked into the copse. I looked around as my eyes adjusted to the gloom. There was clearly no car in here. The whole area was maybe ten thousand square feet. Aren't you impressed that I'm one of those guys who can estimate square footage at a glance? Actually, I'm not. I guessed it was a hundred feet wide and a hundred feet deep and did the math in my head, so just picture a bunch of trees arranged randomly by nature into a perfect square. The copse seemed empty but I walked around to make sure. I thought I saw a flash of metal on the ground. I moved closer and there it was: a motorcycle.

Chapter Twenty

The motorcycle was lying right in the middle of a patch of ivy. The bike itself was a neon green, so it blended in. This may come as a shock to you, but I know nothing about motorcycles. I saw that this one was called a Kawasaki Ninja. That sounded like just the kind of bike Corny would want when he was on a black ops mission like last night.

It also looked like the kind of bike even I could handle. It didn't weigh much and appeared to be designed to be ridden by a small Japanese man.

I couldn't get it started. I quickly deduced that, like the cars I'm familiar with, this motorcycle required an ignition key to start. Kawasaki apparently didn't want a ten-year-old to be able to walk up to any bike on the street and start it with the push of a button. A real theft problem, with some fairly serious liability concerns to boot.

I evidently needed the key but I didn't have a clue where it could be. I'd emptied Corny's pockets before I dumped him in the pond, but couldn't remember what I'd done with all of his personal effects. Did I use a zip-loc bag or one of those impenetrable pouches businesses use to take money to the bank?... and then it hit me: I didn't search his pockets at all. Which meant that his keys—and anything else incriminating and/or helpful—were at the bottom of the pond.

How did I forget to check Corny's pockets? That's Dead Body 101. I needed his cell phone. I needed to know who was calling him and what they knew about his plans. I needed to know if he was in contact with Swanson. I needed any other information he might have with him: names, dates, receipts, whatever. And I needed those goddamn keys.

I left the motorcycle where it was and drove the ATV back to the house. Somebody was going to have to swim down and get the keys and whatever else Corny had in his pockets. And that somebody was probably not going to be me. Since we obviously didn't want anybody else to know, our pool of applicants for the pond-diving job was only two deep.

When we go to a beach, Sarah always likes to *do* something. I don't. I'm perfectly happy just sitting there. I like the beach to be there in the background like a movie set, but I could do without the scalding hot sand and the razor-sharp shells and the cold salty water and the dead sea creatures washing up on shore. For me, the beach is much better as an idea than as a reality.

But not Sarah. She's a strong swimmer. She's built up triathlete lungs, and she hasn't damaged them with frequent intentional smoke inhalation. She'll swim farther out into the ocean than I would willingly go in a boat. Sarah likes to snorkel and explore the coral reefs. She would definitely scuba dive down to a sunken pirate ship and look for treasure if she got the chance.

Although a tremendous ordeal for me, swimming to the bottom of the pond and staying down there for a while would be a breeze for Sarah, except for the dead body. If I tried to go down there, I'd most likely end up keeping Corny company for eternity. It had to be Sarah or no one.

Whatever we did, it was going to have to be after the kids were asleep, so I got back on the "normal day" track. When I came back in the house, the kids acted like they didn't even realize I'd been gone. I was afraid I was going to have to come up with some explanation for Nick, but when I looked in his room, he had a headset on and was conducting some kind of computer battle with his friends, likely against a team of middle-aged pedophiles who intermixed shouts of "Cover the left flank!" with personal questions like "Where do you go to school?"

Sarah came home as I was making dinner in the kitchen. She put her arms around me from behind and rested her cheek against my back. As I mentioned, we're not generally touchy-feely people. Sarah was worried.

I turned around and put a finger against her lips. "Nothing." I got a piece of paper and wrote: DON'T SAY ANYTHING YOU DON'T WANT OVERHEARD. TALK AFTER KIDS IN BED.

Sarah widened her eyes and stared at me. This is a nonverbal communication that she often uses on me in public settings. Like "shalom" or "aloha," it can mean almost anything.

Despite the indecipherable look, she nodded, which I took to mean she understood. We got through the rest of the night like a "normal" night. Sarah and Emily talked throughout dinner while Nick and I smirked at each other. Business as usual. After dinner, I helped the kids with their homework, which consisted of Nick telling me he didn't have any and Emily telling me every single thing that happened in school that day.

Once I got the kids in bed, I went down to my office to do a little Internet research. I typed in "Kawasaki Ninja" on Google and immediately found a YouTube video of a guy showing his girlfriend how to ride. She knew absolutely nothing and weighed about ninety pounds and managed to start it up and drive it around the parking lot. I figured if she could do it, I could do it.

I took some notes and thought about what else I needed to know. I typed in "how to dry out" and Google guessed I was going to type "cell phone" and filled it in itself. Google knows me better than I know myself! I wrote down a few drying tips and then erased my browsing history. I've heard the FBI computer techs can still find everything even after you delete it, so you shouldn't feel all that safe if you're eliminating the trail from a series of incriminating searches, but I didn't want to make it easy for them either.

◇◇◇

I went back upstairs and into the bedroom. Sarah was in her usual position, propped up in bed with her laptop, reading glasses on. I motioned her to join me in the bathroom. She was wearing sweats and a tee-shirt, which in our house counts as lingerie.

I turned on the shower and both faucets and we sat on the floor facing each other, whispering. I knew this wouldn't take long because I can sit comfortably cross-legged for about as long as I can listen to one of Sarah's mind-numbing work stories.

"Do you really think the house is bugged?"

I shrugged. "I don't know. When I was on the phone at my office today, I thought I heard a click. It was probably nothing, but there's no reason to take any chances."

"Why would they bother?"

"They want to know what we know and if we're planning to go to the cops. If they're willing to blackmail me, I don't think they'll be too worried about a little eavesdropping."

Sarah shook her head back and forth and shuddered. "When I think someone might have been listening to every single thing we've said and done…"

"I've been telling you to tone down the dirty talk."

"It's not funny. I feel violated."

"Oh, come on. There's nothing to hear. Like all couples with children, we've trained ourselves to screw in complete silence." Before she could tell me that it was easy for her to keep quiet, I continued. "Look, the idea of someone monitoring everything we do makes me uncomfortable, too. But we need to act normal. As long as they think we're oblivious, we're probably okay."

Sarah nodded. "And we might even be able to use it to our advantage."

I raised an eyebrow at her. "Pretty sneaky, Sis. Remind me not to trust you when all this is over."

She grinned. "I will. It'll keep you on your toes."

"So if we need to talk, we go somewhere where noise will muffle the conversation or go outside. Also, don't say anything over the phone or send texts or e-mails. Got it?"

"Got it."

I took a deep breath. "Okay, that was the easy part."

"There's more?" Sarah's eyes were wide again.

I nodded.

"Oh, my God. What now?"

"It's actually nothing new. It's just follow-up on our earlier project."

"What do you mean 'follow-up'? Should I put a note in my tickler file to get back together with you in four weeks?"

"Unfortunately, no. It has to be tonight."

"That's a pretty quick follow-up."

"This is a very important matter."

She sighed. "All right. What is it?"

"Remember I told you I'd take care of the body and you'd never even know where it was?"

"Yes. And you led me to believe you accomplished that task."

"There's been a new development. Did you notice anything odd about Corny showing up here last night?"

"Like what?"

"Think about it. Corny just appears out here in the middle of nowhere?"

The realization slowly came over her face and she smiled at her own powers of deduction. "How did he get here?"

"Give the lady a gold star. I drove around the property and found a motorcycle in the copse of trees. We need to get rid of it, but there's a problem."

"Besides the fact that you can't ride a motorcycle?"

"Yes, besides that fact. There are no keys."

"Couldn't we just put the motorcycle in the back of the pickup and dump it somewhere?"

"We could, but someone could see me driving the pickup with a bright green motorcycle in the back. That would be hard to explain later. Plus, I want to park the motorcycle in long-term parking at the airport."

"Why?"

"That's what people always do when they need to ditch a car."

"You mean people in books and movies."

"Well, yes," I said. "I don't have any real life experience. But the writers have them do it for a reason. Cars sit there for weeks and no one thinks a thing about it. Remember that time we came back from vacation and our car was in the long-term parking lot under a foot of snow?"

"But why can't we just take it to the airport in the back of the truck?"

"The tags are expired. The last thing we need is to get pulled over. Plus someone might remember the truck with the motorcycle in back. You have to go through the gate and get a ticket. If I drive the motorcycle, I'll be wearing a helmet, so if there are any cameras or anyone remembers the bike, it could just as easily have been Corny. He's a criminal. They'll think he ditched the bike and flew off somewhere with a fake ID."

"Let's say you're right," Sarah said. "And for comedic purposes, let's say you could actually ride a motorcycle all the way to the airport and park it without crashing through the parking garage gate. We still need the keys."

"I think I know where they are."

Chapter Twenty-one

"You know where the keys are?" Sarah asked. "So why bury the lede?"

"You'll see," I said. Sarah and I never have the same approach to solving a problem. The chances of her approving of my chosen burial spot for Corny were basically zero percent. "When I went to get rid of the body, I realized there was no way I could bury him and not have it look obvious. So I needed a big hole that was already there."

"Okaaay."

"The only place I could think of was the pond." Here it comes.

"You put him in the pond?" Sarah didn't disappoint. She was screaming at me while whispering. "That's disgusting! Our kids swim in that pond!"

"I know."

"How about take him to a dumpster *off* the property?" Sarah shout-whispered. "How about digging a hole and burying him *away* from where my kids play all summer long? We've got a million acres and you couldn't find one spot to dig a hole? Is digging too hard for you? What about the big state park down the road where all the dead hookers end up? It takes them *years* to find *them*!"

"Nobody's really looking for them because they're hookers."

"And nobody's going to be looking for Dave, either!"

"Well, it's done. There's no changing it now. Are there any other nits you'd like to pick before we move on?"

"Sorry, I didn't realize not wanting a decomposing body to contaminate my children's swimming area was nit-picking."

"Let's jump to the conclusion of this discussion, where we always end up anyway. You're right and I'm wrong."

"Fine," Sarah said with a satisfied look on her face. At least I think it was. I'm not sure I've ever seen her satisfied. "But what does this have to do with the keys? Wait, let me guess. You threw him in the pond before you checked his pockets."

"I'll admit I forgot to go over my dead body-disposal checklist. You know, it's easy to Monday morning-quarterback. Rational decisions are a little tougher to make when you're on the field."

"So you're saying you choked."

"Yes, I choked. But now we need to focus on getting the keys and whatever else he's got in his pockets. Cell phone, camera, incriminating DVDs that will point to me as his likely murderer, whatever."

"So how do you plan to get that stuff?"

"Obviously, someone is going to have to swim down there and go through his pockets."

"What do you mean 'someone'?" Sarah asked. "I'm not going down there. There are catfish as big as Emily in that pond. They've probably already torn him to shreds."

"Maybe not yet. Those catfish hardly ever move. Look, I'll do it. I'm just not sure I can."

"You *are* pathetic in the water."

"Not to mention prone to panicking."

"And you can only hold your breath for about ten seconds."

"Guilty. And you're always swimming in the ocean where there are actually dangerous creatures. You make fun of me for being too scared."

"That's because you *are* too scared."

"But it would be a cakewalk for you."

"Do we have a decent flashlight?"

"I'm sure Corny's will work underwater. It's like something a Navy SEAL would carry. I think there may even be a couple of cyanide tablets in there in case you get captured. But we'll test it first."

"Okay, I'll do it."

I leaned across, kissed her and batted my eyelashes at her. "My hero."

As she got up from the floor, Sarah muttered, "For my next marriage, I think I'm going to go with a man."

"Good idea," I said. "Mix it up a little."

Sarah found her wetsuit, mask, and swim fins while I tested Corny's flashlight in the bathtub. It worked like a charm. I turned the lights off and even underwater the powerful beam lit up the whole bathroom.

I locked the door and set the alarm and we went outside. I didn't think we'd have any visitors tonight but then again I didn't expect to see Corny last night. I imagined us coming back from the pond to find Swanson sitting on our couch with Emily on his lap. I wasn't taking any chances.

With that thought in mind, I got Corny's gun out of the pickup as extra insurance. I considered taking the ATV, but we were trying to keep a low profile and those things are loud as shit. Our neighbor would probably call the cops and we were definitely not equipped to deal with that. *Oh, hello, Officer. Just down here at the ol' swimmin' hole for a midnight dip.* We decided to walk. I had switched into an appropriate all-black outfit similar to Corny's skulking collection and Sarah was in her wetsuit. It would have been kind of sexy on a pleasanter occasion. When we first moved to the farm, we used to go out at night occasionally and make love under the stars.

When we got to the pond I said, "Okay, just swim out to the middle and then dive straight down. You should be able to spot the boat pretty easily."

"You sank the boat too?"

"I didn't plan to. When I tossed him in, his head cracked a board and it started leaking."

"That's surprising," Sarah said. "That boat was the work of a couple of fine craftsmen."

"True. But body-disposal was not one of the approved uses. There really should have been some kind of disclaimer."

"Yeah, I'm sure it was built exactly to spec."

"Anyway, the boat will help you find him."

"I can't believe I'm doing this," Sarah said and slipped into the water with the flashlight in her hand. From the pier, I watched the beam of light progress toward the center of the pond. I knew there was nothing dangerous in there, but seeing her swimming in that dark water I couldn't help thinking of the opening scene in *Jaws* where a woman is suddenly jerked underwater while swimming in the ocean at night. Unlikely to happen, since catfish never leave the bottom or attack people and don't even have teeth, but I thought it. When she looked like she was in the right spot, I called, "Right about there!"

"Okay," Sarah replied. "I'm going down. If I'm not back up in less than a minute, call the Coast Guard. Or better yet, get your ass in here and save me." She took a deep breath and disappeared under the water. She was back up in ten seconds.

"I see the boat. Where is he?"

"Wedged in the bottom of the boat on his back. You should be able to reach his pockets."

She went back under. I could see the faint illumination from the flashlight moving around beneath the surface. I was counting in my head and got to fifteen before she burst above the water again, coughing and sputtering.

"What's wrong?" I whispered. "Are you okay?"

Sarah was treading water and breathing hard. "I'm okay. I'm going back down." She was down longer this time. My count reached thirty and I was starting to get worried when her head popped up again.

"Goddamn Dave and his skinny jeans," she panted, breathless. "I could barely get his keys out."

"Do you have any place to put them?"

"Yes." She zipped the keys into a pocket of her wetsuit. "There's something in his other pocket. I'm going to try to get that, then I'm done."

"Just do your best. If you can't get it, you can't get it. The keys are the important thing."

Sarah popped back up twenty seconds later holding an old-fashioned flip phone and immediately started to swim for shore. I greeted her with a towel and a hug. "This better have been worth it," she said. "I'm going to have nightmares for the rest of my life."

"I'm sorry."

"It's not your fault. Wait a minute, it's totally your fault."

"I know," I said. "That's why I said I was sorry. How bad was it?"

"It wasn't just the sight of him," Sarah said. "It was the smell. The water smelled like death."

"Was the body already decaying?"

"I don't know. It just looked bloated. But you were wrong about the fish."

"What about them?"

"I don't know what got to him. But when I accidentally shone the flashlight on his face, all that was looking back at me were two empty sockets."

"And you still went back down? Jesus, I would have swum to shore and run straight back to the house without stopping."

Sarah smiled sweetly and patted my arm. "I know you would have, honey. That's why they pay me the big bucks."

We walked back to the house arm-in-arm. I think we were experiencing the same kind of high soldiers feel after a successful mission, if the mission in my case was to stand on the shore next to a pond. Sarah had actually done something.

I opened the door and we went in the house. "I'm going to see about drying off the keys and cell phone. You, young lady, have earned yourself a hot shower. I might even join you—wait, didn't I lock the door and set the alarm?"

"Yes, you did," Sarah whispered back. "Be quiet and listen."

I didn't hear a thing. Not even the dogs were making any noise.

"Stay here." I put my hand on the gun in my jacket pocket and crept toward the kids' bedrooms.

I eased open Emily's door. Sound asleep. Or was someone hiding behind the door? I took out the gun and held it in what would probably be my shooting hand if I'd ever fired a handgun. Safety on or off? No idea. I dove into the room and nearly put a double tap right between Justin Bieber's eyes. Just a poster. You rarely see hardened criminals with that haircut. I shut the door and backed out into the hall.

I tiptoed to Nick's door and put my ear against it. Nothing. I silently turned the knob and pushed the door open. His bed was empty. Did they take him away somewhere? Were they still here? One thing was for sure. I was going to kill Swanson. Even if he didn't hurt Nick, he was dead.

I moved on toward our bedroom. As I got closer, I thought I could hear voices. I didn't want to burst in and cause any nervous gunplay, most likely from me. If everybody kept calm, no one would get hurt, or at least that's what I kept telling myself. Swanson needed me to do something for him. He wasn't going to shoot me. He didn't want to kill me. But I did want to kill him.

I shoved the door lightly forward and crawled in behind it. I read somewhere you're supposed to stay low in a gunfight. Or maybe that's in a fire. No matter, because there was Nick sitting on our bed watching TV. I put the gun in my pocket before I stood up.

"Hi, Dad."

I called to Sarah. "Everything's okay. We're in the bedroom." I walked over to Nick and tousled his hair like a sitcom dad would. "What are you doing up, Sport?"

"Who's 'Sport'?"

"Never mind. What are you doing up?"

"I couldn't sleep and you guys weren't in here so I started looking for you. I thought you might be outside doing barn check, but the door was locked and the alarm was on. I turned it off and looked outside, but there was nobody there, so I just came up here to wait."

Sarah came in the room, wet hair, wetsuit and all. "Do you feel all right, honey?"

"I just couldn't sleep. Have you been swimming?"

Pretty hard to deny that. "Yes."

"In the pond?"

Ditto. "Yes."

"Why?"

I decided to take this one. "Your mother is training for a triathlon. You can't practice in a pool because the actual race is in a lake."

Nick looked at me. "So what were *you* doing?"

"I was helping by, uh …"

"Timing me," Sarah said.

It was all I could think of at the time, but Sarah training for a triathlon was a perfect cover story. The kids would have no trouble believing their mother was starting some kind of selfish project that would take months and constantly inconvenience the rest of the family. It happened all the time.

"Let's get you in bed, honey." Sarah led Nick back to his room.

I went outside and returned the gun to the glove compartment of the pickup. I'd get rid of it later. Then I went back in the kitchen and into the pantry. I scanned the shelves full of recipe ingredients for dozens of meals that will never be prepared. We should empty this room out and just give it all to a homeless shelter once a month. We're never going to use ninety percent of this crap. Lucky for me we don't do that because I found five boxes of Uncle Ben's White Rice. I poured two of them into a big Tupperware container.

Corny's phone was an old-fashioned black flip phone. It had one of those windows so you could see who was calling when it was closed. You had to text using the telephone keypad instead of a typewriter keyboard. Why the hell would Corny have a shitty old phone like this? He always had to have the newest and best products.

The instructions I Googled were very clear that if you turn the phone on when it's still wet, it might short the circuits. I took the battery out and submerged it all in the rice. Apparently rice is a desiccant and will absorb the moisture from the phone, causing it to dry out. The same process causes birds that eat rice thrown at weddings to bloat up and die, if you believe that urban legend, which I do not. I've filed *pigeon murdered by grain of rice* alongside *seagull strangled by plastic six-pack ring* in my folder of bullshit environmental activism. What do you bet whatever Pepsi or Coke did to try to solve the six-pack "problem" was far worse for the environment than the death of the one seagull who was too stupid to pull his head out of a round plastic hole?

I didn't really think the rice would work, but I figured it was worth a shot. I dropped my phone in the toilet once (unused— just the clean drinking water for dogs that fills up the empty bowl) and it dried out in a day or so, but that was probably a lot less likely after twenty-four hours at the bottom of a pond. Whatever information I got from the phone, it wasn't going to be tonight, so I put the lid on and stuck the container on a shelf in the pantry and turned my attention to the keys. I didn't have to ask Google what to do. I dried them with a towel. They hadn't been underwater long enough to rust, so they would work just fine. Of course, starting the motorcycle was going to be the least of my problems.

When I went back upstairs, Sarah was in the shower. I always like a woman in the shower. They're all slippery and soapy and wet. And naked. I resisted the impulse to jump in with her. The warrior celebration mood had been completely destroyed by our insomniac son.

◇◇◇

I talked to Sarah through the shower door. "I'm going to ride the motorcycle to the airport and leave it there."

Even with soap in her eyes, Sarah didn't buy that one. "Are you crazy? You don't know how to ride a motorcycle."

"I rode a moped that one time on vacation. It's basically the same thing."

"It's not the same at all. A moped's just a bicycle with a motor."

"Well, so is this. It's just a bigger motor. Don't worry, I Googled it and took some notes. It's pretty simple."

"You can't learn how to ride a motorcycle from written instructions. That's like saying you Googled how to ride a bull and now you're going to ride Bodacious."

"Look, I'll ride around the farm for a while until I get the hang of it."

"Good idea. That won't make very much noise."

"Corny drove it up here and we didn't hear it."

She considered that while she rinsed the shampoo out of her hair. "So how will you get home?"

"I don't want to take a cab or an über because the driver might remember me. I'll take the shuttle to one of the hotels downtown and walk over to your office. I'll call you to come pick me up."

I went into the front hall closet and dug around until I found an old leather jacket Sarah gave me. I'm sure I would have insisted on returning it if I knew how much it cost, but I kept it because she claimed it was "sexy."

Now, I felt like an idiot whenever I wore it, like I was the older partner of the star of a cop show. The jacket would have gone great with a turtleneck and a shoulder holster. But it seemed perfect for this mission. It was black and I'd always heard motorcycle riders didn't just wear leather jackets to look cool. They protect your skin if you end up sliding along the pavement for a couple of blocks. Unfortunately, I wasn't likely to execute a successful "lay down" where you skid along the ground like a rock skipping on a lake. If anything went wrong, I was going to be catapulted over the handlebars like a projectile. I needed a suit of armor to really do me any good.

I put on the jacket and the cowboy boots I wear when I'm doing my minor farm chores and don't want to get horseshit all over my shoes. I went back upstairs to tell Sarah I was leaving. The mirror in the bathroom was all fogged up, so I wiped a spot clear to check myself out. I had to admit it. By my standards, I looked like kind of a badass. I went back in the bedroom and grabbed some wraparound sunglasses I wear because my doctor told me I really need to protect my eyes from the sun. I went back in the bathroom and checked out the total package. Sure, it was dark out, but I decided the shades really completed the effect. I looked pretty damn cool, if I do say so myself. Not bad for a guy my age.

"The machines don't stand a chance if you're the terminator they sent back to kill John Connor." Sarah had stepped out of the shower and wrapped a towel around herself. I slowly turned toward her and said in what I hoped was an Austrian accent, "I'll be back" and walked out the door.

Chapter Twenty-two

I decided to walk to the copse to get the motorcycle. It took a few extra minutes, but I thought the less noise I made, the better. My plan seemed sound enough, based on my television-based knowledge of police investigations. Nobody notices vehicles left in airport parking unless they've been there for weeks. People leave cars there all the time while they're traveling. If and when the cops eventually found it and traced it to Corny, they'd assume he took a flight somewhere. When they couldn't find his name on any flight manifests, they'd further assume that he used a fake ID, that he was on the run for some reason. He was a shady character, after all, with probably a million reasons to run, if only from cuckolded husbands. Even if the cops managed to pin down the date and had access to some kind of security footage, all they'd see is a guy with a motorcycle helmet pull into the garage. There would be no way to tell it was me. I wouldn't even go into the airport, just hop on a hotel shuttle bus. No one would remember me because there are no records and middle-aged business traveler types are getting on and off those things all night. I decided I should ditch the jacket once I got there, though, so no one would think this particular middle-aged traveler might have ridden a motorcycle. There was no way I was wearing it again.

As Sarah pointed out, my stealth operation wasn't going to work unless I could actually ride a motorcycle. When I got to the copse, I wheeled the motorcycle out into the open field and got out my motorcycle-riding notes. It was too dark to read them, but I figured I didn't need them anyway. I had watched the video. I could figure it out. Hell, I barely took notes in law school and that worked out fine, except for the part where I went on and became a successful practicing attorney, but that failure was much later and unrelated to the lack of note-taking.

From my ATV experiences, I knew that various knobs and switches needed to be in the "on" position. Now that I was out in the clearing, I could see enough to inspect the bike. I found what I thought was maybe the gas knob on the side of the bike. It was already set at "on." I also flipped the ignition switch down to "on." I couldn't find anything else, so according to my calculations, the bike was fucking "on." I was good to go. I climbed on and inserted the key. It went in the lock but the handlebars wouldn't straighten. It was going to be tough to get to the airport making a constant left turn. I jiggled the key and the handlebars unlocked. I turned the key to "on" and a green light lit up on the dashboard. That had to mean "go," even in Japan. I was ready to start this son of a bitch.

As I put on his helmet, I was reminded of a Corny story from college. He claimed he happened upon a naked, passed-out girl in an empty room of the fraternity house one night. Whoever had hooked up with her initially had probably gone to the sleeping dorm to go to bed. Corny put on a motorcycle helmet so she wouldn't see his face if she woke up and proceeded to have sex with her.

Corny's moral code could best be described as situational. If it conflicted with something he wanted to do, he did it anyway. Possibly more disturbing than the act itself was that he was proud of it. He talked about it all the time, like everyone should be impressed with his mad rape skills. In Corny's mind, it was a hilarious story. You know, typical college shenanigans, like the time we came home drunk and broke into the fraternity kitchen and made ourselves breakfast, leaving a huge mess for the cook. To Corny, they were the same kind of thing.

Now I wondered why I was so surprised to discover that Corny was a sociopath, since there had definitely been signs. But when you're looking for somebody to go out drinking with, "nice" is overrated. Give me entertaining over nice any time. It's not only women who like so-called bad boys. It's flattering for both men and women when someone who's a total prick to everyone else selects you for his friend or girlfriend. You think, *this cool guy has nothing but contempt for everyone else but he likes me. I must be pretty cool, too.*

I didn't so much climb on the bike as stand over it with both feet flat on the ground. The thing was tiny. I didn't know if it was small because the Japanese people are small or just a bike for girls and men who couldn't ride a real motorcycle. Either way, I was glad because there was no way I could handle a Harley. I'd be lucky if I could handle this.

I knew from the video that you didn't turn the key to start it like a car, you pushed a button on the right handlebar. I still had to push a button after switching three different levers to the "on" position? There are fewer fail-safes required to launch a nuclear missile at NORAD. We'd hate to have this tiny motorcycle start by mistake and accidentally vaporize Russia. I pushed the button and it fired right up.

The headlight was already on because, like all modern vehicles, the Kawasaki Ninja could tell it was dark outside. If I ever drive a vehicle again that requires me to turn the lights on, I'm sure I'll be cruising around in the dark without even noticing. I knew the clutch was on the left handgrip and the throttle and brake were on the right.

The guy on the video told his girlfriend you shift with your left foot, which makes perfect sense if you're a chimpanzee. For now, I didn't have to worry about it because I only needed first gear.

I pushed the gearshift down to first—first is down, all the others are up, in the traditional number line format we all learned in school of -1, 2, 3, 4—and then eased the clutch out with my left hand while I twisted the throttle with my right. The bike shot out from under me and I ended up flat on my back. Apparently a motorcycle has some kind of shut-off mechanism like a jet-ski, so it stopped after about ten yards. I guess the throttle was kind of sensitive or maybe I needed to hold on better. When you give your horse a nudge in the ribs, he'd run right out from under you too if you weren't gripping him tight with your thighs.

I figured it was a combination of both, so I got back on and this time I held on tight and eased the clutch out as slowly as I could. The bike moved forward gradually and before I knew it I was riding it around the pasture. To me, it was like skiing or riding a regular bicycle: You kind of leaned a little in the direction you wanted to go and it happened. You didn't have to think about it. I drove around for five or ten minutes until I felt like I had the basics down and then I used the hand brake and came to a stop. I was ready for the streets.

On my way down our long driveway, I even managed to get it into second gear, so I felt pretty confident as I exited from private to public pavement. I didn't dare to even glance at my watch, afraid the distraction would cause me to careen off the road, but it was still dark and there wasn't much traffic. I didn't see another vehicle until I pulled up to my first stoplight. I got the bike stopped and just sat there waiting, like the kind of cool customer who might be cruising around on a motorcycle in the middle of the night. When a car pulled up behind me, I didn't even acknowledge it. *Nothing to see here.*

The light seemed to take forever. It was killing me not to turn around. It had to be a cop. Who else would be out at this time of night? I tried to glance down at my side-view mirror out of the corner of my eye, without moving my head, but the helmet blocked my vision.

The light finally turned green and I released the clutch. The engine died. Shit, I forgot to give it some gas. The car behind me honked and I waved it around. As the car pulled past me on my right, I noticed it was full of what looked to my untrained eye to be drunken teenagers. The rear driver's side window rolled down and a stereotypical obnoxious young punk yelled "Learn to ride, asshole!" and threw a full, open beer can at me. I recognized the red, white, and blue can as Pabst Blue Ribbon, a popular choice among cash-strapped drunken teenagers nationwide. We used to buy it for something like seven bucks a case in college.

The can hit me right in the forehead—thank you, helmet—and sprayed all over me. The four fine examples of American youth laughed and peeled out, no doubt worried that a real man on a motorcycle might try to chase them down. But there was no danger of that. I was still able to see out of my helmet, so I waited through another light and then made my way across the intersection.

As I was approaching the next intersection, the light turned green. *My luck is changing*, I thought. *I won't have to execute another panicky stop-and-start in traffic.* But just as I was crossing the intersection, a police car pulled up to the light on the cross street to my right. I was on quite a streak. If the police car turned right and followed behind me, I was screwed. My amateurish motorcycle skills would look an awful lot like driving under the influence to a cop at what-possible-reason-could-a-law-abiding-citizen-have-to-be-out-at-this-time-of-night o'clock. I'm sure I smelled like a brewery, one that made shitty beer for drunken teenagers. If a cop even got near me, he'd have to run my plates and sobriety field-test me to make sure I wasn't drunk.

As soon as I saw the police car start to turn right into my lane fifty yards behind me, I immediately turned right onto a residential street. I didn't know if the cop would follow me, but I knew if he did, I couldn't outrun him. That would take third gear, at least. Even though heroes in movies get away all the time when they're literally surrounded by a battalion of cops, the shittiest graduate of the police academy would be beating me with a nightstick for resisting arrest within thirty seconds. So I had to hide. Right away.

The good thing about a motorcycle is it can pretty much go anywhere. After I passed the first driveway on the left, I turned onto the grass and drove right between the two houses into the backyard. I switched the bike off, laid it down, and dove on the ground next to it, covering my face with my leather-clad arms. I heard some animal noises, but I didn't know if it was a squirrel or the owner of the house had just let his pit bull out for his nightly piss. I thought I heard the cop car cruising up and down the street, but I was too scared to look up. If you don't move, it's almost impossible for someone to see you from a distance in dim light. It's the movement that catches their eye. That's why predators always remain perfectly still before attacking.

So I stayed there for a long time. I don't know how long, but let's just say much, much, much longer than necessary. Anne Frank would have come out of hiding sooner. Truthfully, I doubt the cop car even turned down the street. I just lay there hearing imaginary noises until it had been so long I was afraid I was going to open my eyes and it would be morning.

I risked a glance at my watch and saw it was four a.m. I raised my head and determined the coast was clear. I wheeled the bike back down to the street.

I eventually made it to Airport Road. I wish all streets were named so I'd know where I was going. It would make it a lot easier to find Prostitute Boulevard or Massage Parlor Avenue. The rest of the trip was uneventful, except for the two times I stalled, the straightaways where I managed to get up to fifty miles an hour in first gear, and the time I almost swerved into oncoming traffic because I thought I saw a possum (it was a paper bag). By the time I got to the airport, I was proficient enough to drive into the parking garage in an unsuspicious manner. The little ticket that came out when I pushed the button to raise the barrier arm didn't give me a second glance.

I drove down a couple of levels and parked the Ninja in what I thought was an unobtrusive spot, or to be more accurate, a completely random spot. I didn't know what would make one spot better than another, so I just picked one. It wasn't right near the elevators. That was the depth of my analysis. I left the helmet on the seat. I figured someone would steal it long before the cops found the bike. I threw the ticket in a trash can.

I took off my leather jacket in the elevator and got off at street level. I stuffed the jacket in another trash can and crossed the street toward the terminal. I wasn't sorry to see the jacket go. My motorcycle riding days were over. There was a downtown shuttle waiting at the curb. When I got on the bus, the driver didn't even look up. "Where to?"

"Downtown." I sat down. Maybe my luck was changing. While we were waiting for the other passengers to get on the bus, the doors opened and an out-of-breath woman in some kind of airport uniform came aboard. She was holding my leather coat.

"Sir, is this your jacket?"

"I don't think so," I stammered.

"Yes, it is, sir. I saw you leave it in the trash can outside."

"I, uh ..."

"I knew you really wouldn't want to throw such a beautiful jacket away, so I got it out for you."

"Um, thanks?" I stuck out my hand and took the jacket from her. The other people on the bus looked at me like I was a lunatic. What kind of an asshole would just throw a leather jacket in the trash? I shrugged and sat back down, keeping a low profile and flying below the radar, just like I planned.

◇◇◇

After a few minutes, the bus pulled away from the curb. It was about a third full of weary travelers, most of whom had probably been up all night getting screwed over by the airlines, unless their flight was conveniently scheduled to arrive at four-thirty a.m. As far as I could tell, no one paid any attention to me. I made the same amount of eye contact with the other passengers I would have under normal conditions: none. As I generally do in these situations, I busied myself with my phone so as not to appear rude. A phone is also a handy shield against personal interaction in elevators, when walking down an office corridor toward a coworker, and in my own home.

Even though I was being ignored, I never relaxed. Not because I'm vigilant like a professional bodyguard, ever alert to the slightest discrepancy in my environment, but because I was scared out of my mind. In no way did I think this little mission was over.

But it pretty much was. When we got close to downtown, I called Sarah's cell phone, let it ring twice and hung up. I got off the bus and thanked the driver, who still didn't look up. I walked the couple of blocks to Sarah's office and sat down on the curb. She pulled up thirty minutes later.

Sarah was understandably proud of me. "Jesus Christ! What the hell took you so long? I thought you were lying in a ditch somewhere."

I got in the car. "I spent some quiet time in a random backyard. Otherwise, everything went okay."

"I was just sitting there waiting and waiting and waiting for you to call. I was trying to figure out what I was going to say to the kids. *Daddy's dead. Even though he's never ridden a motorcycle in his life, he had a fatal motorcycle accident at four o'clock this morning.* That would have been easy to explain. I knew you shouldn't have tried to drive that motorcycle. *I* could ride that thing better than you. It was an idiotic plan. Stupid and reckless and unnecessary and..."

I think she kept going, but I didn't hear it. Once I leaned back in the passenger seat, all the adrenaline left me. Before I knew it, I was fast asleep.

Chapter Twenty-three

Over the next couple of days, I watched the local news and scanned the newspaper for any indication that Corny had been reported missing. Despite living in a perpetual state of anxiety, I didn't really expect to see anything. What were his coworkers going to say to the police? *We started to worry when Dave didn't show up for an important extortion meeting.* Maybe Corny had somebody back home who would eventually call the police if he didn't show up, but I figured that wouldn't happen for a while. Corny had to be feeding whoever that was (wife? girlfriend? mother?) a constant pack of lies. The last thing he'd want would be for her to call the police if she didn't hear from him for a couple of days.

So I played it cool, if you call hanging from the ceiling every time the phone rang like that cartoon cat scared by the barking puppy "playing it cool." Sarah didn't have any trouble. Her schedule was full. She didn't have time to think. But everything I did felt unnatural. When I thought about the possibility of being watched, I wasn't frightened—I was embarrassed. I pictured two lifelong criminals sitting in a room full of eavesdropping equipment, disgusted by how little I got done during the day.

Nellie called to find out how the rest of our night went after he and Lang went home. "Tell me what you and Corny did so I can live vicariously through you."

"Sorry to disappoint you, Nellie. Nothing happened. We had a few more and then went home."

"Fine. I didn't expect to get the truth out of you. I tried to call Corny to get the real scoop but it went straight to voicemail. I think I may have an old number for him."

I pictured Corny's phone buried in rice at my house. "Why is that?"

"I noticed he was carrying some kind of old flip phone the other night. That can't be his real phone."

"Why would someone under eighty years old use a phone like that?"

"You ever seen *The Wire*, Bob? Drug dealers use them because they're untraceable. They call them burner phones. But why would Corny use one?"

Oh, I don't know, maybe blackmail, extortion, criminal conspiracy. "Who knows with Corny? Maybe he has a different phone for each girlfriend."

Nellie laughed. "I didn't think of that."

"So there's no way to get the data on one of those burner phones?"

"No. If they were uploading everything to the cloud, it would defeat the whole purpose of having one. Even the cops or the FBI can't get anything from a burner phone."

Dammit. I hoped the rice worked. "Just keep trying Corny. I'm sure he'll eventually get back to you."

"I'm not holding my breath." *Me either.*

My phone rang again. This time it was Lang. "Bobby! Sorry we couldn't stay out with you guys the other night. You know how Nellie's wife is."

"Right," I scoffed. "You would've been there for last call if not for Nellie."

"Well, maybe not," Lang chuckled. "So everything go okay with Corny?"

"Par for the course. If par is eighteen straight triple bogeys and a disqualification for playing the wrong ball."

"That sounds like Corny." Lang paused. "So you guys didn't talk about anything in particular?"

"Not really. Why?"

"No reason. I assume Sarah came home. Everything back to normal?"

God, I hope not. If this is the new normal, I'll be babbling to myself in a rubber room by spring. "Let's just say I'm glad she wasn't around for Corny's visit."

"Did Corny say how long he was staying or where he was going next?"

"This shouldn't surprise you if you've ever been out with Corny, but my memory of the later part of the night is a little cloudy. Why?"

"I tried to call him. His phone keeps going straight to voicemail."

Get used to that. "What do you need him for?"

Lang verbally shrugged. "He said he wanted to talk to me. You know Corny. He's always got something going."

Not anymore.

◇◇◇

I ignored my insecurities and got through the days with the help of the Internet. At night, Max and I patrolled the house like a real-life Shaggy and Scooby, ready to leap into each other's arms at the first creak of a floorboard. Max and I ran in and out of rooms, and made sure doors and windows were locked, and generally accomplished nothing. Just like any other house, if someone wanted to get in, they could get in. Even if they set off the alarm, they could kill us all before the cops got all the way out here in the country. Not to mention they could disable the alarm in about five seconds if they wanted to. The reason alarms and dogs and deadbolt locks normally work is they cause the burglar to just move on to the next house because yours is too much trouble. But if they're coming specifically for you, there's nothing you can do to keep them out.

Nobody came. They easily could have, but they didn't because they really had no reason to. For Swanson, this was still a business deal. His associate Dave seemed to have disappeared, but this was no time to panic. Surely violence toward the innocent family of Bob Patterson would be a last resort. At least that's what I kept telling myself.

After a few more days of self-consciously going through the motions of my life, I was at the office when my cell phone rang.

I didn't recognize the phone number. I thought it was probably the number Swanson called me from before, but I wasn't sure. While I waited for the little chime that would signal a voicemail, I Googled the number and came up empty, which meant nothing. Swanson wouldn't have an easily identifiable number. He probably changed cell phones once a week. No reason to make it easy for the authorities to track his movements or listen in as he conducts his "business." After way too long, my phone finally signaled that I had voicemail.

"Bob, Tom Swanson. I just wanted to touch base and provide you some additional information about our investment opportunity. Please call me at your earliest convenience." Okay, the message wasn't that long, but it seemed like it while I was nervously waiting for it.

I thought about not calling him back but I knew I couldn't avoid him forever. Plus I wanted to know what he would say about Corny. As Michael Corleone once said, "Keep your friends close but your enemies closer." Michael would probably approve of keeping my friend Corny in a pond on my property.

I made the prick wait an hour before I called him back. *I'm a busy man. You can't just get ahold of Bob Patterson on a whim. There are channels. Your girl needs to call my girl, etc.*

Just as with ninety-nine percent of the phone calls I make, while it was ringing I was hoping to get voicemail. There's nothing better when you're making a call you didn't want to make in the first place than when you hear it click over to an obvious recording. Unfortunately, in this case, I got enough rings to get my hopes up—no doubt while Swanson was recognizing my number and excusing himself from the vicinity of his latest victim—followed by the unmistakable pompous assitude of the actual voice of Tom Swanson.

"Swanson." Don't you just hate him?

"Tom, it's Bob Patterson, returning your call."

"Bob, thanks for getting back to me so quickly. I know you're a busy man."

Was that sarcasm?

"What can I do for you?"

"Bob, the question is what can *I* do for *you*? And the answer is: A lot. A helluva lot. Say, have you heard from your friend Dave lately?"

I knew this was coming. I decided I needed to let Swanson know the blackmail was a dead end. "I talked to him a few days ago. I told him he was wasting his time because I already told Sarah about what happened with the girls. She believed me, so the DVD is worthless now."

"I see. A very understanding woman, your wife."

"Yes, she is."

"And what did Dave say in response to your revelation?"

"Not much. He tried to convince me to do the deal anyway, I said no, and that was the end of it. I haven't heard from him since."

"Well, no matter. This deal stands on its own two feet. Dave was perhaps a little draconian in his methods. You need to do this for Bob Patterson. Not to keep your wife from discovering your secrets, but so she'll be proud of her man. This is an opportunity to finally get out from under your father-in-law's shadow. You'll be seen in a whole new light in the community."

"I don't care about that."

"You don't care that the power brokers in this town laugh at you behind your back?"

"No." Nice try, Swanson. They laugh right in front of me.

"You don't mind that the joke around town is that your wife was brought up to overachieve at everything except marriage?"

It was true but I didn't think anyone was really saying it. For whatever reason, my reputation far exceeded my ability. "Look, Swanson, we've been over this before. Sam decided not to do it, and I'm not doing it either."

"That's my point, Bob. It's foolish to pass on a deal so good for you personally just because of your father-in-law, who, I might point out, no longer gets to tell you what to do. He did for twenty years, but now it's your show. Be your own man for once."

"I am my own man. My decision has nothing to do with Sam. The answer is still no."

"But this is a sure-thing, Bob." Why is it Salesman 101 to use a person's first name all the time? People you actually know don't constantly say your name at the beginning or end of every sentence. My wife says my name all the time but it's more as an attention-grabber, like saying the dog's name. *Max! Get off the couch!* Are some people fooled into thinking the salesman is their friend? Would anyone want the salesman to be their friend? I'll bet the net effect on sales is negative. More people are annoyed than are duped.

"Sure-things make me nervous," I said. "You know why? Because they don't exist. Nobody really knows what's going to happen."

"Based on your logic, you could never invest in anything. You're going to do a hell of a job running that trust. Do you want me to help you stock up on mattresses so you'll have someplace to keep your father-in-law's money?"

Swanson had a point but I was unswayed. "I'm sure I'll find plenty of appropriate investments."

"Not as good as this deal. I'll bet not one other investment has crossed your desk with this kind of return."

"You're right. The numbers are actually too good. It seems impossible to me. It's like betting on football. If the line seems way off, it's a sign Vegas knows something you don't."

"So you won't invest because the deal is too good." Swanson laughed, but he didn't sound like he was smiling. It was a disgusted laugh, like the sound you would make as you said *I can't believe you're choosing Yoko over the band.* "I sent some more detailed information over to your financial guy. Give him a call and see what he thinks."

"The answer is still going to be no."

Swanson sighed and his voice got hard. "Bob, don't be a schmuck. This deal will make you rich. I know Sarah has money, but *you* don't. I'd hate to see you pass up the opportunity to provide for your family in the manner they deserve. It'd be a shame to see Emily and Nick have to give up that fancy private school they go to. Where is that, over on Forty-third Street, right? You pick them up about three-thirty every day?"

"What the fuck are you talking about? How do you even know where they go to school?"

"And I'd hate for you to disappoint Sarah," Swanson said. "One day she's going to be so worried about your lack of ambition she's going to lose her concentration and fall off her horse and have a terrible accident."

Swanson was starting to scare me. "Is that some kind of a threat?"

Swanson chuckled. "Of course not, Bob. I'm just pointing out that you have loved ones who are counting on you to take care of them and protect them. Signing off on this deal will do exactly that."

◇◇◇

I hung up and called the young guy who was looking at the Sanitol financials for me. "Eric, Bob Patterson here. You remember I came to see you a few days ago about the Sanitol deal?"

"Of course I remember, Mr. Patterson." Because I never remember anyone until I've met them multiple times, I always overexplain and reintroduce myself more than necessary. Obviously, this guy would remember me.

"What can I do for you, sir?"

"I just got off the phone with Tom Swanson. He said he provided you some new information that might have affected your opinion."

"That's right, sir, he did. I'm in the middle of putting together a complete analysis. I should have it to you sometime tomorrow."

"Can you give it to me in a nutshell?"

"Okay, Mr. Patterson. I don't like summarizing my report because in the financial world everything is qualified. Nothing is black and white. I have to explain the assumptions I made for each conclusion and—"

"I understand that," I said, even though I didn't. "I'm not going to hold you to it. Just give me an idea. Is the new info going to change anything?"

He was silent for a moment, no doubt trying to figure out how to answer my question without committing himself. Finally, he gave up and said, "Not really, no."

"Thanks, Eric. I'll read the full report when you're finished." And then I'll run a marathon and join the astronaut program at NASA.

So my financial guy still had Sanitol as a DON'T BUY and Swanson was still a lying sack of shit. *Second verse, same as the first.*

When I got to my office the next morning, I was surprised to see an e-mail from Eric already in my inbox. He must have stayed up late finishing his report. Of course, it looked like those guys lived at that office. I'm not sure he ever went home, if he even had a home. He probably still lived in his mother's basement.

I clicked on the e-mail. There was an attachment and a short message:

> Mr. Patterson:
>
> After crunching the numbers on the new
> information that was provided, my opinion
> has changed. As you can see from my attached
> report, I now strongly recommend pursuing
> the Sanitol deal. I believe it would be a serious
> mistake to pass up this kind of opportunity. I
> will be out of the office for the next few days.
> If you wish to discuss this further, please con-
> tact me next week.
>
> Eric

What the fuck? I opened the attachment and started to scroll ahead to the conclusion. And then kept scrolling and scrolling because this son of a bitch was over two hundred pages of financial gobbledygook. I recognized a few of the terms and might have been able to fake my way through some of the sections if there were diagrams, but the overall concepts were beyond my comprehension and interest. I didn't know what any of this crap meant.

But then again, that's what I had Eric for. He was supposed to understand this stuff. But why the sudden change? Just yesterday, he had told me that the new info from Swanson didn't make any difference. What could have happened in the last twenty-four hours to make him do a complete one-eighty?

Even though he was allegedly unavailable, I called Eric's cell phone. As expected, it went straight to voicemail. When companies provide cell phones to their employees, they think it gives them the right to call them anytime day or night, so employees learn to turn them off when they really don't want to be bothered so their bosses can't ask them why they didn't answer. I doubt this was the first time some know-nothing superior kept badgering Eric at home about his work, although if he came to Bennett Capital straight out of college, I probably *was* his first boss who actually knew nothing.

I eventually abandoned the scrolling and dragged the little bar on the right side of the page down to the bottom. I got to the conclusion of Eric's report, and even I could see he had completely changed his tune. I didn't understand the details, but it was pretty clear that Eric now thought Sanitol was the second coming of some very successful company I didn't invest in when it was trading for pennies a share. This wasn't just a minor change of opinion. Eric had gone from "I'm not really interested in boys" to "Oh my God, there's Justin Bieber!" overnight. It made no sense.

I left my name and number on Eric's voicemail. Operating under my normal business procedures, this would have ended my portion of the interaction. I tried to call him, he didn't answer, I left a message. My work was done.

But somebody who "gets things done" would do more. My wife would find out his home phone and try him there or call some of his coworkers. If she wanted something from someone, she would track the bastard down. I once worked for a senior law partner who would hunt you down all over the office if he wanted to see you. He would open the bathroom door and shout "Patterson, you in there?" at the stalls. I wanted to pull my feet up where he couldn't see them, but I was afraid he'd crawl under the stall and find me. I'd blurt out a meek "Yes, sir. I'll be in your office in five minutes." The guy was an insufferable prick and I hated to work for him, but I'd hire him in a second if I was in legal trouble. If everybody likes your lawyer, fire him.

I thought about calling Eric's coworkers or his girlfriend, or more likely his mother, in an effort to get ahold of him, but I decided it wouldn't do me any good anyway. He would presumably just say it was all in his report, and I wasn't smart enough to question him about the details. What I really needed to know was what happened to Eric to change things since yesterday. I knew he wasn't in his cubicle. I should just go over there and read his e-mail. Who was going to stop me? But unlike my capable wife or that effective lawyer, I'm not the confrontational type. I needed to look at his computer secretly.

Doesn't a company have a right to look at their employees' e-mails that were sent or received on company computers? Even if true, I didn't exactly run Bennett Capital and I sure didn't want to involve Harriet if I didn't have to. Plus, a technophile like Jacobs would have his computer password protected, so I'd need some kind of administrator status.

The answer to my problems was staring me right in the face. On the bottom right hand corner of my monitor was a sticker that said *Innovative Business Systems*, a little company conveniently run by a close personal friend and frequent drafter off my good fortune.

For whatever reason, Kevin Nelson had gotten involved in the computer lab in high school and understood programming. In college, he helped us all pass the computer science classes necessary for our business degrees.

For a nerd, Nellie was a cool guy. He generally used clear tape on his glasses and his tennis shoes often had the correct number of stripes, although I thought his *Dungeons & Dragons* character, Sir Nelsington the Wizard, a level five Paladin, was a little overrated. He drank his share and held his liquor as well as the rest of us, which is to say, not all that well. He fit right in with our mediocre starting rotation when we went out chasing tail.

So, even though I don't really know what his company does, Nellie is my computer guy. When I'm buying a new computer or setting up a wireless network at home, I basically just turn the job over to him.

"Bobby!" He answered his cell phone right away. When I answer my cell phone, I always just say "Hello." I don't like to broadcast the fact that I check who it is before I answer. Nellie, being of relatively sound mind and body, probably didn't worry about things like that. Plus, nerds aren't self-conscious. Their obliviousness to social custom is what makes them nerds. They're so focused on their particular passions they don't waste time on things like fashion or popularity, which makes them good at what they do.

"Nellie, I need your help."

"Don't beat around the bush, Bob. Get to the point."

"I need to take advantage of your unmatched computer skills."

"Has it occurred to you that I'm running an actual business here?"

"This is a paying gig," I said. "The trust will pay your hourly rate plus any expenses you have."

"I don't have an hourly rate."

"Make one up then. You'd be shocked what the trust pays our attorneys per hour. No matter what we pay you, we'll be getting more bang for our buck than we get from those jackals. Plus this job actually *is* your regular business. Didn't you set up the computer system at Bennett Capital?"

"As a matter of fact, I did," Nellie said. "Should I be afraid to ask why you want to know?"

"Maybe a little," I said. "So you must be set up as an administrator or something so you can get into every part of the system in case you need to change the protocols or update the settings or whatever the hell you do."

"That's right. I could theoretically have access if necessary for legitimate business purposes. So?"

"I need to look at an employee's e-mail account."

"That would fall into the category of not necessary or legitimate."

"It is in this case."

"I can't just go poking around in people's personal correspondence even if I am the administrator. It's a violation of their privacy rights."

"It's not private if they sent and received the e-mails on company computers. The Fourth Amendment only protects you against searches if you have a reasonable expectation of privacy."

"Great," Nellie said. "The one day you happened to show up at law school…"

"I'm an expert on searches," I said. "The rest of law school didn't apply to me personally, but there was a very real chance I was going to get pulled over with weed in the car or something. I mastered that criminal law shit."

"I'm glad it's led you to such a lucrative career."

"If you're a criminal lawyer, you have to defend criminals. The only criminal I want to defend is me."

"The way things are going, you may get your chance."

"I need you to do this. It's not illegal and it might be crucial to the future of Bennett Capital."

"You know I'd do anything for the Bennetts," Nellie said. "When Sam hired us to set up the network for Bennett Capital, it really put my company on the map. I'd probably be making house calls for the Best Buy Geek Squad if it wasn't for Sam."

"I guarantee you Sam would have wanted you to look at these e-mails."

"All right," Nellie sighed. "I can get in the system remotely from here, but give me a couple of minutes. It's not a matter of just hitting a few keystrokes. I have to look up usernames and passwords and log on through a bunch of doorways set up to keep the bad guys out. In the movies, a fifteen-year-old kid can hack into the National Security Agency in about ten seconds. In real life, these things take some time, even if you know the passwords."

"Real life sucks."

"You don't even know what real life is. I'll call you back."

"Thanks, Nellie. I owe you one."

"You won't think that after you get my bill."

I "worked" for a while. Fifteen minutes later, Nellie called back.

"Okay, I'm in." I could hear him typing furiously, like a woman about to tell you the rental car you reserved is unavailable.

"Can you look at all the e-mails for a particular account?"

"Yes, I'm doing it right now. I've always wanted to get a look at your wife's inbox."

I forgot Nellie could get into Sarah's account. "Yeah, well, if I were you I'd hit 'Refresh' a lot."

"Why does she send so many e-mails to her tennis instructor?"

"Knowing Sarah, she's helping him start a new tennis club. If she was fucking him at thirty-five dollars an hour, it would be a lot cheaper." Of course, I could just look at Sarah's laptop whenever I wanted to, which I don't. My already fragile ego would be even further damaged by confirming that her daily e-mail correspondence dwarfs my annual work product.

"I'm just kidding. I would never look at employee e-mails. The corporate bullshit would drive me insane. Not to mention getting my ass fired."

"I know you wouldn't."

"I'm making an exception in this case because you said it was important. But if you do anything that causes Bennett Capital to pull my contract, I'm coming to live at your house when my wife kicks me out."

"It's a deal. We can sleep in the basement and make popcorn and stay up super-late—"

"Enough. This is serious. Who am I looking for?"

"Eric Jacobs."

"Okay. *What* am I looking for?"

"E-mail received yesterday afternoon or evening, especially from someone named Swanson."

More typing. "There's a couple from Swanson. Let's see…the first one says 'attached is additional information blah blah blah Sanitol blah blah blah.' It's got some pdfs and excel spreadsheets attached that look like some kind of financial information."

"Okay. What about the next one?"

"This one's shorter. It just says 'more info to help you make a decision' and has a jpeg attached and a link to what looks like some kind of news article. Hang on." This time no feverish typing, just a few mouse clicks. "The jpeg is just a picture of a house."

How is a picture of a house more info? Was Swanson trying to bribe Jacobs? "What do you mean 'a house'?"

"You know, a place where people live who didn't marry a billionaire's daughter? It's like a mansion, but smaller."

"I know what a house is. Why is Swanson sending a picture of a house to Jacobs? Is there anything special about it?"

"No, it's just a regular house, nothing fancy, probably three bedrooms, one-car garage. I don't know, I'm not a realtor."

"Is there an address?"

"Yeah, it's across town. I'll look it up." I could hear the keys on Nellie's laptop clacking.

"Can you do that? I thought you had to use a reverse directory or something that only cops have."

"Does your TV only get the '70s channel or something? I guess you're right if Mannix or Baretta is trying to track down a suspect, but here in the twenty-first century you can just Google an address and the name will come up if the address has ever been on the Internet, which most have. Here we are. Wanda Jacobs, sixty-four years old."

It had to be Jacobs' mother's house. I could feel myself starting to sweat. "What about the link?"

"It's coming up. It's a newspaper story. The headline reads 'No Suspects in Rape, Murder of Grandmother.' There's a picture of the house where it apparently happened."

My neck muscles tightened. "Is it the same house?"

"No, it's just kind of similar. Typical, middle-class house, like you might see an old woman living in." I could hear him scrolling. "Let's see. This crime was a couple of years ago in Pennsylvania. I don't know what the connection is."

I let out a sigh of relief. "There isn't one."

"Then why send it to him?"

As a warning: *We know where your mother lives. Bad things sometimes happen to old women who live alone.* "Don't worry about it. Thanks for your help. I owe you one."

"I'll add it to the list."

Chapter Twenty-four

Even after Corny hinted that Swanson was behind Sam's death, I still thought of Swanson as just a businessman. Not above a little blackmail or some ham-handed threats, but not running around raping and killing people. Evil, but in a corporate way. A criminal, but a white-collar criminal. Now a more sinister picture was emerging.

For lunch I decided to walk down the street and get a sandwich. As I was about to cross the first intersection, a big black sedan with tinted windows pulled up to the curb and stopped right in front of me. I can't tell one car from another, but it looked like the kind of car a diplomat with a driver would ride around in. Two huge guys in dark suits and sunglasses got out. They looked like pallbearers at an NFL lineman's funeral, the kind of guys who never look right in a suit because their necks are too big. They even had that scary long blond hair like those bad-ass white linebackers on the Packers, the kind of maniacs who still make the tackle even after their helmet gets ripped off. They stopped and stood right in front of me.

The one on my left spoke first. In the NFL, they call the middle linebacker the Mike linebacker. He needs to be stout enough to hold up against the power running game. This one was the slightly larger of the two, so in my mind I named him "Mike."

"Mr. Swanson wants to see you," Mike said in a surprisingly high voice undoubtedly caused by his shrunken steroid testicles.

"Of course he does." I got in the car.

◇◇◇

I've always managed to defuse potentially volatile situations with words. I may be scared, but I'm not scared to talk. Danger paralyzes my body, not my mouth.

The testosterone twins got in the front. Mike drove. I sat in the back by myself. Apparently they could tell just by looking at me that I wasn't going to try anything. They were right, but I tried to find out what I could.

"So where are we headed?"

The thug in the passenger seat answered. He was a little smaller, so I decided to call him "Will," which is what NFL coaches call the weak side linebacker, who needs to be more athletic, able to drop into pass coverage. Will had more of a regular voice, but give him a few more years on the juice and his ball sack will look like a two-year-old's just like his partner's. "We're going to see Mr. Swanson."

"I know." I smiled. We're all buddies here. "But where is that?"

Mike this time. "You'll find out when we get there."

"Okay." Just like the magazines say, girls, if you want to get him talking, ask him about himself. "So, you guys ever play any ball?"

"Ball?" asked Will.

"Ball. You know, American football?"

"High school," Will said.

"Just high school? I figured you guys for college at least, maybe the NFL."

Back to Mike. "We were smaller then." They took turns like it was doubles ping pong.

"I guess some high schools have crappy anabolic steroid programs." The ones that lose all the time.

"Yeah." I guess if they were glib, witty conversationalists, it would have broken the stereotype, but stereotypes are stereotypes for a reason. Most intellectually curious people have a hard time lifting weights and staring at themselves in the mirror for eight hours a day. Still, I hadn't learned anything, so I kept trying.

"So what do you guys do for Swanson?"

"Whatever needs doing." I gave up keeping track of who said what. It made no difference.

"So it could be anything?"

The stupid one glanced at the other stupid one. "Mr. Swanson hasn't asked us to do anything yet that we wouldn't do."

I had a feeling these guys weren't asked to do too much. Drive Swanson around. Glare at people. Show off your hair and your muscles. Don't open your mouth. Let people presume you can handle yourself. Even minor scrutiny would reveal that these guys weren't all that tough. But in this case they just had to be tougher than me.

I decided I wasn't going to learn anything from these idiots. No way Swanson would tell them anything important. Plus, they were about as talkative as my son if you ask him how things went at a school dance. *It was okay. Kinda boring.* But if you ask my daughter the same question, make sure your schedule is clear for the next couple of hours.

◇◇◇

I stared out the window as we drove. I was hoping for a modern office building, where I might land on a huddle of smokers if I was tossed out the window. But no, we were headed into some kind of industrial park with huge warehouses full of God-knows-what. You can easily picture the place if you're one of those unenlightened souls who still has a television. It was a typical bad-guy-selected meeting place to which the hero has been ordered to "come alone," but unless you're Dirty Harry, you probably shouldn't agree to the meet.

We pulled up to a nondescript industrial building with no name or other markings indicating ownership. They all looked the same to me. Big, prefabricated (so much easier than fabricating the metal right on-site!) metal buildings with slanted metal roofs. Huge barns, really, like the practice facilities for college football teams. There was a large overhead door, probably used for massive shipments of whatever the hell they were manufacturing or assembling or storing in there. There was also a regular human-sized door next to the overhead door. We went in that one. It wasn't quite NFL linebacker-sized, but by turning sideways, my large blond escorts were able to squeeze through.

The door was metal and heavy, what I think of as a fire door, thick enough to hold back the flames from the inevitable arson after the business goes in the toilet. If it was closed and locked, there was no way I could break through it if I had to get out of here in a hurry.

The space was almost completely empty. It was like going to a New Orleans Costco during Hurricane Katrina. Just about cleaned out. You'll have to come back for your hundred and forty-four rolls of toilet paper and seventy-two-ounce bottle of ketchup another time. There was some scattered junk at the far end. Old furniture, toys, sports equipment. The previous tenant probably didn't have time to grab all their stuff while they were being forced out at gunpoint by Swanson's goons.

We went up some steps that led to one of those second-floor offices that stick out from the warehouse wall. They put them up high with big plate-glass windows so the Japanese supervisor can look out and make sure no one leaves the Mitsubishi assembly line to use the bathroom. In most warehouses, no one really stands there, but the workers know someone *could* be watching so they work a little harder than they otherwise would. Whatever they were planning to do in here, I was pretty sure Swanson wouldn't be the guy doing it. He was a "keep your hands clean" kind of guy.

Swanson was sitting behind a beat-up old metal desk looking over some spreadsheets. Because this was a blue-collar work area, he had shed his suit jacket and rolled his sleeves up a quarter of the way to show he was a man of the people. He looked like a politician at a barbecue fund-raiser trying desperately to look like a regular guy, despite his blow-dried anchorman hair, winter tan, and capped teeth. He even had the requisite yellow Live Strong bracelet to show that he was a humanitarian as well as a jock. I wasn't convinced.

Swanson looked up and smiled that phony smile of his at me. "Bob! Thanks for coming to see me."

"I had a choice?"

He seemed genuinely surprised, almost as if he had normal human thoughts and feelings. "What? Did my associates give you a hard time?"

"No," I admitted.

"I apologize for their lack of sensitivity. I may have to send these boys back to charm school." He glared at the two blond monsters, now looking sheepish, like scolded yellow labs if yellow labs lifted a lot of free weights. "Now go downstairs and wait."

I watched them shuffle meekly out the door and then turned to Swanson. "I've never understood how people like you boss around behemoths like these guys. I always expect the three-hundred-pound nose tackle to snap his puny coach's neck when he's yelling at him."

"It's called command presence, Bob," Swanson said. "I may look like a normal successful businessman, but I'm ex-military."

"In what capacity?"

"I could tell you, but—"

"Yeah, yeah, I know, then you'd have to kill me."

"That's right, I would," Swanson said and gazed evenly into my eyes until I looked away. "Now sit down, Bob. We need to talk."

I sat in an office chair with stuffing coming out of holes in what used to be maroon leather. "What are you doing in this shithole, Swanson? Doesn't seem like your style."

"I forgot that you've never really worked for a living, Bob. You don't actually *make* things in a nice office building. You make things in a place like this, outside of town because of all the noise. Lots of space for moving things in and out, equipment and oil and grease everywhere. Production is a messy business, Bob."

"So what are you making here? It looks pretty empty to me."

"We're going to be building our sanitation machines here, Bob. That's what I brought you down here to show you."

Did this guy ever give up? Swanson was like a honey badger in a fifteen-hundred-dollar suit. If the honey badger got mani-pedis, two-hundred-dollar haircuts, and teeth-whitening treatments.

"I'm not going to change my mind."

Swanson smiled his usual mirthless smile, which apparently fools adults but undoubtedly frightens small children and animals. "I know you think you won't, Bob. But I also know you're skeptical about our numbers, so I wanted to give you a personal demonstration of the product so you'll know I'm not full of crap."

That ship had already left port with a full load, but I figured I might as well let him show me and get it over with. I wasn't exactly being held by force, but I didn't think they'd just let me walk out. Plus in this neighborhood, I'd probably stumble onto a ransom exchange. I was likely in more danger outside than I was in here. "Fine. Show me."

Swanson got up from behind the desk and I followed his tasseled reindeer-skin loafers down the metal steps to the warehouse floor. He kept his hands off the railing, as if he was afraid to touch it except through his handkerchief. It was like watching Prince Charles go down a fire escape, but he eventually made it all the way to the bottom.

We walked over to the far diagonal corner of the warehouse. On the cement floor sat a gray metal box about four feet tall and a couple of feet wide and deep. I hadn't even noticed it before because it was so small. It looked like something my lawn guy might use on my yard, not some device that was going to revolutionize the sanitation industry. There was a yellow hose running into it from a faucet in the wall and what looked like your basic green garden hose with one of those spray handles coming out of it. I was more convinced than ever that Swanson was overselling his product.

"This is it?"

"You bet it is," Swanson said. "All you need is water from a tap and this thing will clean up any mess you can imagine. It's three thousand times the sanitizing power of chlorine, and perfectly safe."

"Come on. That can't be true."

Swanson waved over a middle-aged guy in blue coveralls with "Jim" written in cursive on the left chest. "Jim, show my associate here what this baby can do."

Jim went over to the pile of junk across the warehouse and came back with a can of oil, a can of paint, and a bucket. The scene was similar to the old traveling vacuum salesman bit where he would impress the housewife by dumping various things on her carpet and then vacuuming them up. That's all Swanson really was. A door-to-door Fuller Brush man.

Jim poured thick motor oil all over the floor, then grabbed the hose coming out of the machine and sprayed the oil with it like he was hosing off the deck in his backyard. Within about thirty seconds, the oil was gone. It just disappeared. By the time the water reached the drain about ten feet away, it was perfectly clear.

I didn't say anything. It did seem kind of amazing, but they clean up toxic waste somehow, right? Or they just say they do and then some community downstream from the factory ends up with an unusually large number of Siamese twins.

Next Jim poured bright yellow paint all over the floor. Same result. No trace of paint anywhere when he was finished with the hose. Swanson looked at me for some kind of reaction but I just shrugged. Swanson nodded at Jim. He picked up the bucket. I could see that it was full to the brim with blood. Some kind of animal blood, I hoped.

"You guys heading over to Carrie's prom later, Swanson?"

"Pay attention, Bob." Jim poured blood everywhere. The smell was sickening. Just seeing it spreading on the floor was horrific to me, which I'm sure was at least part of the point of this ridiculous exercise. *This could be your blood, Bob.* To complete the effect, Swanson took out a sharp knife and dipped it in the puddle. Blood dripped off of it like a horror movie poster.

Jim came over and rinsed off the knife and then the floor. The blood washed away just like everything else and the smell was gone.

"That's not even the best part, Bob. Watch this." Swanson took out a plastic spray bottle, like you might use to water a plant or get the cat off the couch.

I knew he wanted me to ask but I couldn't help myself. "What's that?"

"You ever watch those crime shows? CSI or whatever?"

"I don't own a television."

Swanson raised an eyebrow but continued. "Anyway, this is Luminol. When you spray it over an area that's had blood on it, it emits a blue glow. Even if there are just minute traces. The crime scene techs use it all the time on those shows. They almost always find something. It's virtually impossible to get rid of every trace of blood. Until now."

Swanson squirted Luminol, if that's really what it was, on both sides of the knife and then sprayed a big circle on the ground where the blood had been. He signaled for one of his many henchmen to cut the lights.

Nothing. Total darkness. I thought about making a run for it, but I couldn't see any better than anyone else, so the darkness really wasn't my friend. But there was definitely no glow. I didn't know Luminol from Lemon Pledge, but I Googled it later. Apparently police investigators actually do use it to find blood.

For all I know, there was water in that bottle, but it was an impressive display, nonetheless. I could obviously test it myself pretty easily, or more likely get someone to do it for me, so Swanson didn't really have much to gain by lying, at least in this one specific case. Ergo, the Sanitol sanitizer actually worked.

The lights came back on and Swanson held up the knife. "You could operate with that knife."

"I guess, if you're performing surgeries in an abandoned warehouse with a kitchen knife. Most people prefer to go to a hospital."

"Seriously, Bob." Swanson gestured to the floor. "All that blood. Gone without a trace. If O.J. had had one of these machines, he'd never even have been arrested. Weeks of testimony about blood and DNA never would have happened because there wouldn't have been any at the scene."

"Yeah, it's a shame a cold-blooded killer had to sit through his own trial and acquittal and then a subsequent civil trial. He deserved better."

"You know what I mean, Bob. This machine could have changed history."

Swanson was right. If that little display of magic blood-removal was on the level, this thing was awesome. I wish I'd had one with me the other night in the barn with Corny. Maybe I could borrow it for a couple of hours. But just because I could use it for my own nefarious purposes didn't make it a sound investment. The numbers were still too good to be true.

"Swanson, I don't know what you think you just proved. I guess you'll make a fortune selling this thing to auto mechanics and painters and butchers, but I assume they're already cleaning up with something. I suppose hospitals could use it, too, but I'm guessing they've got to go through some elaborate process to get it tested and approved first. What makes this so special?"

"It's true there are other companies offering sanitizing solutions, but ours is cheaper and more effective."

"It cleans stuff," I said. "I get it. But you haven't shown me how it's going to make us all billionaires."

Swanson sighed audibly. I understood. I can be exasperating. Sarah sighs like that whenever I'm winning an argument, right before she declares a mistrial on the rarely cited grounds of "I don't want to talk about it anymore."

"Bob, I must confess I thought you'd be an easier nut to crack. Nothing in your history indicated you would show this kind of resolve or interest or even a pulse. But it's clear to me now that we—or should I say your fraternity brother, Dave—underestimated you. Badly."

I kept my face passive but smiled inwardly. Underestimated for once! I'm almost always overestimated.

"A guy like you," Swanson continued, "should have leapt over the table to grab the pen out of my hand to sign up for this deal. But you didn't. So now we're going to have to take your knowledge and input on this project up another level. Especially now that I know that, despite all appearances to the contrary, you're not afraid to get your hands dirty."

"Looks can be deceiving, Swanson. You can't judge a book by its cover. Wait, how are my hands dirty?"

Swanson looked me in the eye like a poker player about to turn over a full house. "You think I haven't noticed the conspicuous absence of your old buddy, Dave?"

"So? What does that have to do with me?"

"I know you killed him."

Chapter Twenty-five

In the book *Outliers*, Malcolm Gladwell describes what he calls the "10,000-Hour Rule." The idea is that tremendous expertise in any field can only be achieved through at least ten thousand hours of diligent practice. Even the most talented people have to put in the work before they can master their craft. As examples in lieu of actual evidence, he notes that the Beatles performed live for ten thousand hours before they hit it big and Bill Gates spent ten thousand hours programming on a high school computer before he created Microsoft.

While the Beatles had their live performances and Bill Gates had his computer time, I've gotten the necessary reps sitting in board meetings and business planning sessions completely unprepared. I have been startled out of my reverie on, let's say, a shitload of occasions by a question posed directly to me on a subject about which I know nothing.

Swanson couldn't possibly know what had happened to Corny, but he knew he was missing and there was a chance I had something to do with it. I'm sure his plan was to spring this accusation on me and watch me closely. He'd know it was true by my guilty reaction. What he didn't know was I was the John Lennon of faking my way through answers to questions out of the blue. By now, with all of Gladwell's practice hours under my belt, I've put in the work. My heart rate doesn't shoot up and I don't stammer and fumble for words. The heroes in these kinds of stories often have hidden talents that really come in handy just when they need it. I guess this was mine.

I stared right back into Swanson's eyes. Well, actually his left eye. I have a hard time staring at both of a person's eyes at the same time. Let's just say I looked calmly in his direction. "Are you saying Dave is dead?"

"That's exactly what I'm saying. And you know it as well as I do."

"I do not know it. What happened to him?" Guilty people always make a mistake when they don't ask questions when informed of tragic news. If you didn't know anything about it, you'd want to know what happened.

"You killed him, that's what happened to him."

"That's ridiculous. I couldn't kill Dave even if I wanted to. You've met us both. What odds would I get? They'd have to take the fight off the board in Vegas because no action was coming in on me."

"I don't know how you did it, but I know you did."

"What makes you think he's dead? The police haven't contacted me and I haven't seen anything in the paper."

"He's missing and Dave wouldn't run off. He's not that kind of guy. So somebody got to him. I know it wasn't me, so that leaves you."

"So what you're really saying is you don't know where Dave is and you have no idea if he's dead or alive."

Swanson took a step toward me, putting his face closer to mine than I prefer another man's face to be. "That's right. I don't know for sure. But I have no doubt that Dave paid you a little visit on your farm and never came back."

A little too close for comfort, but he'd admitted he didn't know. "Wrong again, Swanson. Maybe Dave just had a change of heart. Maybe he finally got sick of doing the dirty work for rich pricks like you."

"Then I'm sure you won't mind if I make a little anonymous phone call to the police telling them they might find a body on your property." Shit. Can the police really get a search warrant just based on an anonymous tip? If so, I've got a few people I'd like to have body-cavity searched. Starting with Swanson here.

I called his bluff. The last thing Swanson wanted was the cops involved. "Go ahead. I've got nothing to hide."

"Bob, you've been blackmailed before, so I'm not going to bore you with how it works, but murder is like the holy grail of extortion. I needed some more leverage on you, and now I've got it. It's like you're doing my job for me."

"There's no leverage if I didn't do anything."

"That's true, I suppose, although irrelevant." Swanson chuckled to himself and shook his head back and forth with a little grin on his face like a parent pretending to be disappointed but actually proud of his child's misbehavior. "You know, Bob, I didn't think you had it in you. In a way, you're a better fit for this company than ever. Come on back up to the office. I have a few more things you need to hear."

We climbed back up to Swanson's temporary office and sat down in the same chairs. "Can I get you anything?" Swanson asked. "We have water." He pointed behind me to one of those old-fashioned water coolers with a five-gallon jug that some poor bastard had to lug up the metal stairs and then flip upside down into the base without spilling it. One of the linebacker twins could probably do it without much trouble. They weren't much good for anything else.

Despite what I thought was a successful deflection of Swanson's questions, my throat was a little dry. It's not that I didn't get nervous at all. I was just able to fake my way through it. I got up and went over to the cooler. Although undetected by the casual observer, I still might get a little cotton-mouth. After a brief search of the water cooler, I found the hidden cup dispenser. They never want to make it too easy on your typical dehydrated factory worker. Otherwise, they'd be hanging around the water cooler all day, except for the ten hours they spend on the line.

I pulled out a cup. Perfect. The kind shaped like a little cone. You have to do all your drinking right there at the cooler since you can't set the cup down. Why in the hell would anyone make any kind of a liquid container with a pointed bottom? It's what a kindergartener would come up with if he tried to make a cup out of construction paper. Were employees hoarding water at their workstations?

I sat back down. "You get enough to drink?" Swanson asked.

"Yes. I like to drink my water in a series of shots."

"Good. Like I said downstairs, Bob, I didn't think you had it in you. But this newfound…I don't know, ruthlessness of yours has convinced me that I need to lay all my cards on the table."

"I'm no more ruthless than I ever was, but let's hear it. I want to get this over with and get out of here."

"Do you acknowledge this is a fantastic investment if the projections are accurate?"

Where was he going with this? "That's a big if."

"You're having a hard time believing those numbers?"

"Legitimate businesses don't make those kinds of returns."

"Right. But this one does."

I was puzzled. "So…what are you saying? This is an illegitimate business?"

Swanson put his finger on his nose. "Bingo. That's exactly what I'm saying."

"I want nothing to with anything illegal."

"That may have been true before you murdered your old friend, but it appears your moral compass is becoming a little more flexible." Swanson held up a hand as if to signal *Stop* or *Heil Hitler.* "Don't say anything. I know you deny it. Let's just agree to disagree on that for now."

I should have gotten up and walked out of there right then. It was a long trek back to my office, but I was fortified with a couple of tablespoons of water and I probably could have made it. But now that Swanson was allegedly coming clean, I needed to stick around. I wasn't necessarily going to believe any of it, but I definitely wanted to hear it.

"What do you know about meth?" Swanson asked.

"Meth?"

"Yes, methamphetamine. Also known as speed, glass, ice, boo, crank, jet fuel, tick-tick, trash, scootie, and chicken feed."

"I know what it is. I've seen *Breaking Bad.*"

"I don't know how to tell you this, Bob, but that show is not a documentary. Let me give you a little crash course." Swanson opened a file folder on the desk in front of him. "Meth is the second most popular drug in America, after marijuana. In rural areas, it's number one with a bullet, and it's moving into the suburbs. It's the drug of choice for white people."

"A legitimate white people problem."

"I guess, for them. But not for us. Approximately twelve million Americans have used meth. That's a lot of customers."

"What, did you send out a consumer survey?"

"I did some research, just like any businessman would before entering a market."

"You really need a PowerPoint for this."

Swanson smiled. "I thought about it." He waved a hand at his surroundings. "But we don't really have a modern office environment here."

"I can see that. So why is meth getting so popular?"

"First of all, meth is better and cheaper than cocaine. Highs can last eight to twelve hours instead of twenty to thirty minutes."

"Jesus. Who'd want it to last that long? It would take me a month to recover."

"More bang for your buck," Swanson shrugged. "Second, it can be made from common household products. You can use cold tablets, paint thinner, camping fuel, fertilizer, iodine, drain cleaner, rock salt, battery acid, even kitty litter. There are thousands of recipes on the Internet."

"Just about every one of those things sounds like something you'd never want to put in your body unless you were trying to kill yourself in the most painful way possible."

"That's why people use mostly cold tablets, if they can get them."

"But even that messes you up pretty bad. I've seen those *Faces of Meth* pictures on the Internet. You'd have to be crazy to even try it."

"Not necessarily. At first, meth is similar to an ADD drug. It gives you incredible focus and energy. Users are often people working long hours at grueling blue-collar jobs, young parents with small children struggling to get through the day, or people looking for an escape from their miserable lives."

"What are you, their industry spokesman?"

"I'm merely trying to explain why someone would use it. You asked."

"They must see what happens to other people when they keep using."

"Well, at first they're just looking for a pick-me-up, but when they take meth, they feel fantastic. Among other things, it produces bursts of energy, euphoria, heightened concentration, high self-esteem, and enhanced sex drive."

"I could actually use all of those myself."

"Exactly." Swanson chuckled like we were just two old friends having a good time, but I was getting tired of this.

"Okay, I'm up to speed on meth." Swanson started to laugh again but I cut him off. "No pun intended. So what's your point, Swanson?"

"Let me give you a little background history."

"What for?"

"Hear me out. It's relevant. Meth first became popular with outlaw motorcycle gangs in the seventies. Back then it was called crank because they smuggled it in motorcycle crankcases. In the nineteen-eighties, the Mexican syndicates moved in, mostly in the Southwest. Today the Midwest and the East Coast are supplied almost entirely by thousands of mom and pop enterprises. And that situation cries out for change."

"Why?"

"Because these people don't know what they're doing. If they're not killing their customers with their drugs made from paint thinner or drain cleaner, they're killing themselves in lab explosions. Someone competent and organized could dominate that market."

"So why hasn't anyone?"

"Because it's too messy. Literally, not figuratively. Cooking meth gives off a strong smell, like ammonia or cat pee. That's why it's usually made in Cletus and Jolene's trailer out in the middle of nowhere."

I was beginning to see where this was headed. Swanson continued. "It's almost impossible to get rid of the smells and the residue from a meth lab."

"So it would be a pretty big advantage to have some kind of a portable system that could really clean up a lab." I got there.

"Yes, it would. No big organization has moved in because without a way to clean up, it's just not worth it. If it's not the smell, it's the garbage that gives meth labs away. You're tossing dozens of trash bags outside a small house or trailer every single week. All the cops have to do is dig through your trash and when they find rubber gloves, aluminum foil, funnels, glass beakers, and hot plates, you're screwed."

"How do you clean the hardware up? Your little sanitation machine isn't going to vaporize a glass beaker, is it?"

"No, the Sanitol sanitizer just disposes of the chemicals and makes sure all traces are completely gone. We've got something else for the big stuff, which I'm looking forward to showing you."

"So the reason the Sanitol projections are so impressive is that you're really selling the sanitizers to your own meth labs."

"And a gold star for little Bobby. Dave owes me fifty bucks, if we can ever find him. He bet me it'd take me a week to get you to understand our operation."

Good luck collecting on that one. "What does the creator of this magic solution think of your plans for his invention?"

"He doesn't know anything about it. He's a scientist who works in a laboratory. We don't bother him with real world issues. But it's a tremendous business model. Our market is growing. Unlike most drugs, which appeal largely to men, nearly half of all meth users are women."

"Excellent. Equal opportunity destruction of lives. Meth is like the Title IX of addictive substances."

"And we don't lose customers."

"Except when they die."

Swanson continued without missing a beat. "A poor economy doesn't affect our business. Demand is inelastic. Our customers will lie, cheat, steal, fuck, suck, or kill to acquire the disposable income to purchase our product. There's no down cycle. The worse the economy, the better we do because more people are desperate for an escape. It's really the perfect business, if you can get past any ethical qualms you may have. And now that your elimination of your old friend has shown us what kind of man you are, I don't see why you wouldn't climb aboard."

"What kind of man am I?"

"A moral relativist, someone whose values are adaptable depending on the time, place or situation. Or if you prefer, a pragmatist. I don't mean any of these terms to be pejorative. You've earned far more of my respect than I ever thought you would."

"That's an interesting theory, but since I didn't kill Dave, it doesn't hold up. Why not just get someone else? There have got to be people who would kill for this kind of return."

"Not everyone is like you, Bob. They're not actually willing to kill to get what they want. But be that as it may, most of the other investors—hell, all of the other investors—I could approach are smarter than you. They would have the same concerns you had about the numbers. No, I'm afraid you're it."

"Then you're out of luck because I'm not going to do it."

"Hear me out, Bob. You're looking at this the wrong way. We're the good guys here. We're performing a public service. We're helping people."

"Oh, please."

"These poor creatures are going to do meth whether we're involved or not. The only difference is now their product will be made by professionals who aren't meth-heads themselves. Before, they didn't know whether to snort it or put it in the corner to get rid of their rat problem."

"Any drug dealer could claim the same thing."

"Think of it like Prohibition. People still drank anyway, but they were forced to drink black-market booze that might blind or kill them. Then the ban got lifted and look where we are today."

"Yeah, a country full of alcoholics."

"Sometimes you need a drink and sometimes other people need a little boost to focus and get their work done. We're really like doctors prescribing medicine for an entire nation of people suffering from adult ADD."

"Somehow I don't think a real doctor would agree with that diagnosis."

"The point is that even though what we're doing is technically illegal—"

"It's not 'technically' illegal," I interrupted. "It's one hundred percent, beyond a shadow of a doubt, banned in every state, illegal."

"But it's not immoral," Swanson said. "We will produce a much better and safer product than the hillbilly meth these idiots are making now. And we'll clean up after ourselves. I'm sure you wouldn't be surprised to learn that meth labs wreak havoc on the environment. By helping us sanitize these labs, you'll actually be saving the world, Bob."

"I'm sure I'd receive a humanitarian award from Greenpeace. My meth lab work will overshadow its 'save the whales' campaign."

"Even if you don't buy that it's helping, you have to concede that it's not hurting anything. Someone's going to do it. It might as well be you."

"Things haven't seemed to work out that well for the *Breaking Bad* guy."

"Again, Bob, that show is not real life," Swanson replied with a dismissive wave of his hand. "But even if it was, the guy's a rank amateur. He's a fucking high school science teacher, for Christ's sake. We're professional businessmen."

Swanson went on. "But you don't need to worry, Bob. We're not going to get caught. Our competitors get caught because they're idiots. And Al Capone went to federal prison for tax evasion. But we're going to be paying our taxes, Bob. And if anything ever does go wrong, you'll never be tied to it. You were just an institutional investor. You never had any idea what was going on. You don't even know what's going on in your real business."

"But it would still be blood money."

"There's an old saying, Bob. 'Behind every great fortune, there is a great crime.' Let's go back downstairs."

Chapter Twenty-six

I followed Swanson down the stairs and over to the other far corner of the warehouse. Random junk was strewn about. A few good-sized rocks, a leather belt, diapers, tennis balls, wood two-by-fours, Kotex and tampons, aluminum and tin cans, steel wool, a cantaloupe, a tennis shoe, a leather shoe, women's pumps, a couple cans of paint, a wet army blanket, that pink fiberglass insulation, a plastic water bottle from the water cooler, and a wood-framed couch.

"What's all this, Swanson? You do some shopping at Casey Anthony's post-acquittal yard sale? Or did you have to foreclose on one of your 'customers' for nonpayment?"

"You know, Bob, it's hard to believe you're not more successful with that sparkling wit of yours."

"Unfortunately, there really aren't that many high-paying jobs that call for a guy to stand around making snarky comments. I may just have to start a blog."

"You're not going to have to worry about money once we get this operation off the ground, Bob. This last little demonstration is the icing on the cake. If this doesn't convince you, nothing will."

"My money's on 'nothing.'"

Swanson walked over to an open area in the middle of all the junk. "This little baby," he said with a malevolent grin that seemed inappropriate when I finally heard the words he was about to speak, "is called a Muffin Monster."

He was standing next to a small piece of equipment that didn't even come up to his knees. It was a metal rectangle on four legs, painted army-green, no more than a couple feet wide and three feet long with a motor attached to one end. There was a smaller rectangular opening in the top and you could look down into the guts of the thing, which appeared to contain a row of silver metal coils. Maybe you cooked muffins in there somehow. My sister used to bake cakes with a light bulb in her Easy-Bake Oven.

"So part B of your master plan involves selling meth muffins at bake sales all across the Midwest?"

"Oh, no. The Muffin Monster doesn't *make* anything. It destroys things."

I walked over for a closer look. It looked like something you might see on the sidewalk outside a hardware store that people buy for lawn care or gardening or cleaning or any of the other home improvement projects I know nothing about. My family has learned that it's easier and cheaper to hire that kind of work out to professionals.

"What does it have to do with muffins?"

"Best I can tell, it's called a Muffin Monster because it's like a fairy-tale monster that can eat anything and still shit out a muffin."

I tried to give Swanson a look that told him I thought he was out of his mind, but by this point that was my default expression. "So it does make muffins."

"Not really. They're usually installed in sewer lines to shred anything that gets tossed in there that would clog a pipe. But it will grind anything it gets its teeth on into such small pieces you could form it into a muffin if you wanted to."

"I've had a few bran muffins that tasted like they might have been made from sewage."

"You wouldn't want to eat one of these, I assure you. In addition to normal bodily waste, you wouldn't believe what people flush down the toilet or throw in the sewer. That's why they make these things so they can chew up anything."

"It doesn't look like much just sitting there."

"Like a woman, you can't get the full impact until you turn it on."

"Is this being filmed before a live studio audience?"

"You're not the only one who can come up with a clever quip."

"I'm the only one in this warehouse."

Swanson walked over and plugged the machine into an orange extension cord. The parallel coils began spinning toward each other, the left one clockwise, the right one counter-clockwise.

"Those spinning cylinders are two rows of sharp, reinforced-steel cutters," Swanson said. "It's low-speed, to keep objects from bouncing off it before they can be grabbed, and high-torque for tremendous cutting power. The two counter-rotating shafts turn at different speeds and the cutters overlap to pull objects in and shred them with a cutting and grinding action. Each shaft is made up of a stack of individual steel cutters, each with five teeth. It can apply over seven thousand pounds of cutting force at peak load."

"Spare me the sales pitch. I'm not looking to purchase the home model." *Although it might have come in handy the other night.*

"It might have come in handy the other night," Swanson said. He and I were spending so much time together we were starting to think alike.

"Whatever," I said, "let's see it eat something."

Swanson picked up a tennis ball and tossed it into the opening on top of the machine. It briefly rolled along the line between the two spinning cylinders until it caught. It was instantly smashed flat and pulled down into and through the tiny gap, and was gone. Swanson reached underneath and pulled out a metal receptacle like a little wastebasket and dumped the contents on the floor. It was just yellow fuzz and shredded bits of rubber.

"Big deal," I said. "My dog does that twice a week."

"Can your dog do this?"

Swanson grabbed a couple of rocks the size of baseballs and dropped them into the Muffin Monster. Then he dumped out the contents of the wastebasket and it was just ashes, as if grandma's urn had gotten knocked over in a lame situation-comedy.

Swanson then fed a thick, wet, army blanket through the monster's jaws. The machine never caught or paused, it just kept munching until the blanket was gone, leaving only a pile of fuzz and fiber.

"How does it work?" I asked.

"Each of those cylinders is a bunch of razor-sharp, hardened steel cutters kind of like a Chinese throwing star or a circular-saw blade. The points are angled toward the direction they're spinning so they grab at anything they can get their teeth on and force it down between the spinning cylinders. There's only a few millimeters of space between the two rows of blades, so whatever it's got ahold of just gets chopped and ground until it's small enough to fit through. The result ends up in the wastebasket."

"So it's kind of a combination industrial shredder, garbage disposal, wood chipper, meat grinder, and trash compactor."

"Exactly," Swanson said. "Although not its intended purpose, it's the ultimate eliminator of evidence. It destroys physical objects forever like a paper shredder destroys documents." Swanson grabbed a glass beaker and placed it on the spinning blades. Instant glass powder, as fine as unmixed Kool-Aid. He fed some copper tubing into the opening and nothing but copper-colored shavings came out the bottom.

"I get it, Swanson. This machine allows you to eradicate any meth lab evidence in a hurry."

"In conjunction with the Sanitol sanitizer, yes. Once the sanitizer washes all this stuff away, there's no chemical residue or incriminating evidence of any kind left. This thing can even get rid of signs there were ever people there at all."

Swanson signaled to the linebackers and they lifted the couch and brought it over to the Muffin Monster. They had to break it up a little to fit the pieces into the opening, but when they were finished, no couch. No sign there had ever been a couch.

"If we decide one of our locations is compromised, we can literally erase it from existence in a couple of hours. The DEA will never make a case against us."

◇◇◇

Swanson may have been an asshole but he was right about the Muffin Monster. It was freaking awesome. If you walked by one outside your local hardware store, you wouldn't think anything of it. Until it was plugged in and turned on, you'd have no way of knowing you could be dragged into it inch by inch until you were a puddle of goo ready to be hosed down the drain. I didn't even want to be in the same room with the thing. It was like a Stephen King novel, the Muffin Monster just sitting there day after day, patiently waiting and waiting until you or your cat or your child forgot about it and accidentally got too close.

"I don't know how good you are at making the product, Swanson, but you seem to have a knack for destroying things."

"That's not all, Bob. We can also use the Muffin Monster to safely dispose of other 'problems.'" Swanson's one of those people who can make air quotes with the inflection in his voice.

"What problems would those be?"

"Observe." He walked over to the junk pile and rummaged around for a minute. He came back with a man's leather belt. I can't really tell one belt from another, but it looked suspiciously like one of mine, a Christmas present from Sarah that I would never have bought for myself because it cost way too much and a belt is a belt. He fed it smoothly through the machine. "The Muffin Monster is very effective at getting rid of articles of clothing we wouldn't want found."

"I'm sure it is, but it's actually kind of an anticlimax after the couch. I wouldn't close with it."

"Oh, I'm not finished." Swanson dug around in the junk some more and came back with a pair of black women's pumps, again naggingly familiar. I don't really know one women's shoe from the next, but I remembered Sarah had bought a pair just like this one. It stuck in my mind because these shoes cost four times as much as the already outrageous normal price of women's shoes because they had bright red soles. "You're paying a premium for the bottom of the shoe?" I asked her. "That's like paying extra because you like the underside of a rug."

In the shoes went. The Muffin Monster gobbled them up like candy. The next item Swanson selected was a red, white, and blue basketball, the old ABA style popularized by Dr. J and his giant seventies afro. Nick's favorite ball looked just like it. Obviously, I was beginning to sense a pattern here, but all of these things were fairly generic items. They were similar without question to my family's belongings, but not necessarily the prized possessions themselves. I also have to admit it was pretty cool the way the monster grabbed that basketball, completely flattened it and sucked it down into its belly in about two seconds.

But the next thing Swanson brought back from the pile, there was no doubt. It was not kind of the same or similar to or the same brand as Emily's favorite stuffed animal. It *was* Emily's favorite stuffed animal. I know because I've tucked her into bed with it every night for the last year. It was a stuffed beaver her brother, Nick, gave her for her eighth birthday. Nick dressed it in a flat-billed baseball cap like rappers and suburban white kids wear for street cred and named it Justin Beaver. So, naturally, Emily loves it and she can't go to sleep without it. Max is also fond of him and as a result Justin has a mangled beaver tail and a missing right eye. Just like the beaver Swanson was now holding above the gaping jaws of the Muffin Monster.

"All right, Swanson!" I yelled. "You've made your point."

Swanson looked at me, fake-puzzled. "What are you talking about?"

"It's one thing for you to destroy some of my family's impersonal belongings, although I may be underestimating Sarah's intimate feelings for those shoes. It's another thing to destroy my daughter's favorite stuffed animal. She loves that thing like a real pet."

"How do you know it's hers?"

I walked over to Swanson, reached out and squeezed the furry creature's left paw. Nick's voice echoed in the warehouse. "Happy Birthday, Emily. This is Justin Beaver. Like, baby, baby, baby, oh. Like baby, baby, baby, no!" That's right. He even sang that last part.

"My son got this for my daughter at Build-a-Bear. They put a voice chip in the paw with a personal message. I get the message, Swanson. You're threatening my family."

Swanson looked offended. "I haven't threatened anyone."

"Whatever. Call it what you want. It doesn't matter. But you or one of your henchmen have obviously been in my house."

"I don't know what you're talking about," Swanson replied innocently.

"I'd like to leave now."

"Of course. You can leave whenever you want, Bob. No one is holding you against your will."

"It's kind of a long walk from here, Swanson."

"Oh. You're looking for a ride."

"Well, considering you had the Aryan Linebacking Brotherhood bring me here in the first place…"

"Fine. But before you go I want to make sure you truly understand what our operation is capable of here. Come over here where you can really appreciate the power of this machine."

I walked over and stood next to him, but a couple of steps back from the Muffin Monster. I still felt like it was something I might trip and fall into. I treated it like a cliff overlooking an abyss. I didn't want to get too close to the edge.

"Just look at those spinning steel blades," Swanson said. "Can you imagine what that would do to flesh and bone?"

"I've been imagining it for the last fifteen minutes. If you're trying to convince me this machine is an instrument of horror, you've succeeded."

I noticed the linebackers were suddenly standing right behind me. They each grabbed one of my arms and held it.

"Sometimes the reality," Swanson said, "is far worse than the human mind will allow itself to imagine."

"Not for me." I struggled futilely. One of them could have easily held me. Two was overkill. "You wouldn't believe what I can imagine."

"I can believe that," Swanson said, "having gotten to know you over the last few weeks. But you still need a demonstration."

I closed my eyes and waited for one of my hands to be forced down toward the jagged teeth. Nothing happened. I opened my eyes. Jim in the blue coveralls was walking toward us wearing rubber gloves and holding a large brown rat by the tail. The rat was very much alive, stretching to bite and scratch him, but it couldn't penetrate the gloves.

I wasn't particularly looking forward to seeing Swanson's little "demonstration," but it sounded a lot better than carrying part of my body back to the city in a bucket. Swanson nodded and Jim brought the rat over to the Muffin Maker.

I'm sure the rat didn't know what he was being lowered into, but he knew he didn't want to go there. He struggled, but there's not much you can do when you're being held by the tail. I don't know which part of his body touched one of the spinning cutters first, but it didn't matter much. Like everything else, the rat was immediately flattened and forced down into the tiny space between the twin rows of whirling blades. I'm sure he was killed almost instantly.

The linebackers looked as green as the Packer uniforms I imagined them wearing. Jim looked like a guy who was just following orders. Swanson was the only one who looked like he was enjoying himself. He probably pulled the wings off flies and burned anthills with a magnifying glass when he was a kid. Maybe he still did.

Swanson pulled out the wastebasket and carried it over near the drain. He turned it upside down and dumped out a bloody, pulpy mess. Jim hosed the gore down the drain with the sanitizer and Swanson sprayed the area with Luminol. The whole thing took less than five minutes.

Swanson yelled "Hit the lights!" and someone did. We all stared at the spot where the rat's liquefied remains had puddled.

"Look at that, Bob," Swanson said. "No traces of blood. No traces at all."

Chapter Twenty-seven

I rode back from the warehouse in the backseat of the black sedan with Justin Beaver on my lap. My hulking escorts didn't say a word, not even to each other. They didn't even turn the radio on. They just stared straight ahead. I probably should have been pumping these guys for information or turning them against their boss or something, but I couldn't think of anything to say. I'd been in a state of constant fear for days. I wasn't two steps ahead of Swanson with an ingenious plan I haven't told you about yet. I was being played like a ~~violin~~ computer program that simulates music. No one plays real instruments anymore.

This was about the time I needed an ace in the hole, that one previously unmentioned friend of mine who used to be a green beret before he got kicked out of the army for assaulting his superior officer for needlessly putting his men in danger. Or that old high school buddy who is now a career criminal but respects me because I took the blame for something he did when we were kids. The problem with the ace-in-the-hole plan is I don't know anyone like that.

So when I got back to the office, I called the one person who is always willing to give me advice whether I want it or not.

"Hi, honey," Sarah said.

"We need to talk," I said. Normally this would have elicited a list of all the things Sarah had on her plate at the moment, but she must have sensed something in my voice because she just said "Pick me up in front of my building in an hour."

As soon as she got in the car, she said "Did something happen?"

"Sort of. Give me a minute to park and I'll tell you the whole story." I drove a couple of blocks and parked in the back of a fast food parking lot that was mostly empty at this time of day. My stomach reminded me that Swanson had interrupted my lunch, not that I had any appetite left after watching him make rat gumbo.

I turned and faced Sarah. She stared at me wide-eyed. "First of all, the kids are at school, everyone's fine."

She exhaled. "That's a relief. I assumed they were or you would have come out with that right away, but I'm glad to hear it."

"Here's what happened. Swanson had a couple of his goons kidnap me."

"What do you mean? They blindfolded you and threw you in the trunk?"

"Maybe 'kidnap' is the wrong word," I said. "A car pulled in front of me as I was walking across the street and two line-backer types got out and told me Swanson wanted to see me. They didn't exactly force me into the car, but if I refused, I'm sure they would have. They took me to a warehouse where they have their operation."

"They let you see where it was?"

"It's not a secret lair inside a volcano. It's just a warehouse."

"What was in it?"

"Not much. They had clearly just moved in."

"What did Swanson want to show you?"

"How his sanitation system works. But he really wanted to explain how the financials work. You know how the numbers seemed too good to be true?"

"Yes. I look at puffed-up projections all day long and I've never seen any that good."

"It turns out there's a simple explanation. They're going to use the sanitation equipment to clean up meth labs."

"That's their great business plan?" Sarah asked. "Marketing and selling directly to meth labs? That's a real stable wholesale market."

"They're not selling to Jimmy Don and Faylene cooking meth in their double-wide while their kids drink goat milk out of test tubes. They're setting up their own labs. Eliminating the middleman."

"So all that profit they project comes from selling illegal drugs."

"A lot of it, anyway. From what I saw, the sanitation system could be successful in its own right, but not to that level."

"Drug dealers don't normally print up prospectuses, but if they did, they'd look pretty impressive."

"Swanson explained the whole setup to me. On paper, purely as a line item on a financial statement, meth is a dream product. Cheap to produce, huge profit margin, no marketing expenses, inelastic demand. Other than the lab explosions, destruction of human lives, and possible lengthy prison sentence, it's a slam dunk."

Sarah shook her head. "This all just sounds unbelievable to me."

"I know," I said. "I'm not normally inclined to believe in conspiracy theories. Nobody can keep their stories straight and their mouths shut. But it's different with a criminal enterprise. It's right there in the name. It's *organized* crime. And they have a great system for keeping people quiet. The threat of having your tongue cut out does wonders for a person's ability to keep a secret. So I definitely believe Swanson's story is within the realm of possibility."

Sarah thought for a moment. "Why would he tell you all this?"

"He knew I didn't trust the numbers so he wanted to prove to me they're real."

"Surely he must know there's no way you'd invest now."

"Swanson has somehow gotten the idea that I am of dubious moral character."

Sarah raised an eyebrow at me. "Somehow?"

"He claims he knows I killed Dave."

I'm not sure I'd ever heard anyone actually gasp before, but Sarah gasped out loud. "Omigod! How does he know?"

"First of all, let's remember that I did not kill Dave. Your horse did. Second, I don't think Swanson does know. He knows Dave's missing, so he took a shot in the dark. I've got a pretty good poker face, so I think I hid my reaction pretty well."

Sarah smirked. "Oh, really? Then how come you never win at poker?"

"I'm talking about a poker face in real life. I fool you all the time."

"Maybe you just think you do."

"Anyway," I continued, "there's no way he really knows anything. There's nothing to know. He's just trying everything at this point. He tried getting your dad and then me on board as legitimate investors. That didn't work. Then he tried the blackmail scheme with the girls. That didn't work. Now he's upped the ante on the blackmail to murder. At the same time, he's thinking 'Maybe I just need to lay all my cards on the table. If Bob would ruthlessly kill his old friend, why would he have a problem selling meth?'"

"Because it's illegal?"

"So is murder."

"You didn't kill anyone."

"But he thinks I did."

"Wait a minute," Sarah said. "There's more, isn't there?" She looked around the car. "What's Emily's Justin Beaver doll doing in the backseat? What haven't you told me?"

"Swanson also made some vague threats against the entire family."

"How do you make a 'vague' threat? Did he threaten us or not?"

"He poured blood on the floor and cleaned it up with the sanitizer," I said. "There were no traces of blood left behind."

"And you think that was a threat?"

"I think he meant it both as a selling point for the product—*with the new Sanitol sanitation system, you'll be able to eliminate your competitors without a mess*—and as an implicit threat—*or we could just kill you if don't cooperate.*"

"How is that a threat against the family?"

"He showed me this machine called a Muffin Monster that will grind anything to bits. They shoved a whole couch through it and then just washed it down the drain."

"What do they need that for?" Sarah asked.

"To dismantle labs and get rid of the evidence."

"How does that make things worse?"

"He hinted that he could grind up other things as well."

"Like what?"

"Like something that looked an awful lot like that belt you gave me for Christmas. And those shoes of yours with the red soles."

Sarah's eyes flashed with anger. "That son of a bitch shredded my Christian Louboutins?"

"It sure looked like them. And Nick's red, white, and blue basketball." I decided not to tell her about the rat. Sarah would beat a rat to death with a shovel if she saw one in the barn, but the idea of someone else hurting an animal made her sick.

"But you saved Justin Beaver," she said.

"I wasn't sure it was really our stuff until then."

"Wait a minute." Comprehension dawned across Sarah's face. "Those bastards have been in our house?"

"That would appear to be the case," I said.

"That changes things. That changes everything. Violating the sanctity of our home crosses a line."

"I agree," I said. "We have to come up with some kind of plan. But everything's on the table now. Everything."

"Everything?" Sarah asked.

"The first thing we need to consider is just doing the deal."

"We can't do that. What about all the lives meth ruins?"

"Swanson's actually pretty persuasive about that," I said. "We're not really hurting anybody. They're going to do meth anyway. Why not provide a safer product?"

"That's a pretty big rationalization," Sarah said. "By that logic, we should start pushing drugs at the junior high school."

"I agree that 'ethical drug dealer' is a bit of an oxymoron, but we'd also stop people from having to turn their houses into meth labs. It would probably save some children's lives."

"I don't think I could ever convince myself this is some kind of benefit to society."

"I'm just laying out the arguments here," I said. "But what about the money? Other than the minor detail that it's an illegal operation, Sanitol is going to be a cash cow for somebody. Why not us?"

"Because it would be wrong?"

"I don't disagree. But when it comes down to it, I'm basically being forced, upon threat of bodily harm to me and my family, to make a boatload of money. That's not the worst resolution to this shitstorm."

"But would the threat go away once you invest?" Sarah asked.

I considered that. "No. The man's a criminal. Why would he pay me anything at all? In addition to being a drug dealer, I'd be pissing your dad's hard-earned money away and the family wouldn't even be any safer."

Sarah looked at me with a determined stare. "So what do we do?"

"Now that Swanson's told me everything, he can't let us just walk away. In fact, that's probably one of the reasons he told me. He's blocking the exits, giving me no choice but to say yes."

"But you do have a choice."

"Yes, but Swanson can't be left standing. He has to be in jail or dead."

"What about his partners in crime?"

"I don't think there's some vast conspiracy. The linebackers are just hired hands. They won't be out for revenge or anything. And whoever else is behind this whole setup will just move on. We'll be too hot to touch at that point."

Sarah nodded. "Okay. What do we know?"

"We know they've been in our house. That's why I wanted to talk in the car. They could be listening to everything we say at home."

Sarah was quiet for a moment. "Does it seem strange to you that Swanson destroyed the other stuff but let you keep Emily's stuffed animal?"

"No, I took it from him. He was about to—oh, shit." I grabbed Justin Beaver and examined him closely.

"Does it look tampered with?" Sarah asked.

"How could you tell? Some high school burnout stitched it up right in front of us at the store. It's not like I can tell if the fine craftsmanship has been altered."

"There's only one way to find out," Sarah said.

I spoke directly into the doll's face. "Swanson? Can you hear me? Stop masturbating to your own reflection in the mirror and answer me." I looked at Sarah. "Nothing."

"That's not the way I meant." She handed me a nail file from her purse.

"Sorry, Emily." I split Justin Beaver down the middle of his chest like an autopsy.

I dug around in the stuffing, but I could find nothing but the little chip with Nick's message. "Looks clean." I tossed Beaver into the backseat. Just one more casualty in America's war on drugs.

Sarah rolled her eyes in the manner females have mastered by the time they're five years old. "You can't tell if the toilet seat is clean and you're declaring this doll free of bugs?"

"That's correct," I said.

"So we don't think we're bugged here, but we think we are at home."

"Right," I agreed. "So if we have any advantage at all, it's that we know Swanson's listening at our house, but he doesn't know we know."

"He doesn't know we know because we really don't know."

"The key is making sure Swanson doesn't know we know."

"How are we going to do that?" Sarah asked.

"We're going to need to work from some kind of script."

More eye-rolling. "You're barely convincing when you're telling the truth. I can't wait to see you try to act."

"What about you?" I asked. "The kids and I laugh behind your back about your phony nice act whenever you answer the phone."

"That is not phony, but anyway, people buy it, so what's the difference?"

"Nothing," I said. "And if we screw this up, what's the difference? Even if Swanson knows we know, what's that going to do for him? I know we know and I have no idea what we're doing."

Chapter Twenty-eight

After dinner that night, I approached Sarah in the kitchen. "Now that the children are in their rooms, we need to talk."

She nodded vigorously. "About what?"

"About what we are going to do with that dead body."

"Why now?"

"I had a meeting with Tom Swanson today."

I waited for Sarah to respond. She gave me her wide-eyed stare and made some hand gestures I didn't understand. "Go on."

"Sorry," I said. "I thought it was your tur—you were going to say something."

Sarah glared at me. "I wasn't. Now go on with what you were saying."

"Swanson knows."

Sarah let out an exasperated sigh. "Knows what?"

"That I killed Corny—I mean Dave."

She waited again for me to continue and then rolled her eyes. "And?"

"And what?"

"Is that it?"

"I think so," I said, trying to remember. "No, wait. He also knows the body is here. On our property."

Sarah nodded encouragement and helped me along. "Soooooo?"

"So we cannot just leave it there," I said. "We must get rid of it." Sounded perfectly natural to me.

Sarah still nodding, seeing the finish line. "How?"

I pretended to think. "Hmmmm. I am going to be traveling all day tomorrow. Madison has got me going to a bunch of meetings a couple of hours away. I will not be back until late tomorrow night."

Sarah waited until she realized I was finished. "Then what?"

"Then we will get rid of the body." I hesitated. "I have a plan."

Sarah was silent for a few seconds, then shook her head in disgust. "Will anyone ever find it?"

"No one will ever find it."

◇◇◇

Afterward we huddled in the bathroom with the shower on. I wondered if Swanson and/or his team of eavesdroppers were suspicious of our lengthy late night showers. I hoped they were imagining us having wild monkey sex in there.

"I haven't seen acting that bad since Dan Langham asked you what you thought of his wife's new boobs," Sarah said.

"They were lopsided," I said. "It was like staring at someone who has a lazy eye. What was I supposed to say?"

"I don't know. Do you think they bought it?"

"I do," I said. "If you can only hear the voices without seeing the faces, it's hard to tell if it's phony. That's why it's so much easier to lie on the phone."

"Like when you call and pretend you're working late when you're really going to a bar with your friends."

"Exactly."

◇◇◇

I didn't really go out of town. Because I had a plan. I took the kids to school in the morning, but instead of going on to work, I doubled back home.

I pulled off the driveway and drove west across the grass to the copse of trees. I knew I'd be basically hidden, as Corny's motorcycle had been. A search of the entire property would discover me, but why would anyone do that? They knew I was out of town for the day. If they were listening. And if they bought my Keith Hernandez on *Seinfeld*-level performance. And if they would react the way I wanted them to. Like drunken plans made at two a.m. to get up super-early and play golf with your buddies, my plan didn't look quite as good in the light of day.

But I was stuck with my plan, so I settled in to wait. Although Sarah and I had unfortunately not created a complicated system of audibles last night, I had made some preparations. I packed granola bars and water bottles. I brought my phone and a car charger. I had some books and magazines as well as the Internet on my phone to keep me busy. I didn't think the waiting would be too hard. I waste time like this every day.

I didn't call anyone. I didn't e-mail anyone with my phone. I didn't know what or who Swanson had access to. I just waited. Finally, around five, my phone rang. It was our home phone, which we never use except to field calls from telemarketers during dinner.

I took a deep breath and answered. "Hello?"

"Bob?" It was Sarah.

"Yeah, honey, I'm really busy. What is it?" I said, cleverly perpetuating the ruse that I was off on business somewhere.

"I need you to come home as soon as you can."

"You sound funny. Is there someone in the room? Do you have a gun to your head?"

"As a matter of fact, I actually do." Her voice sounded shaky, as one might expect from someone who apparently had a gun to her head.

I wasn't doing so great either, but I tried to focus. "Are you on the house phone in the living room?"

"Yes."

"Try to keep him there so I'll know where you are when I get there."

"Okay."

"I'll be there…as soon as I can."

I choked and couldn't remember what I should say, but Sarah was still on top of things. "When will that be? Aren't you out of town?" *Objection. Leading.*

Oh, right. I'm out of town. *Sustained.* "Yeah, it's going to be three or four hours. Maybe eight or eight-thirty."

"Okay."

"Put Swanson on the phone," I said.

"What?"

"Just do it."

Swanson's smug, I've-got-you-by-the-short-hairs attitude came through loud and clear even over the phone. "What can I do for you, Bob?"

"I have a very particular set of skills," I said. "Skills I have acquired over a very long career. Skills that make me a nightmare for people like you. If you let my wife go now, that will be the end of it. I will not look for you, I will not pursue you. But if you don't, I will look for you, I will find you, and I will kill you."

No, wait, that was Liam Neeson in *Taken.* I, on the other hand, have a particular set of skills that are a nightmare for the people who employ me. What I actually said was "Swanson? Don't do anything stupid. You know if you hurt Sarah, there's no way in hell I'm ever doing any kind of deal with you. It's in your best interests to make sure she's safe."

"True enough for the time being, Bob. But at some point I'm going to be so sick of your bullshit I won't care anymore. So if I were you, I'd get my ass home as fast as I could."

Swanson handed the phone back to Sarah. "Call when you're getting close."

"I will," I said, but I wouldn't. I hoped Swanson would relax for the next few hours, maybe even until my next phone call, which would never come.

Chapter Twenty-nine

Some people are just naturally confident. They don't feel pressure like the rest of us. They always think they're going to come through. It doesn't even occur to them they might fail. In everyday life, these people are known as assholes. They have a much higher opinion of themselves than they deserve and they generally fuck everything up. They insist on taking the big shot or handling an important task and then they blow it. But extreme successes also come from the superconfident pool. You couldn't become Tiger Woods or Ted Turner if you didn't believe in yourself, even against all odds. You're still an asshole, but a very successful one, and those guys get stuff done.

This situation called for one of those ruthless, overconfident sociopaths. Someone with no nerves and no doubts, certain of success even against impossible odds. Someone we all knew would come through in the clutch. Instead, what we had was me.

I made my way toward the house. I doubted anyone was watching but just in case I crawled through the grass when there wasn't any cover, dragging my duffel bag full of supplies. Crawling is actually very tiring. I don't know how babies do it. If only I had participated in more corporate retreats featuring obstacle courses that foster team unity, I could have excelled at the fast crawl. I finally reached the barn and peered around the corner to get a look at the house while I caught my breath. It takes a long time to traverse a quarter mile when you're alternately crawling and serpentining, so it was already approaching that time of the evening real novelists wax poetically about but I call getting pretty dark.

Swanson's black sedan was parked in the driveway. There was no reason to hide it. He didn't fear anything from me. I could see one of the linebackers, the one I called Mike I think, patrolling in front of the house, in a half-assed attempt to follow orders, but most of the time he just leaned against the house fiddling with his phone. He was not what you would call vigilant. This was clearly no heavily guarded compound, but then again I wasn't exactly a Navy SEAL, so maybe it evened out. I assumed the other line-backer was around the back of the house or inside with Swanson.

A couple of years ago we had a mountain lion scare in our area, which was curious because there are no mountains around here. Panicked people were e-mailing around these pictures of three mountain lions feasting on a deer carcass. Of course it all turned out to be a hoax, but at the time manly men like me armed ourselves so we could defend our homesteads against the feline hordes descending upon us. Sarah, however, didn't like the idea of killing a kitty, so instead of real guns we got a couple of tranquilizer dart guns, handguns that fire darts with a CO_2 cylinder, supposedly at a range of up to thirty yards. I didn't have any illusions that I could actually hit a mountain lion sprinting toward me and leaping for my throat, but I thought maybe I could open the front door a crack, shoot one, and then call animal control. Last night I loaded them and grabbed all the darts we had and packed them in my bag.

I got out both guns and a couple of spare darts for each and put them in my coat pockets. I didn't exactly go charging wildly across the grass. When I watch one of those movies where huge armies meet in hand-to-hand combat, I always wonder how they get anyone to go in the front. When they yelled "charge," I'm sure I would have been down on one knee pretending to tie my Roman sandal.

I'm good at rationalizing my inability to act, so I decided I needed to do some recon. I remembered reading somewhere the most important part of any military operation was intelligence-gathering before the fact. Once they collected all the data on his location, killing bin Laden was the easy part. In my case, there was no easy part, but I did know the lay of the land. I'd literally been walking around out here in the dark for ten years. What I didn't know was how many were here and what they were doing. I decided simply to observe until I spotted someone else or detected some kind of pattern to what appeared to be pretty haphazard sentry duty.

After fifteen minutes, the other linebacker came around from behind the house. They chatted for a few minutes. In an old war movie, they would have spoken English with a German accent, as all Germans do when talking to their fellow soldiers, and shared a cigarette as we watched through fake binoculars framing the scene. They didn't seem concerned. They didn't look around at all. They clearly weren't on the lookout for enemy combatants. They were just staying outside because Swanson told them to.

Since they had no schedule and their movements were random, there was no point in trying to time it, so as soon as Will went back around the house, I was on the move. I made myself go before I had time to think about it. Now that it was dark, I knew you couldn't see anything from the front of the house. There are no streetlights on a farm. You can see a little if you get away from the house, but looking out from bright lights, you see nothing but darkness.

I circled around and came up behind Mike. The shades were drawn. I couldn't see into the house, but I didn't think anyone could see me either. Plus they weren't expecting me for another couple of hours. Being the coward I am, I wanted to shoot him in the back. Even with a dart gun, I wasn't sure I could pull the trigger if he was looking at me. Plus I might miss if he was moving. I pulled out one of the guns, aimed for center mass, and fired.

At first I thought I'd missed him entirely, but I could see the orange tailpiece sticking out of his lower back. He grunted but didn't go down. He reached behind him and yanked out the dart and looked at it. He didn't seem upset, but then again, he's probably used to needles. Finally, he turned completely around and saw me. He wasn't mad and he wasn't hurrying. He just kind of nodded to himself like *Oh, that explains it. That idiot who wouldn't shut up in the car shot me with a dart. I will now pick him up by the throat.*

As he approached, I fumbled another dart into the gun and hoped the CO2 would fire again. Mountain lions aren't really all that big. Even the largest males are only a couple hundred pounds, more like wide receivers and cornerbacks than linebackers. One mountain lion-sized dose was not going to do it for a monster like this guy.

I kept the gun fairly steady by my standards, but I somehow managed to miss his center mass entirely and hit him in the thigh. The dose didn't even have time to take effect, but he went down like a guy who just got shot in the leg. He yanked out the dart and gave me a hurt look as if to say, *What did you do that for? I thought we were friends.* Or maybe it meant, *I'm going to drag myself over there and snap your neck like a pencil.* Either way, I wasn't interested, so I stayed a comfortable distance back. He tried to pull himself toward me, but his movements got slower and slower. He looked like he was moving underwater. After a minute or so, he collapsed. I left him there and tiptoed around to the back, probably making twice as much noise as I would have by walking normally.

I peeked around the corner of the house. Will was sitting in one of our deck chairs with his back to me. I didn't want to try to shoot him while he was sitting down. I didn't know if the dart would even penetrate his thick skull and anyway, the target was too small. I picked up a rock and tossed it over his head into the trees, thinking I would shoot him in the back when he got up to investigate. I don't know if he saw the rock sail over his head or just sensed me behind him, but he jumped out of the chair and spun around to face me.

I had the second gun in my hand and aimed it at his chest. Will kept coming, showing no fear of the gun, like animals do because it's something they've never seen before. I fired and he didn't even slow down, most likely because the dart missed him entirely. Will snatched the gun from my hand, spun me around, and locked his forearm across my throat.

"You're early," he whispered in my ear. "We thought you were out of town."

"Traffic was light," I croaked.

"I'm sure Mr. Swanson will be glad to see you. But tell me why I shouldn't break a couple of your bones for trying to shoot me?"

"Because you'll be too sleepy?" I asked and plunged one of the darts from my pocket into his thigh, which appeared to be the Achilles heel of blond, steroid-fueled ex-linebackers. The drugs don't work instantly, but both guys went down right away from the pain.

Will let go of my neck as he collapsed. I leaned down and jabbed another dart into his thigh right next to the first one. Even if it didn't knock him out, he'd be dragging that leg around like an anchor for the next few days. He struggled to get up, but he couldn't get his movements in synch. He seemed to be trying to form words, but with him it was hard to tell. From what I'd seen, he always struggled to form words. Like his fellow henchman, he was out cold within a couple of minutes.

For my first tactical assault, I thought things were going pretty well. My only regret was I didn't have a comrade-in-arms on this slipshod SWAT team to whom I could make vague, undecipherable hand signals, like two fingers pointing to my own eyes.

I left the two sleeping giants where they were. Tying them up wouldn't accomplish anything. Dogs, horses, and boats routinely escape my efforts to tie them to something, so I assume a couple of full-grown men with opposable thumbs wouldn't have any trouble.

I reached in my pocket to reload. I was down to my last dart. Okay, mountain lions were one dart and linebackers were two. What did that make Swanson? If you put khakis and loafers on the mountain lion, there wouldn't be much difference except the mountain lion would have a better personality. But I couldn't be sure one dart would do the trick and even if it did, he wouldn't be knocked out instantly. If I shot him with a dart, he could still kill Sarah and me before the drug took effect. I needed a better weapon.

Corny's gun had been sitting in the pickup since the night he'd paid us a visit. I opened the passenger door and looked in the glove compartment and sure enough, there it was, all black and ominous-looking and within easy reach of our two young children. I pointed the gun at a tree, closed my left eye, and sighted down the barrel with my right. I slipped my finger around the trigger and imagined squeezing it tight. It seemed easy enough. I could do this.

I stuck the gun in my pocket and walked quietly over to the sedan. The keys were in the ignition. I didn't know if I wanted them to be able to leave or not, but I took them anyway and threw them into the bushes by the house. Maybe I could use them as a bargaining chip later. I circled back behind the house at a jog. I was still early enough to surprise Swanson, but time was running out. Plus, I didn't know how long his goons would be out of commission or if they were supposed to check in on a regular schedule or what.

I came around the far side of our guest house, where I couldn't be seen if Swanson happened to be looking out the window, and slipped inside. I leaned against the front door and exhaled. Getting here was the hard part, but this guest house was my home court advantage, the only reason my plan had a chance in hell of working. I obviously couldn't just burst through the front door with gun blazing. Sarah was going to try to stay in the living room but who knew where they'd really be?

What Swanson didn't know was there was an old underground tunnel between our guest house and the main house. I don't know if it was supposed to be some kind of a bomb shelter or just a way to get to the other part of the property during the winter. Whatever its original purpose, the kids loved it and I'm sure they'll use it for all kinds of teenage hijinks one day.

I went down into the unfinished basement under the guest house. I'm sure you can picture it. Cement floor. Bare light bulb hanging down. Worthless crap you should have thrown out years ago lying around. There was a door set in the far wall. You'd imagine that it contained a water heater and a furnace and other things so unappealing that you'd build a wall to separate them from something as shitty as an unfinished basement, and you'd be right. But if you squeezed past all the equipment that regulates the climate inside the house and knew what you were looking for, you might notice another smaller door in a recess in the wall. It looks like somewhere you wouldn't want to go, some kind of a crawl space full of spiderwebs and rats, and possibly tiny human skeletons left by the previous owner who may very well have been a serial killer because no sane person would put a door there.

Once you open that door and squeeze yourself in, it's actually pretty nice. It's basically just a corridor about seventy-five yards long, maybe ten feet wide and eight feet high. If you encountered this exact walkway going from the parking garage to an office building downtown, you wouldn't think anything of it. I wasn't sweaty and jumpy because of the tunnel. It was because of what was waiting for me at the end of the tunnel.

It was pretty much the same situation under the main house. A small door opened into the room with the furnace and water heater, a room that no one in our household would have reason to visit except to point it out to a repairman. It was pitch black, so I lit a match, which provided almost enough light for me to make out the bare outlines of my own hand. I felt along the wall through what I assumed were brown recluse spiderwebs and rows of sleeping bats. I found the light switch and made my way to the finished part of the basement.

I avoided the video games and DVDs and dirty plates and half-full Coke cans and tiptoed up the basement steps with Corny's gun in my hand. I kept an eye out for the trail of shoes and socks that Emily leaves around the house as a series of booby traps for me in the middle of the night.

I was confident they couldn't hear me upstairs. I knew you needed to avoid the middle of the steps to keep them from creaking. I pressed my ear to the door at the top of the stairs. Silence, but that didn't necessarily mean anything. For all I knew, Swanson was standing right on the other side of the door waiting for me. There was nothing to do but open it and take my chances, so I did.

Chapter Thirty

The kitchen was empty. I crept toward the living room and stopped outside the open doorway. I could hear muffled voices, one male and one female. From the tone of the conversation, it was hard to imagine Swanson had Sarah in some compromising position, holding a gun to her head and shielding himself with her body. That meant it was go time.

If I ever truly *had* to do something, it was this, right now. So I took a deep breath and walked into the room pointing the gun in front of me. A famous study says a homeowner's gun is forty-three times more likely to kill a family member than a criminal. That number is undoubtedly even higher if I'm the homeowner in question. Accordingly, my first goal was not to shoot Sarah. My second goal was not to shoot myself.

Swanson and Sarah were sitting on the couch with mugs of coffee on the table in front of them. In his usual polo, khakis, and loafers, and to the naked eye unarmed, Swanson looked like a neighbor who just stopped by for a chat. Sarah flashed her eyes at me and since we've been married for almost twenty years, I had no idea what she meant.

Swanson stood up. "Bob, what do you think you're doing? I'm just here to talk." He took a step around the coffee table.

I started to say I leveled the gun at him, but let's go with I pointed the gun in his general direction with a wobbly hand. "Stay right where you are."

Swanson took another step. "Or what? You're going to shoot me?"

"Yes. I am."

Swanson paused and put his hands up in a placating gesture. "Okay, take it easy. I'm not going anywhere." He snuck a look toward the windows, trying to see if his henchmen were coming to the rescue.

"You're down a couple of linebackers, Swanson," I said. "You're going to have to go to your nickel package."

Swanson smiled, which was not the reaction I was hoping for. Quivering in fear, yes. Begging for his life, hopefully. Soiling himself, ideally. Smiling, no.

"So it's just you and me then, Bob." He took another step, smiling all the way.

"Well, us and Sarah." I gestured toward her with the gun. "She's right over there. You've been sitting and talking with her?"

"I'm sure you'd prefer to keep this just between us men." Swanson was now about ten feet away from me.

Not really. I needed all the help I could get, women, children, animals, whatever. But admitting that would have detracted from the manly, commanding image I was trying to project, so I said, "Yes, I would. Do not take another step."

The problem with holding a gun on someone in real life is there's no reason for them to obey you unless they believe you're actually going to shoot them. The mere fact of holding a gun does not suddenly put the rank amateur in charge. People familiar with gunplay know it's hard to point a gun at another human being and pull the trigger.

Swanson continued to move toward me. I knew the one thing I couldn't do was let him get close enough to grab the gun. Before you even realize what's happening, he'll be clubbing you over the head with it and then raping your wife in front of you while you're tied to a chair.

My hand was shaking, but I knew I had to start shooting before he got any closer. He started to take another step. "This is your last warning. One more step and I'll shoot."

Swanson stopped and glanced at the gun. "It's going to be kind of hard to shoot me with the safety on, Bob."

"Nice try, Swanson. Apparently you and I have seen the same movies. We must have a similar Netflix queue."

He took another step, so I shot him.

Or I would have shot him except the safety really *was* on. I pulled the trigger and nothing happened. I looked down at the gun and by then Swanson was taking it out of my hand like a kindergarten teacher taking scissors from a five-year-old. "Here, give me that before you hurt yourself."

Swanson flicked the safety off and motioned me over to the couch. I sat down next to Sarah. We hugged each other like it might be the last time because it might. Sarah had tears in her eyes, but she looked determined.

"I must say you surprised me, Bob," Swanson said. "Well, until the end there. That was in line with my expectations for you. But getting past my guys and pulling a gun on me. I have to admit I'm impressed."

I had another card to play. "Swanson, before this goes any further, you should know that I've taken the precaution of outlining your scheme in a letter to my attorney."

Swanson burst out laughing. "Oh, no!" he gasped, in faux outrage. "Not your *attorney*. Dan Langham's been doing a *great* job looking out for your interests so far."

What was that supposed to mean? "The point is, if anything happens to me, he has been instructed to open the envelope in his safe and contact the police."

"You're right, I guess that settles things, Bob. I give up." Swanson held the gun out to me butt-first. When I reached for it, he pulled it back like a kid punking someone on the playground with a fake high-five. "Unsubstantiated allegations against a respected member of the community by a guy who has disappeared. I'm sure the cops will do a fantastic job following up that important lead. 'We can't find Bob Patterson? Oh, well, dead end!' If they could pin anything on me, they already would have."

Swanson was crazy enough to believe a white-collar executive could dominate the meth market, but in this case he had a point. The letter wouldn't work. I'd already be dead by the time Swanson was under suspicion. It would only benefit me as posthumous revenge, like a woman who gets a restraining order against her ex-boyfriend but he kills her anyway. Plus, I hadn't had the foresight to actually do it.

"The envelope to your lawyer thing always works in the movies," I said.

"I hate to break it to you, Bob, but this ain't the movies," Swanson said. "In real life, the bad guys win."

"Now let's get down to business," Swanson said. "I understand you've hidden a body on your property."

"I don't know what you're talking about," I said. We still didn't want Swanson to know we knew about the bug. I didn't know what difference it would make, but we had to hold on to whatever edges we had left. "What makes you think there's a body?"

"It doesn't matter how I know. I just know."

I looked at Sarah. "I didn't tell him anything," she said. "Not that there's anything to tell."

I waved her off. "Don't worry about it. Come on, Swanson. I'll show you."

Sarah stood up. "I'm coming, too."

"You most certainly are not," I said. "Swanson, she can stay here. She won't try anything as long as you've got a gun on me."

"Do you think I'm an idiot?" Swanson asked. "Sarah's coming with us."

We went out the back door, Sarah and I leading, Swanson following a few steps behind. We almost tripped over the unconscious mass of steroids on its back on the patio. Swanson took out a flashlight and shone it on Mike's face. "Is he dead?"

"No, just sleeping."

"How long will he be out?"

"Long enough."

Swanson walked across the patio toward our barbecue grill. "I want to show you something before we go to the body." He moved the flashlight beam along the ground until it found a familiar green metal rectangle. "Bob, you remember the Muffin Monster."

"Yes, I do." The thing was small enough I didn't even notice it in my own backyard.

Swanson aimed the flashlight a little to the right. "And its partner in crime, the Sanitol sanitizer. We're going to be able to clean up any messes that may become necessary tonight, Bob, if you know what I mean."

"I knew what you meant before you even said it."

Sarah stared at the two innocent-looking machines. "These things are the key to your evil plan? I use more dangerous equipment in my garden."

"Let's hope you never have to find out how deadly they can be." I took a step toward Swanson. "Don't threaten my wife."

Swanson pointed the gun at me. "Back off, Bob. You know, you two should be glad I brought my little toys. It will actually be to your benefit if we can dispose of Dave safely."

"I'm glad you're so concerned with our welfare, Swanson."

"I'm not your enemy, Bob. I want us to work together as partners."

"Then what do you need the gun for?"

"Because it looks like you still need some convincing." He waved us forward with the gun. "Now let's go take a look at that body."

◇◇◇

We marched obediently ahead, just like you're supposed to when someone points a gun at you. "It's Sarah who needs convincing," I said. "She doesn't fully appreciate the merits of your business plan."

Swanson smiled at Sarah. "What I'm offering your hesitant hubby here is an opportunity to make a lot of money with virtually no risk and do some good in the process."

"But you're talking about producing and selling methamphetamine," Sarah said. "How could that possibly be helping anyone?" We were walking past the barn in the direction I came from earlier, the opposite direction from the pond.

"Because we produce a much higher quality product than the meth monkeys do. And our labs are safer. Fewer explosions and fewer children exposed to the chemicals."

"But you do intend to sell meth to the general population," Sarah said. I kept quiet. This was her show.

"Uh, yeah." Swanson looked at Sarah like she was an idiot. "That's how we make our money."

"What happens if we don't go along?"

"Now that you know the details of our plan," Swanson said, "you'd have to be disposed of. If you're not with us, you're against us."

"You're the one with the gun," Sarah said.

Swanson looked puzzled. "True, but it's odd that you would feel the need to say that out loud." He cocked his head like a Labrador and listened intently to the darkness around us. "What's that noise?"

I finally spoke. "I don't hear anything." But I did. There was a faint buzzing coming from overhead. It could have been cicadas. Sometimes when you walk outside at night it sounds like they're gathering their entire force of insect soldiers for a massive attack on our house. But this was different. It was the wrong time of year, for one thing. And it wasn't nearly as loud.

We all looked up. Swanson frantically searched the sky. It was dark, but you could just make out a form hovering about fifteen feet above our heads. Just hovering. It was made up of four equal circles, like a cloverleaf interchange seen from the air or something you would draw with a spirograph. If you didn't know better, you'd have thought it was a flying saucer. I did know better, but Swanson didn't.

"What the fuck is that?" he shouted.

"That, Swanson," I said, "is the Parrot AR Drone Quadricopter. It's controlled by an iPhone and has an infrared HD camcorder on board. It's like the drones the U.S. military sends into places like Afghanistan to gather intelligence or assassinate terrorists. It just recorded your helpful synopsis of your scheme. You evil geniuses just can't resist telling everyone how smart you are. I'm sure the authorities will find it interesting."

Swanson didn't look as dazed and defeated as I had hoped. "That's assuming they ever see it, which they won't."

He held the gun straight over his head, pointed it at the drone and pulled the trigger. Nothing happened. "What the hell?" he said, examining the barrel. "Is the safety on again?" He moved the switch back and forth and pointed the gun skyward again. Click. Nothing.

Swanson ejected the clip and examined it in the darkness. "Jesus Christ, Bob. It's not even loaded?"

"You tell me." Maybe Corny wasn't such a bad guy after all. He clearly never planned to shoot me if he didn't even bring any bullets. Or maybe he just knew he wouldn't need a loaded gun to handle the likes of me.

"You brought an unloaded gun on a mission to save your wife's life?"

I shrugged. "I assumed it was."

"With or without a loaded weapon, I'm going to wait for that thing to land and then smash the shit out of it. Are you going to stop me?"

"It's too late for that," I said. "It's already transmitted a video feed to the iPhone and been uploaded to a secure server in the cloud."

Swanson stood still, absorbing the information. "I don't believe you, but it doesn't matter anyway. I still need you to show me the body."

"Why?"

"I need to see for myself what happened to Dave."

"What do you care?"

"I didn't say I cared," Swanson said. "I said I need to see the body."

"Well, forget it," I said. "There is no body. I just said there was to trick you into coming here."

"You knew the house was bugged?"

I nodded. "That's right."

"Bullshit."

"Why is it bullshit?"

"Because you don't know anything about technology or computers or infrared cameras."

"I know how to use the Internet." I said.

"And that's all you know," Swanson said. "All you do all day is goof off. That's why we targeted you in the first place. We needed someone who would just go along with the plan."

"But you didn't choose me. You chose Sam."

"That was just a matter of going where the money was. But Sam was a tough old bastard and it became clear pretty quickly he wasn't going to budge, so we looked around at our options. And lo and behold there you were: the hapless son-in-law. We brought Dave in because he knew you in college. He confirmed our initial analysis that you would be a human rubber stamp and we moved on with the plan."

"But you couldn't have known Sam would have a heart attack."

"Yeah, we actually could," Swanson said.

That got Sarah's attention. "What does that mean? Nobody could have predicted that."

"Let's just say we may have given Sam a nudge in the right direction." Swanson said.

"What do you mean 'we'?"

"Our organization is far-reaching. We've got techies to bug your house and hack your e-mails, and a team of operatives across the country willing to do whatever is necessary to get the job done."

Sarah's eyes were blazing. "If what you're saying is true, how'd you do it?"

"Easy as pie." Swanson had a smug grin on his face. "We just swapped out his digitalis for a much stronger dose and then sat back and waited. It's the same way that male nurse in New Jersey killed all those people. They overdose, but all they have in their system is stuff they're supposed to be taking."

Sarah wanted to be sure Swanson wasn't lying. "Wouldn't the increased dosage be discovered at the autopsy?"

"No, but even if it was, they'd probably blame the pharmacist," Swanson said.

"But how could you know I'd be named trustee?" I asked.

"We got some expert legal advice from your friend Dan Langham."

"You got Lang to change Sam's will?"

"He explained to us that Joan would still be in charge of the money unless Sam died before the end of the year. All that marital versus family trust business."

A sickening realization suddenly punched me in the gut. "Wait a minute. Are you saying this whole scheme to kill Sam came about just because I was the son-in-law?"

"That's exactly what I'm saying," Swanson said. "It's really *your* fault Sam's dead. If his daughter had married a better man, he'd still be aliv—"

Swanson was interrupted by a fist in the face from my wife. "You son of a bitch!" she screamed. "I'll kill you!"

Sarah's ring cut the bridge of Swanson's nose and he fell on his back more from surprise than the force of the blow. Or maybe I'm not giving Sarah enough credit. She jumped on top of him and started pounding his face. Blood was flying everywhere. She was sitting on his chest whaling away. I could have pulled her off but I didn't. Swanson deserved the beating and Sarah deserved to be the one delivering it.

Swanson finally managed to push her off and they both got to their feet, breathing hard. Swanson's face was a bloody mess. His nose looked like it might be broken. One of his fake teeth was chipped. Sarah wiped the hair out of her eyes and inadvertently smeared blood across her forehead like war paint from the blood of the vanquished.

Swanson stared at Sarah, seething with anger. "If you weren't a woman…"

"You'd what?" I asked. "Get your ass kicked even worse?"

"Shut up, Bob," Swanson said. "What kind of man lets his woman fight his battles for him?"

"I don't know, but it's got to be better than being the kind of man who gets beaten up by that same woman." I pointed at the drone in the sky. "Give it up, Swanson. You're on tape confessing to murder. You're going away for a long time."

Sarah chimed in. "And with your pretty boy looks, you're going to be very popular in prison."

"The video's already been sent," I said. "The cops are probably on their way right now. You might as well turn yourself in."

"Like hell." Swanson glanced around looking for a way out. He started to run toward the house where the sedan was parked.

I yelled after him. "I disabled the car on my way in, Swanson."

Sarah looked at me. "You know how to disable a car?"

I shrugged. "The keys were in it. Now they're not. I'd call that 'disabled.'"

Swanson made a U-turn and raced back toward us, his three-hundred-dollar loafers now caked with mud. I braced myself for what looked like an attack but he veered away and headed for the barn, the one place I didn't want him to go. Sarah and I chased after him. As we neared the door, we heard a loud roar and Swanson came flying out of the barn on the ATV headed straight for us. Sarah and I had to dive out of the way like border checkpoint guards when someone crashes through the barrier gate.

I helped Sarah up and we watched as Swanson tore across the grass toward the driveway. He would need to make a sharp right to get on the paved surface, but he was only increasing his speed.

"Uh, honey?" Sarah asked. "Did you ever fix the throttle on the ATV?"

I stuck out my hand. "I don't believe we've been properly introduced. I'm Bob Patterson."

"I'll take that as a 'no.'"

"I've been meaning to," I said. "But I've been kind of busy with this whole mortal threat to my family thing."

The ATV's engine continued to howl as Swanson approached the driveway. There was no way he was going to make the turn at that speed. There's a huge hundred-year-old oak tree at the head of the driveway. The trunk of the tree has got to be at least eight feet in diameter. If you drove a Hummer into it at fifty miles an hour, it wouldn't even budge, so I was pretty sure the ATV stood no chance. Swanson sped across the driveway and hit the tree dead on. The impact flung him forward headfirst into the trunk.

I told Sarah to go to the barn to check on Nellie, who had been up in the loft operating the drone. I ran over to Swanson and rolled him over onto his back. There were bits of tree bark embedded in his bloody face, but it was hard to tell how much of his damage was caused by the tree and how much by Sarah. He was badly injured but he wasn't dead. The ATV was on top of him and he appeared to be paralyzed, at least temporarily.

"Call 911, Bob," he croaked. "We can still work this out."

"You know," I said quietly, "this all came about because you thought I was a pushover."

"True, Bob...I underestimated you...you're not a killer."

"I've learned it all from you, Swanson."

"What have you learned?" Swanson gasped.

I kneeled down and took Swanson's face in my hands, my palms on his cheeks. I leaned in close and whispered. "Behind every great fortune, there is a great crime."

I twisted Swanson's head violently with both hands. There was a sharp *crack* and then silence, except for my own heart pounding in my chest and Sarah's approaching footsteps.

Chapter Thirty-one

"Do you think we should move?" I asked Sarah. "It seems like it's awfully easy to get yourself killed around here."

"I don't think we need to move," Sarah said. "Those two deaths were so ridiculously improbable, not to mention convenient, it's hard enough to believe it happened even twice."

"Right," I said. "Like in *The World According to Garp* when he buys the house with a still-smoking plane sticking out of the roof because the odds of it happening again are astronomical. I think we're safe from now on."

I got the pickup and we threw Swanson's body in the back. It was becoming our own personal meat wagon. I found his gun and flashlight in the grass. The gun was bent and didn't look like it would fire, not that I had any bullets. I threw it in the back of the truck. The flashlight was in perfect shape. Those things are indestructible. They should have commercials where people try to break them like the gorilla and the Samsonite luggage. I was keeping this bad boy. I put it in my pocket.

"What about the ATV?" Sarah asked.

"It's destroyed," I said. "We'll have to get someone to haul it away."

"How do we explain the accident?"

"I'll say I was driving it."

"Then why aren't you hurt?"

"Guys who sell scrap metal for a living don't ask as many questions as suspicious wives. Half the junk that ends up in their hands is probably stolen. But if he asks I'll tell him I managed to jump off just in time."

We hid the pickup behind the barn for now and went inside. The horses were standing there in the dark like they always were. A trap door above our heads opened and a ladder slid down to the floor. Nellie descended the ladder carrying an iPhone.

"Where's the drone?" I asked.

"I landed it outside after Swanson took off on the ATV. I was able to control it pretty well. Not like Nick can, but not bad for an old guy."

I had considered having Nick operate the drone but Sarah squashed that idea immediately. She also nixed my plan of tying Emily up in the yard as bait like the goat in *Jurassic Park*. Seriously, though, I only thought about it for like one second. I am an excellent father.

"What about the video?" I asked Nellie. "Did you get it?"

"I got it," Nellie answered. "It's right here on my iPhone. You want to see it?"

"Sure."

Nellie pulled the video up and hit play. The first thing you could see was the ground falling away as the drone rose into the air. It looked more like a video game than real life. After a few minutes, you could make out three separate individuals even in the dark. As the camera got closer, you could even hear us talking. Swanson said his lines like an evil genius explaining his scheme for world domination to James Bond as he's hanging upside down over a shark tank. Just before the drone flew away, there was a crystal-clear shot of Swanson pointing the gun straight at the camera and pulling the trigger.

"Nice shot, Tarantino."

Nellie grinned. "All these years of filming childhood events my family will never watch has finally paid off."

"Don't erase it. Actually, send it to my phone."

"Roger. And I need it for back-up documentation for my enormous bill."

"Isn't the video already uploaded to the Internet?" Sarah asked.

I looked away. "I, uh, actually, I lied about that."

Sarah was not happy. "You're kidding."

"You don't have Internet access out here in the barn," Nellie said. "Although I'd be happy to get you all wired up. I'm thinking of buying a boat."

"Let's try to leave *some* money in the trust." I turned to Sarah. "The uploading to the Internet thing was just a bluff, like the envelope to the lawyer."

"Yeah, that worked like a charm," Sarah said. "In fact, your whole plan was ingenious. Especially how you let Swanson take your gun to give him a false sense of confidence."

"My *unloaded* gun," I corrected her.

"But you didn't know that at the time."

I put my arms around her and looked into her eyes. Both of them. "Look, if you really want to, we can have a full debriefing at a later date. But what's the difference? Chalk it up as a win and hope we never have to do anything like that again."

Sarah hugged me tight. "You're right. I'm proud of you."

"Good. Now you and Nellie get out of here while I get rid of this dead body."

◇◇◇

I looked out of the barn toward the house. No movement that I could see. We hustled over to Sarah's car and she and Nellie got in and drove away. I walked to the front of the house. The first guy I tranquilized was still lying on his back. I leaned down and lightly slapped his cheeks a few times. I was thinking about going into the house for a pitcher of water to toss in his face when his eyes started to flutter and he let out a groan.

I wasn't worried about what the bench-press brothers might do to me when they woke up. Unlike in the movies, if you get knocked unconscious for a couple of hours, whether by a drug or a blow to the head, you don't wake up feeling fine. These guys weren't going to be looking for revenge. They were going to be looking for a toilet to puke in. And I sure wasn't worried about them going to the police. What were they going to say? This guy killed our boss while we were in the middle of a home invasion?

After a few seconds his eyes focused and he saw me. "You guys need to get out of here," I said. "Swanson confessed to murder. The cops are on the way."

"Gnnnnnh," he said.

"Don't worry, I'll keep you out of it. I know you guys didn't do anything. But who knows what Swanson might say? You need to get out of town as fast as you can and don't look back."

I helped him to his feet and led him around the back to his unconscious doppelganger. "See if you can rouse him. I'm going to go find your car keys." I took the flashlight and searched the bush I thought they landed under. They were right there, but it somehow took me ten minutes to locate them. By that time, the two behemoths were already sitting meekly in the car. I leaned in the window and handed whoever was driving the keys.

"Seriously, go straight home, pack your things and hit the road. Swanson's going down and you don't want to go down with him. If anyone asks, I've never seen you guys. Good luck and Godspeed."

"Thanks, Mr. Patterson," the driver said. "We owe you one." He put the car in gear and drove slowly down the driveway. His headlights bounced back and forth as he corrected left and right to stay on the path. I don't know how the darts correlate to alcoholic beverages, but these guys had to have had at least the equivalent of a couple of six-packs. Hopefully they'd sober up before they got pulled over. I didn't want these idiots trying to talk their way out of a traffic stop. But I had other things to worry about. For the second time in the last week, I was on dead body cleanup duty and this time the bodies had to stay gone for good.

Swanson had mentioned the Muffin Monster is used in sewer lines to make sure the pipes don't clog. In fact, it's specifically designed to shred waterlogged objects into little bits, but I don't know how many dead bodies that usually entails. It probably depends on the city.

I only had two bodies, and I knew the Muffin Monster would work underwater, but I ultimately decided I would have to take care of this nasty business on land. My kids swim in that pond.

Not to mention the difficulty of dragging the Muffin Monster out into the middle of the pond and feeding two bodies into it without drowning. I was going to be lucky if I could get Corny to shore.

I went into the garage to look for one of those orange extension cords you use to plug things in outside. I found a 200-footer I purchased with the idea of snow-blowing the entire driveway in front of the house. Huh. Still in the packaging. I got Sarah's mask and fins from the house.

I tossed everything in the back of the pickup and drove behind the house. I wheeled the Muffin Monster close and was able to wrestle it onto the tailgate and slide it into the truck bed. I got back in the pickup and drove over to the pond.

I unrolled the extension cord and plugged one end into the dock socket and the other end into the Muffin Monster. I pressed the start button and was relieved when the blades started turning. Now all I had to do was retrieve a dead body from the middle of a freezing cold pond in the dark.

I stripped down to my underwear. Even though I knew there was nothing really dangerous in our little pond, the human brain is conditioned to imagine monsters lurking in the darkness. Like anything else frightening or unpleasant (death, a social outing with Sarah's coworkers, etc.), I tried not to think about it. I'm good at that. Most people are.

I put the flashlight in my mouth and swam until I saw the sunken boat. Not a very good hiding place. Pretty easy to find, even at night. I swam down and dragged Corny out of the boat. The body was bloated enough that I never could have gotten it out except that a lot of the flesh was missing, thanks to the efforts of whatever creatures feed themselves by scavenging at the bottom of a pond. I spent some time on the surface breathing in and out and trying not to puke, and then made my way to shore.

I dragged Corny up onto the dock and collapsed onto my back. I just lay there for a few minutes staring up at the sky and getting my wind back. I got up and sloshed my way over to the pickup and opened the tailgate. Yaaah! There were two eyes staring at me from the truck bed. I almost shit myself. How could I have forgotten Swanson? John Wayne Gacy or the Green River Killer might lose track of a body here or there, but Swanson was fully fifty percent of the dead bodies I'd ever encountered. And he was brand new. He should have been fresh in my memory.

I drove as close as I could to the wooded area near the pond and hauled the bodies, the Muffin Master, and the sanitizer into the trees as far as the extension cord would go. You can imagine the rest. It was as horrific as you would expect. I don't know if it scarred me for life, but let's just say I'm not going to be making my own sausage anytime soon.

I sprayed everything in the area with the sanitizer. I even went around and washed off the areas where my dart-gun victims had fallen to get rid of any traces of blood or tranquilizer. While I was at it and since I was already wet, I hosed myself down with the sanitizer as well. I left the two machines on the porch, spotless and evidence-free. It was three in the morning. Sarah and the kids had been asleep for hours. Disposing of a couple of dead bodies took a lot longer than I thought it would. I went inside and showered and went to bed.

When my head hit the pillow, the adrenaline drained from my body and I started to fall asleep almost immediately. That was the most physical activity I'd had in one day in at least twenty years. But I kept thinking about the Sanitol sanitizer. It was an amazing machine. Anything can be free of contaminants in thirty seconds with virtually no cleanup. I should probably carry around a plastic bottle of the stuff in the glove compartment in case I ever get pulled over after a couple of drinks. Just a quick spray in my mouth and *Why, no, Officer, I haven't had anything to drink at all.* The possibilities were endless....

Chapter Thirty-two

The next morning, Sarah tapped me on the shoulder before the alarm went off. No, not that kind of tap, although after last night's backbreaking labor my ability to take the field would have been a game-time decision anyway. "Is everything taken care of?" she whispered.

"Yes."

"No one will find them?"

"No."

"You're sure?"

"I'm sure." Sarah put her arms around me and hugged me from behind in the rarely used woman-as-the back-spoon position, which is rarely used for a reason. She's just too small for it to work effectively. It's like she was riding a horse and refused to let go even when it decided to lie down on its side. I rolled over and faced her. I don't know what that's called, but it's better.

Sarah pulled my face close to hers. "I know what you're doing and I know you're not finished."

"Why didn't you say anything?"

"Because I trust you. I always knew you'd rise to the occasion and do whatever had to be done to take care of your family. You've always had it in you. You couldn't see it, but I could. You think I'd marry some loser?"

"No, but everybody makes mistakes. I thought maybe you fucked up just this one time."

Sarah smacked me lightly on the nose. "Stop."

"I know you're right. I've been feeling sorry for myself because I haven't accomplished enough personally, instead of being grateful for all I have. That's going to change."

"The kids and I love you just the way you are."

"You're going to see a new man around here. Starting today."

"I like the old man just fine," Sarah said and reached for me. I was upgraded to probable and placed on the active roster.

I got the kids off to school, went to work, and tried to act normal again. As I faked my way through the day, my mind kept running through the recent string of unsettling events. Something wasn't adding up. Maybe it was because the first ending in these kinds of scenarios is never the real ending. Hell, sometimes the second ending isn't the real ending. The hero has to suddenly realize the whole scheme has been manipulated by the last person you would expect or the one whose betrayal would hurt the most. Ideally, both.

In this particular case, if you looked at who had means, motive, and opportunity, it really pointed to one obvious person. Who could have controlled the whole thing from behind the scenes? There was really only one answer.

I left the office, got in the car and drove with a specific destination in mind. After about ten minutes, I pulled into the driveway of…my own house.

I went into the pantry and opened a Tupperware container and there buried in the rice was Corny's cell phone. Next to it on the shelf was a bottle of Stallion Spray—the weapon I used to kill Corny.

I said up front that my entire life is a lie. Why wouldn't it be me?

In the end, who profited from all this? Whose accomplices, and the only other people in on the conspiracy, are both now conveniently dead? Who had access to my father-in-law? Who else really had any reason to want me in charge? Who has come out of this entire fiasco smelling like a hero, despite a long history of not coming through in the clutch?

As Hollywood has told us, the rich white guy is always the murderer. But don't get the wrong idea. While I did have access to my father-in-law, I didn't kill him.

I knew Corny would be visiting to check up on me, so when I went out to do the night check, I brought along the Stallion Spray, the same bottle Officer Tate later found in the back of our pickup. Stallion Spray is a solution made of urine from a mare in estrus, used to get a stallion worked up so you can get a "sample" without an actual mare around. I sprayed it all around Rex's stall. Rex is almost impossible to control under the best of circumstances and the smell of a mare in heat turns him into a bucking bronco. All I had to do was get Corny in the stall and he had no chance.

It was easy enough to lure Swanson to my property by pretending with Sarah to discuss disposing of Corny's body. I wouldn't say everything went according to plan, but we did get Swanson on tape incriminating himself and he did end up dead. By my hand.

◇◇◇

Once I'd committed my crime, it was time to get my fortune. I took Corny's phone into my office. At first I just stared at it. Even though I hardly ever saw him when he was alive, I kind of missed Corny, or at least the memory of him. I couldn't think about the old college days the same way anymore.

I dialed his voicemail. The first few messages were from the girls after our night out together. I had no hard feelings toward them. They were just doing their jobs and we actually had a pretty good time together.

> *Natalie: Hey, Dave, I thought you were a cool guy.*
> *Why are your old college friends so lame? Call me*
> *when you*—Delete.

> *Lexi: Dave, next time can you get someone younger*
> *so we can at least have fun before the frame job?*
> *That Bob guy was a stiff. Remember when he tried*

to dance? I thought he was having a stroke. Ha ha h—Delete.

There were a few messages from Lang.

Lang: Hey Corny, call me and let me know how everything went with Bob the other night.

Lang: Corny, where are you? What the hell happened when you were out with Bob?

The rest were from Swanson. Apparently this was Corny's work phone. No messages from concerned family or friends, if he had any of either.

Swanson: Dave, I get that being around Patterson makes you want to kill him, but don't. We need him. Delete.

Swanson: Seriously, Dave, don't hurt Bob. You don't want all our hard work to go to waste, do you? Delete.

I was beginning to miss Corny less. This trip down memory lane wasn't doing much for my ego either. Next were a bunch of "where the hell are you?" messages from Swanson, which I promptly deleted. Then it got interesting.

Swanson: Dave, I don't know what you're trying to pull, but running away won't save you. I know about the missing money and I will hunt you down and kill you wherever you go.

Swanson: Dave, you can't hide from me. Return the money and everything's square. Otherwise, you're a dead man.

I'd suspected that Corny was stealing from Swanson. Corny had dropped a few hints that this was his last gig and there had to be a reason Swanson was so adamant about seeing the body. But Corny's body wouldn't get him his money back. Or would it?

I tried to remember what happened to Corny's keys after I took his motorcycle to the airport. My usual go-to plan: find what I was wearing when I had them last. I went down to the hall closet and my leather jacket was hanging there, waiting patiently for the next time I wanted to embarrass my daughter. The keys were in the pocket, right where I left them to make it easy for the police if they ever searched the house.

There was the usual assortment of keys on the ring. Vehicles, apartment/house, possibly office. One in particular caught my attention. It said 2896. But what did it open? PO Box? Bus locker? Safe deposit box? There was no way to know. This was going to take all my deductive powers. I turned the key over and on the back it said "If found, return to U-Store-it" with an address where Corny grew up, a small town in Iowa. How does someone like Corny come from a place like that? Nature versus nurture, I guess.

I eventually made it to U-Store-it. Fortunately, all I needed was the key. No one tried to stop me. Quite a secure operation they're running there. Some serial killer is going to be pissed if he misplaces the key to his "storage shed." Inside the storage unit were five large duffle bags full of cold hard American cash, which at least for the moment, is still worth something in the current world economy. Corny had apparently been planning for his retirement, but unfortunately for him, that day was never going to come.

I still had one more loose end to tie up. I drove to the law offices of Daniel J. Langham, Esq. His secretary showed me in right away. Almost as if he had been expecting my visit.

"So what can I do for you, Bob?" Lang asked. "What's so important I had to cancel paying clients to see you in the middle of the day?"

"You'll find somebody to invoice. The first lawyer I worked for told me not to worry about overbilling because you never bill the client for all the times you're thinking about their case when you're on the toilet or in the shower."

Lang smiled at that. "I always forget you used to be a lawyer so you know all our tricks. Have a seat."

I slid into one of the chairs in front of his desk. We both sat there wordlessly, each waiting for the other to start. I read somewhere that the best interviewing technique is to remain silent until the other person gets nervous and tries to fill the emptiness by talking. It wasn't working so far, but Lang was an experienced lawyer who wouldn't fall for th—

"So what's this about?" Or maybe he would. From what I've seen, he's not an especially *good* lawyer.

"If you're waiting to hear from Swanson, you can forget it."

Lang's expression didn't change. Years of handing outrageous legal bills to clients has at least taught him how to keep a straight face. "Swanson? The guy who wants you to invest in his company? What does that have to do with me?"

I ignored the questions. "I know you changed the will. On some level, I always knew, but I didn't want to believe it because you were my friend. Now I know you were involved from the beginning."

"I honestly have no idea what you're talking ab—"

I cut him off. "I kept trying to think of ways that didn't involve you. But Swanson needed me as trustee. Even if Sam had truly wanted me, how would Swanson have known?"

"Maybe he assumed you would be named because you're the only son-in-law."

"That might be true in other families where the son-in-law is a high-powered executive and the daughter is a housewife. But it's the opposite here. Sarah's the high-powered executive, not to mention his own flesh and blood. No sane person would assume I would be named trustee."

Lang looked uncomfortable. "So?"

"So the only people who knew Sam's intentions were Sam himself and his estate lawyer. Who also happened to be friends with the son-in-law and the crazy fraternity buddy who showed up out of nowhere. Remember, you were the one who spotted Corny and got us all together."

"I mean, I guess I saw him first...."

"And you were with us the other night at the bar."

"Nellie and I were both there...."

"And, if I remember correctly, you made Nellie go home early."

"We left at a reasonable hour because we have wives and families. I don't know what you remember, but I certainly didn't 'make' Nellie go home."

"No, you pretty much did. It was almost as if you wanted Corny and me to be alone."

"Why would I want that?"

"So he could arrange a meeting with his pretty friends. And then afterward you kept trying to call Corny on his burner phone. Nellie also tried to call him, but on his regular phone. How would you know to call that number? The only messages were from people involved in this scheme. Swanson, the girls, and you."

"Corny must have given me that number when he came into town."

"Save it. I've known all this for a long time. What I didn't know was who actually killed Sam. But when Swanson told me how they did it, everything clicked into place."

Lang looked defeated. "How'd they do it?" he asked quietly.

"Swanson said they switched Sam's heart medicine for a higher dose. At first I thought Swanson was the mastermind behind some huge, secret organization that could get to anybody, but when I realized that wasn't true, I thought about who would have access to Sam's medicine cabinet. I didn't think Swanson or his two goons could pull it off."

Lang stood up. "Surely you're not suggesting that I—"

"You mentioned at the will reading that Sam's trust paid for his prescriptions, so I knew you were aware of what he was taking. And then you slipped up that night at the bar when you said you liked Sam's sauna. You've been to Sam's house quite a few times, but there's no reason you'd be up in the master bathroom."

Lang slumped back down in his chair. "I was hoping the alcohol would make that one slip out of your brain."

"Another half hour and it would have. Here's what I don't understand. Changing the will is one thing. But murder is another."

Lang sighed and shook his head. "By then I was in too deep. I made the mistake of telling Swanson about the estate tax loophole. He said we had to get it done by the end of the year and I was the only one who could do it."

"But how could you kill him? He was your friend."

"Swanson threatened me and my family. I was scared of him. Sam was old, and we have our entire lives ahead of us."

"When did you do it?"

"It was actually over a month ago. That Patrons Party the Bennetts gave before the benefit. You and Sarah were there."

Somehow this shocked me. "You murdered Sarah's father right in front of our faces?"

"It didn't seem like it at the time. I didn't even know if it would work."

I shook my head in disgust. "Keep telling yourself that. What exactly did you do?"

"I went to use the bathroom when I knew it was occupied so I had to go upstairs to find another one. I bypassed the hall bathroom and went back to use the master bath. If anyone noticed, I'd just say I got confused. I opened the medicine cabinet. I knew the prescription from the trust and the bottle was right there. I switched the pills with some Swanson had given me and headed back downstairs. It was a big party. No one noticed me at all."

"Maybe you could convince me at some point it was too late to extricate yourself, but how do you explain pointing them to me in the first place? Apparently they thought I was some kind of easy mark. I wonder where they got that idea?"

Lang shrugged. "I admit I told them about you."

"We're supposed to be friends."

Lang jumped up angrily. "You can be an infuriating person to be friends with. You haven't done a damn thing and yet you think you're better than everyone else."

"I don't think that at all. I think pretty much the opposite of that."

Lang sneered. "Oh, come on. Guys like you are all the same. You were born on third base and think you hit a triple."

"You couldn't be more wrong. I think I was born on third base and got picked off by the pitcher."

Lang ticked off a list on his fingers. "You married the perfect woman. She's smart and beautiful and, as a bonus, she's incredibly wealthy. You don't really work. Everybody likes you. Everything's so easy for you."

"I'm sure it's been tough for you growing up with no alternative but to toil away in the coal mines."

Lang's voice shook with anger. "It *has* been hard for me! I've had to work for everything I've gotten. You think I like busting my ass for sixty hours every week?"

"No, but I wouldn't have thought you'd spend all the rest of your time feeling sorry for yourself." I thought for a minute. "You drew up the documents for them. Did they tell you to give me no pay for all that trustee work?"

Lang smiled weakly. "No. I thought of that myself. I figured you've been getting paid for doing nothing all these years, this would even it out. Look, at first they were just paying me to steer Sam in the right direction. Then when Sam dug his heels in, they wanted me to hook you up with Corny. I just figured it was another angle. I never knew it would lead to killing Sam."

It was time to get to the point. "Rationalize all you want. You're screwed now. I have Swanson on video admitting everything." *More or less.* "He implicates you in all of it." *Not untrue.* "I have it here on my phone…" *waving it in front of his face…* "and it's stored in the cloud. So it will be a simple matter to prove Sam's will was doctored. At a bare minimum you're going to get disbarred and kicked out of the firm."

Lang had tears in his eyes. "It would crush my father if I disgraced the firm he spent his life building. I'll be humiliated. My wife will leave me. And what will I do for a living? I only know how to be a lawyer."

"You'll be lucky if you don't spend the rest of your life in jail. Meanwhile, for your last act as my lawyer, I want you to go to Swanson's backers and tell them he's out of the picture. It turns out that Swanson was all hat and no cattle. This big criminal enterprise he talked about to intimidate everyone didn't exist. I tracked his techie down. His vast surveillance operation was one teenage computer nerd who taught himself to hack into people's e-mail so he could see what the other kids in school were saying about him. His army of enforcers consisted of Corny and two dimwitted body builders who weren't even especially mean or tough. It was nothing but bluff and bluster."

"So you think they'll just walk away?"

"The inventor and investors didn't know anything about what Swanson was doing. He was off the reservation, acting on his own. Tell them he confessed to a criminal scheme on camera. They'll be glad to get out without being implicated themselves."

"I'm not sure that video would even be admissible in court."

"Maybe not, but with some push, it could become a huge YouTube hit. And they're not going to walk away empty-handed. Because they'll have all that unneeded property and equipment, I'll buy it from them at a fair price and run Sanitol as a lawful business."

"What if they won't go for it?"

"Make it happen. I'll give you a week."

Lang came through. He could be persuasive when he wanted to be. But I was still determined not to let him get away with murder. I was hesitant to involve the police and risk incriminating Sarah and me, so I wracked my brain for a solution that wouldn't compromise me or my family. Lang saved me the trouble. He crashed his Lexus into a bridge abutment and was killed instantly. It was two in the morning and he had a blood alcohol content of 0.26 percent. His wife said he had been depressed and drinking heavily. She'd been trying to make him get help. I don't know if it was suicide or a drunken accident, but I felt like justice was served. No, I didn't cut the brake lines or anything. His fear of exposure and, I like to think, shame, eventually overwhelmed him.

Corny's retirement money was enough for a down payment on a bank loan to secure the Sanitol deal. The profits won't be obscene like Swanson envisioned, but we'll do fine. We can sell that sanitizer to every legitimate business on the planet.

I made the deal personally, not on behalf of the trust. I resigned as trustee and Joan replaced me, which is as it should be. It's her money, after all. Now I run Sanitol.

A renewed sense of dedication didn't suddenly make me capable of managing a large company. I brought in Harriet to run the place. I'll be holding down my usual figurehead position. But I'm working harder at it.

I'm no longer living a lie. Maybe I never was. This is who I am. Or if I'm still living a lie, it's a better lie, one of my own choosing. I'm like a lot of successful businessmen now. I've capitalized on an opportunity and hired people better than me to handle the details. There are plenty of smart, hard-working people out there, but far fewer visionaries and leaders like I'm pretending to be. Steve Jobs didn't assemble those iPhones himself.

Approximately nine months later, little Samantha Patterson was born. Maybe we weren't careful enough, maybe subconsciously we wanted another child, maybe we just beat the contraception odds, maybe it was fate. I don't know. But I do know that if Sam hadn't died, his beautiful new granddaughter wouldn't exist, because the exact sequence of events leading to her conception would never have occurred. I could never regret that, and I have no doubt Sam would agree with me.